KEEP ME SAFE

"You providing me sanctuary is payment enough if you feel you're in my debt."

"Count on it," he vowed. "You're coming home with me, Ramie. I formed a security firm with my brothers after Tori's abduction. I swore never to be without the right tools to ensure the safety of my family. We hire only the best."

"I need the best," she said in a low voice filled with conviction. "Because he's always only a footstep behind me. No matter where I go. No matter what I do. And until he's taken down, all the women he kills will be my fault. I can't live with that guilt any longer."

Caleb emitted a soft curse as he slid his hand underneath her chin, framing it between his thumb and the rest of his fingers. His gaze bored into her unwaveringly.

"I *will* protect you, Ramie. I don't make promises I can't keep."

By Maya Banks

MAYA BANKS

KEEP ME SAFE

A Slow Burn Novel

AVONBOOKS

An Imprint of HarperCollins*Publishers*

This is a work of fiction. Names, characters, places, and incidents are products of the author's imagination or are used fictitiously and are not to be construed as real. Any resemblance to actual events, locales, organizations, or persons, living or dead, is entirely coincidental.

First Avon Books mass market printing: December 2016
First Avon Books paperback printing: October 2014

ISBN 978-0-06-249587-7

14 15 16 17 18   QGM   10 9 8 7 6 5 4 3 2 1

To May Chen
for being tenacious and allowing me
to write a story that has lived
in my mind for many years
xoxo . . .

ONE

CALEB Devereaux turned out of the sharp switch-back and onto the driveway leading up to the tiny mountain cabin, swearing when he hit pothole after pothole. Fury and impatience simmered in his blood but the anticipation of having finally found Ramie St. Claire after an exhaustive search kept his mood from being completely black.

Ramie was his sister, Tori's, only hope.

The moment Tori was kidnapped, Caleb had begun his search for Ramie St. Claire. She certainly wasn't the first person on most people's go-to list when looking for a loved one. Ramie was psychic and had been helpful in locating victims in the past. While many would be skeptical, Caleb absolutely believed in Ramie's abilities.

His own sister had psychic abilities.

He and his brothers, Beau and Quinn, had always been extremely overprotective of their baby sister. With good reason. Caleb was the head of a veritable empire. Security was always top priority. They'd always feared kidnapping for ransom, but in their worst nightmares they'd never imagined that Tori would simply disappear and be at the mercy of a madman.

There'd been no ransom demand. Simply a video of Tori bound hand and foot and the maniacal laughter of her captor as he told Caleb to kiss his sister goodbye.

He just prayed he wasn't too late. God, don't let it be too late for Tori.

It infuriated him that Ramie St. Claire had simply dropped off the map three months ago. No trace of her, no forwarding address. No evidence that she even existed. How could she simply disappear when she was such an invaluable aid in finding kidnap victims and missing persons? How selfish of her to simply refuse, by her actions, to help anyone.

He'd worked himself into a rage by the time he finally pulled up to the small cabin that looked as though it wouldn't weather the upcoming winter at all. He wasn't even certain there would be electricity. Only a person determined not to be found would live in a place like this.

He got out and strode to the ramshackle front door, his fist up and pounding. The door shook and rattled under the force of his knock. Only silence greeted him and it sent his blood pressure soaring.

"Miss St. Claire!" he roared. "Answer the goddamn door!"

He beat on the door again, shouting for her to answer. He likely looked and sounded like the madman holding his sister, but at this point he didn't care. He was beyond desperation. It had taken every resource available to him to finally track Ramie down. No way in hell he was leaving until he'd gotten the information he'd come for.

Then the door swung open and he was greeted by the sight of a petite woman with wary gray eyes. He was momentarily taken aback, going silent as he stared at Ramie St. Claire for the first time in person.

The photos he'd seen of her didn't do her justice. There was a delicate air to her as though she were recovering from an illness, but it in no way detracted from her beauty. She looked . . . fragile. He felt a brief moment of guilt for what he was about to ask her to do, but he brushed it away. There was no price too high to pay for his sister's life.

"I can't help you."

Her softly spoken words slid like velvet over his ears, a direct contrast from the anger her refusal caused. He hadn't even made his request yet and she was already giving him the brush-off.

"You don't even know what it is I want," he said in an icy tone that would wither most people.

"It's rather obvious," she said wearily, fatigue drooping her eyelids. "Why else would you come all this way? I don't even want to know how you found me. It's obvious I did a piss-poor job of covering my tracks if you managed to find me here."

Caleb frowned. Had she been ill? Was that why she'd dropped out of sight, so she could recover? It didn't matter why now that he'd found her. He didn't care what her reasons were.

"With your abilities why would you purposely make yourself difficult to find?" he demanded. "My sister's life is at stake here, Miss St. Claire. I'm not merely asking you to help me. I'm not leaving until you do."

She shook her head adamantly, fear chasing the lethargy from her eyes. "I can't."

There was quiet desperation to her words that told him there was more to her refusal than what appeared on the surface. Something was wrong and yet he couldn't summon any regret for forcing her compliance. Not when Tori's life hung in the balance.

He reached inside his jacket and pulled out Tori's scarf. The one item they'd found at the site where she must have been taken. In the parking lot of a grocery store beside the open door of her car. He should have never let her go alone. He'd failed her. Failed to protect her. Failed to ensure proper security.

Ramie immediately backed away, a desperate cry on her lips. He shoved forward, forcing the scarf into her hands and holding her and the scarf so there was no escape. She emitted a broken sob and she looked up at him, stricken, her face going unnaturally pale. Her pupils flared and then clouded, pain and devastation clearly outlined on her features.

"No," she whispered. "Not again. Oh God, not again. I won't survive it."

Her knees buckled and she would have gone down, but he caught her, ensuring the scarf never lost contact with her hands. He watched in horror as Ramie's body sagged, slipping from his grasp despite his best effort to support her weight. She was simply lifeless, as limp as a rag doll. He quickly followed her down to the floor, determined that she not lose her grip on Tori's scarf. But it didn't seem to matter now. Ramie was somewhere else.

Her eyes glazed over and her body began to twitch spasmodically. She curled into a fetal position, the fragility of such a self-protective measure gutting him. She moaned softly and then began to weep.

"Please don't hurt me again. Please, I'm begging

you. I can't take any more. If you're going to kill me, just do it. Quit torturing me."

Chill bumps spread rapidly up Caleb's nape as Ramie's voice, which sounded nearly *identical* to Tori's, filled his ears. Dear God, was he witnessing what was happening to his sister through Ramie?

The scene Ramie was painting was horrifying. Not only for the fact that his sister was even now enduring the absolute worst. But from all appearances, Ramie was suffering with her.

He'd certainly done his research on Ramie St. Claire's abilities but there was little information beyond her astonishing success record. No mention of *how* she managed to help victims or what it did to her. God help them all. What had he *done*?

Her body jerked and it took only a moment for Caleb to realize what was happening. It was too unmistakable. Bile rose in his throat and he had to suck in steadying breaths to keep from heaving the contents of his stomach on the floor. Tears burned his eyelids as he helplessly watched his sister being raped through the window of Ramie's awareness.

Ramie's weeping tore at his heart and he gathered her into his arms, not knowing what else to do but rock her gently. "Tori?" He whispered his sister's name experimentally, not knowing if a link had been established through Ramie. "Can you hear me? It's Caleb. Tell me where you are, honey.

I'll come for you. Hold on please. Don't give up, no matter how bad it is."

Ramie's head jerked sideways and the imprint of a hand immediately appeared on her cheek. Caleb was horrified, unsure of what to do now that he'd crossed a line he couldn't come back from. He tried to push back his guilt, telling himself that anything that helped him recover his sister was worth it. But was torturing an innocent woman worth it?

He hadn't given her a choice. She'd told him no and yet he'd forced this on her not knowing the heavy toll it would take. He had no idea how her powers worked and now that he did he was sick to his soul. No wonder she'd been so resistant. No wonder she'd told him she couldn't do it anymore.

"Ramie. Ramie!" he said in a more forceful voice. "Come back to me, Ramie. Come back so you can tell me how to find her."

Ramie's eyes were opened but so distant that he knew she wasn't here. The imprint of the hand on her face was bright and vivid, red against deathly white skin. There was a look of such defeat and despair in her eyes that once again he found himself battling tears.

Suddenly she hunched inward, her entire body jolting as though absorbing a blow. She wrapped her arms around her stomach and he realized that she'd been kicked. Or rather Tori had been kicked.

It was a horrific, helpless feeling to know that two women were being victimized, one because of *him*.

Then she simply rolled away, her cheek lying against the cold floor, her eyes fixed and vacant. She was completely still and terror gripped him. Was Tori dead? Oh dear *God*! Had he just witnessed his sister's *murder*?

"Ramie! Wake up! God, *please* wake up. Tell me how to find her. Tell me that she's still alive!"

He picked Ramie's slight weight up, swearing because she was so thin and fragile, weighing nothing in his arms. He carried her to the worn sofa and carefully laid her down, not wanting to hurt her any more than she'd already been hurt.

He sat on the edge, gathering her icy hands in his, rubbing, trying to infuse warmth. He had no idea what to do. Should he take her to a hospital?

Then after several long moments, she blinked and seemed to come out of her trance. Pain immediately swamped her features and she began to silently weep again, each tear cutting him to ribbons.

"Is she still alive?" he asked anxiously. "Do you know how to find her?"

"Yes," Ramie said dully.

Hope surged in his heart and he found himself nearly crushing her hands in his.

"Tell me where," he urged.

Slowly and painfully she whispered the location down to the minutest detail. Chills once again slithered up his spine at the precision with which she described not only the location but the kidnapper. She even provided a license plate number.

He picked up his phone and immediately called his brother, relaying the information that Ramie had provided. When he was done, he stared helplessly down at Ramie, grateful and yet deeply regretful for what he'd just subjected her to.

"What do I need to do to help you?" he asked softly.

Resignation dulled her eyes even further. "There's nothing you can do," she said in a flat voice. "Just go."

"The hell I'll just leave you here!"

He was already calculating in his head that he could simply bring her with him. He could get her the care she so obviously needed at the same time Tori was receiving what she needed.

"Your sister needs you. Just go. I'll be fine."

The lie was so obvious, but it seemed to be all she could muster. He was torn between rushing to be with Tori and staying to ensure Ramie would be all right. But how could she be? Two women would live with this for the rest of their lives. His precious sister and the woman he'd forced to help him, never knowing the price she'd pay.

"Please," she begged, her voice breaking. "Just

go and leave me be. I gave you what you wanted. I helped you, now go. It's the *least* you can do."

Caleb stood, wiping a hand over his hair and down the back of his neck in agitation. "I'll go, but I'm coming back, Ramie. I'm going to make this up to you."

"You can never take this back," she whispered. "There's no making up for what's been done. Just go and take care of your sister. She needs you."

She closed her eyes, tears seeping from her eyelids. How could he just leave her like she asked? And yet how could he not go and ensure that his sister was safely recovered? He'd never felt so torn in his life.

"If you have any humanity whatsoever, you'll leave and never tell anyone where you found me," Ramie said hoarsely. "Please, I'm begging you. Just *go*. He plans to kill her tomorrow. At dawn. You don't have much time."

Her words proved to be the impetus, driving him to action. But goddamn it, he would make this up to her. Somehow, someway.

Regret swamped him. Worse was the fact that even knowing now what he hadn't known before, he couldn't say he would have done anything differently. Not when it meant the difference between Tori's life and death. But at least now he better understood Ramie's resistance. No longer did he look at her and think she was selfish and cruel. Now he realized her disappearance had been self-preservation. He didn't know how she'd survived this in the past. He just prayed he wasn't the tipping point in pushing her so far over the edge she'd never recover.

Caleb closed his eyes and then gently touched her cheek. "I'm so sorry. You'll never know how much. My family and I owe you more than I can ever repay. I'll go for now and pray to God I'm not too late. But I'm coming back, Ramie. Count on it. I'll make this up to you if it's the very last thing I do."

TWO

RAMIE dragged herself toward the end of the couch, lacking the strength to even make it to her feet. Caleb had departed just a few minutes earlier. Not that he'd introduced himself. But his name had been a strong presence in Tori Devereaux's mind, her anchor to reality as her captor pushed her further and further to the brink of insanity.

She could summon pity and even understanding for Caleb's actions. She could even forgive what he'd done. But she'd never be able to forget. That was worst of all. The images, the memories, engraved permanently in her mind.

Tears burned a trail down her cheek. She felt hollow and empty. Not even like a person. She'd been stripped of all humanity time and time again.

She pushed herself upward, forcing her way through the horror and pain that flooded her. Because the connection to Tori Devereaux didn't end when the scarf was taken away. Ramie was still very aware of what she was enduring. The link could last an hour or a day. Ramie could only pray it ended soon.

She had to run. Had to get as far away as possible and this time make sure no one could find her. So *he* couldn't find her. Because if Caleb Devereaux had found her, then the man stalking her could as well. Never again could she go through what she'd just experienced. She wasn't sure she'd ever recover. Too much, too soon, too fast. She hadn't even healed from the last time she'd located a victim and now she'd been forced to do it all over again.

Numbly she shuffled like an old woman to the tiny bedroom of the cabin. She couldn't even summon hate for what Caleb had done. She understood desperation. Had encountered it time and time again. Who was to say she wouldn't do the same exact thing if she had a loved one whose life hung in the balance?

But no, there were no loved ones for her. She supposed at some point she had a father and a mother. Somewhere. But she'd been abandoned when she was just a baby and had become part of the system. Bouncing from family to family with no real roots.

The discovery of her powers had only alienated her many foster parents. They looked at her with fear, like she wasn't a human being with feelings. And the last foster home where she'd been placed had ended in horror and violence.

Ramie had lived her life alone ever since. She'd never been able to bring herself to trust someone enough to become involved with them. Being isolated didn't bother her. She embraced it.

Except . . . every once in a while, she grieved for what she'd never had and never would. A normal life. Friends and family. All the things most people took for granted. Ramie would never make that mistake. If she were ever blessed enough to have family or friends, she would cherish every single day and never take life for granted. It was impossible for her to do so because she'd witnessed death and unimaginable horror over and over again.

Where to go now? Where could she be assured no one would find her? She simply wanted to disappear.

For good this time. And pray that this time she'd do a better job of covering her tracks. Of hiding. Of making certain no one could find her. Because if the one man who'd focused all his concentration on destroying her ever found her, she would die. And her death wouldn't be quick and merciful. She would die an agonizing death, spending her last breaths praying that each one would be her very last.

THREE

CALEB received word as his plane touched down that Tori had indeed been found at the location Ramie had provided. His brother Beau grimly filled him in on her condition and even though Caleb had known through Ramie exactly what happened it was still a fist to his stomach to know his baby sister had endured such horrific treatment at the hands of her captor.

What pissed him off all the more was that Tori's kidnapper had not been arrested. She'd been alone, in a completely normal house in a peaceful, family-oriented neighborhood just outside of Houston, when the police had burst in and found her chained in the bathroom.

She'd been treated like an animal, barely kept alive with minimal food and water. According to Beau she'd lost a lot of weight and was severely dehydrated. Worse was the fact that Beau had completely broken down on the phone while trying to relay Tori's condition.

Beau was solid. Of the four Devereaux siblings, he was the hardest nut to crack. Never showing his emotions, his features always set in stone. And he'd broken down in tears while talking to Caleb. It was a testament to just how truly terrible Tori's condition was.

Quinn, Caleb's youngest brother, had remained with Tori at all times, riding with her to the hospital, where Beau now awaited Caleb's arrival.

When Caleb strode into Tori's hospital room, he was quickly met by Beau and was motioned outside. Caleb shook his head. He was going nowhere until he saw his sister. He had to see Tori with his own eyes, no matter how bad it was. He needed that reassurance, to know she was alive and finally safe from further harm.

Quinn glanced up from his position at Tori's bedside, anguish in his eyes. Caleb quietly approached, not wanting to disturb Tori's sleep.

"They gave her something so she would rest," Quinn said softly. "She was hysterical and who the hell can blame her? God, Caleb. What she went through."

Quinn choked out the last words and then went

silent, his gaze drifting back to their sister, a glossy sheen in his eyes.

Caleb took in Tori's haggard condition, the deep shadows underneath her eyes, her pallor and the fact that she was far too thin. He sucked in his breath when he saw a handprint on her face to match the one that had appeared on Ramie's when he'd forced Tori's scarf into Ramie's hands. Guilt surged through him all over again.

Tori was here. Hurt, damaged, but *here* with family and a support network. Ramie was alone in a high country cabin with no one. She'd endured the same treatment as Tori and yet she had no one to help pick up the pieces. It just hardened Caleb's resolve to return as soon as Tori was taken care of. He couldn't take back what he'd done, but he could damn well try to make amends. At least make sure she was taken care of and not alone.

"How the hell did you do it?" Beau asked in a quiet voice. "How were you able to pinpoint her location so quickly when we weren't able to find a trace of her before now?"

"Ramie St. Claire," Caleb said simply.

Quinn's surprise was obvious. But then he knew through Caleb that she'd gone off the grid and presumably was refusing to help anyone again. "You got her to help?"

"I didn't give her a choice," Caleb returned quietly. "What I did to her. God, I had no idea. I hunted her down and when she refused to help me, I forced Tori's scarf into her hands and she went straight into the pits of hell."

Beau's expression became savage, anger flaring in his eyes. "Why would she tell you no? What the hell is *wrong* with her that she would refuse to help save someone's life?"

"Because of what it does to her," Caleb murmured. "I didn't *know*. I had no idea. How could I have? And what's worse is that I can't honestly say I wouldn't have still done the same exact thing I did, but at least now I understand *why* she said no."

Quinn cocked his head, confusion in his gaze. "I don't understand. What does it do to her? I thought she was just able to track victims, locate them by touching an object that belonged to them or that was associated with the crime scene."

"She tracks them because she becomes part of them," Caleb said. "I put her there. Just as if she were the victim. Everything that Tori endured? Ramie endured it too. I saw a handprint matching the one on Tori's cheek appear on Ramie's cheek. Ramie was raped as surely as Tori was."

Quinn paled, astonishment and disbelief reflected in his eyes. Beau visibly flinched and the anger that had been present in his eyes just moments before subsided as he stared back at Caleb. Then he closed them, fatigue evident when he next spoke.

"Son of a bitch," Beau muttered. "That's a hell of a note."

"Tell me about it. I feel like a complete bastard for subjecting her to that and even worse of an ass-hole for knowing I'd do it again if it meant having Tori safe and out of the hands of a killer."

"Jesus, what are you going to do? I mean, how is Ramie now?" Quinn asked.

Even more guilt plagued Caleb. He'd been so desperate to get to Tori, to call in her location, that he'd simply done as Ramie had begged. He'd left her alone.

"I don't know how she is," Caleb admitted. "I left her. She begged me to. And my focus was entirely on Tori. But once we get Tori home and on her way to healing I'm going back to make things right with Ramie."

"We all owe her a huge debt," Beau said, his gaze sweeping over their sleeping sister.

"Yes, one I fully intend to repay," Caleb vowed. "What did the doctor tell you?" he asked, changing the subject from the uncomfortable topic of Ramie St. Claire. "How long will Tori have to remain in the hospital?"

"A few days at least," Quinn replied. "She has multiple broken ribs and numerous contusions."

He winced as he said the next. "They need to make sure there's no permanent internal damage and they want to rehydrate her and make sure she's ready to be discharged before doing so."

The three men went utterly silent when a soft moan escaped Tori's lips. Her forehead furrowed and an expression of pain marred her face. She twisted restlessly and tears slid down her cheeks.

Caleb was there in an instant. "Tori, honey, it's me, Caleb. You're safe now. Beau and Quinn are here too."

Slowly, her eyelids fluttered open and then anguish and despair swamped her eyes, turning them to liquid aqua-colored pools. But worse was the shame crowding her eyes. It gutted Caleb that she would be ashamed of what she had no control of.

"Caleb," she croaked.

He cupped his hand over her forehead and pushed back her hair in a soothing motion. "Yes, honey, it's me."

She licked her lips and swallowed, the medication slowing her and making her sluggish.

"How did you find me?" she whispered. "I thought no one would ever find me. That I'd *die* there. He *told* me I would die. He was going to kill me. God, if you hadn't gotten there when you did. He was going to kill me and I prayed that he *would*."

Her words ended in a sob and Quinn buried his face in his hands as Caleb hugged Tori gently to him. Beau stood at the end of the bed, his expression murderous, eyes filled with rage.

"I went to someone like you," Caleb said gently, leaving off the part of Ramie being reluctant—with good reason—to help him. He'd never tell Tori that he'd forced Ramie's compliance.

Tori's brow furrowed and she stared up at him with a puzzled expression. "Someone like me?"

"Well, not exactly," Caleb said, injecting a smile just for her. "After all, there's only one you. But I went to Ramie St. Claire. She's been helpful in finding missing persons before. I gave her your scarf and she was able to locate you."

Tori looked stunned. Her mouth drooped open in astonishment and confusion wrinkled her brow. Then tears filled her eyes.

"If only she could have helped sooner," Tori whispered.

Caleb swallowed and avoided the gazes of his brothers. No matter that he'd just told them what Ramie endured and why she refused, they were condemning her for not being available earlier.

"I owe her so much," Tori choked out. "I'll never be able to repay her. Can I at least thank her? When this is all over with and I go home?"

Caleb swallowed the knot in his throat and he

wiped at a tear from her cheek with the pad of his thumb. "We can only try."

"I'm scared," Tori said, her voice cracking.

Her fingers dug into the thin sheet covering her, but Caleb could see how badly her hands were shaking.

Caleb gently pried the sheet from her fingers and then curled his hand around hers. "What are you afraid of, honey?"

Her grip tightened on his hand, her torn nails digging into his skin. "That he'll come back for me."

Her words fell ominously over the small room and his brothers glanced Caleb's way, fury—and fear—evident in their gazes. Her kidnapper hadn't been arrested. He was even now out there, free, possibly hunting his next victim. Or would he come after Tori since she was the one who got away?

"Listen to me," Caleb said in a low voice. "I know you're scared. God only knows you have the right to be. But me, Beau and Quinn are going to protect you. You'll be under constant guard until this asshole is found and arrested and he pays for what he did to you. I swear it on my life."

"You can't all put your lives and jobs on hold for me," Tori said.

"The hell we can't," Beau clipped out. "You are our number-one priority, Tori. Nothing else is as important."

"We won't let that bastard near you," Quinn said firmly. "And we're going to use every available resource to find him and put him away for life."

Tori didn't look convinced but she nodded and then closed her eyes, the medication pulling her into its embrace.

Caleb kissed her forehead. "Get some rest, honey. We'll be here when you wake up. You need to focus on getting better so we can take you home."

FOUR

CALEB stood in the doorway of the cabin where he'd last seen Ramie, a grim expression marring his face. The cabin was completely empty. Abandoned and looking as though no one had ever been there. She'd left no stamp or fingerprint on the place. Nothing that signaled her presence. He dragged a hand through his hair and closed his eyes as frustration took hold.

He'd fulfilled his vow to Ramie—and himself— to return for her. But she was gone.

He couldn't blame her. Didn't fault her for running hard and fast. If he'd found her, who was to say others wouldn't? And while before he'd considered her selfish, now he understood fully why she was no longer willing to put herself through the agony of finding missing people.

The question plaguing him was whether he

should let it go and walk away, leave her to the peace she wanted. Or did he pursue her again, find her and atone for what he'd done?

He wasn't the kind of man to ever give up. His entire life was a study in relentless pursuit of his goals.

Born to an extremely wealthy, old oil money family whose fortune had only grown for generations, Caleb had taken over the reins of the family at a very young age.

His parents had openly flaunted their wealth. Been involved with society, lived larger than life, and he was convinced that at least his father was involved in shady activity. Their deaths had been suspicious, clouded by the question of whether they were accidental or actual murder. It was a question that to this day wasn't answered.

But from the moment Caleb had taken over the family and inheritance, he'd systematically begun removing them from the grid. Lowering their profile and maintaining avid secrecy. He'd always maintained an extremely high level of security, but it was obvious that it hadn't been enough. Now his focus would be on security and tightening it so that what had happened to Tori would never happen again. Or to Ramie if he could help it.

Caleb's gaze swept over the interior of the cabin, looking for any clue, any sign to point him in the right direction. He already knew the answer to the question he'd posed to himself. He would go after Ramie and from there she would be in the driver's seat. Whatever she wanted, whatever she needed, would be at her disposal. If Caleb had his way, she'd never lift a finger for the rest of her life. Nothing was too much or too big in light of the fact that she'd saved Tori at great personal sacrifice.

Hell, she'd probably kick him in the balls if she ever saw him again. He certainly deserved it even if he couldn't say that he still wouldn't have forced her compliance if he'd known what it did to her. And that ate at him. Knowing he'd do it all over again if it resulted in the same outcome. Tori alive. Safe.

He checked his cell phone for a signal and grimaced when "no service" glared back at him. He walked back out to his SUV and slowly navigated his way back down the mountain. As soon as he had a reliable signal he punched in Beau's number and waited for his brother to answer.

"You find her?" Beau said in greeting.

"No," Caleb said quietly. "How is Tori? Was she okay with me leaving so soon?"

"She's fine. Quinn and I are with her every minute of the day. She's not sleeping worth a damn and she refused to take medication until Quinn finally leaned on her and forced the issue. She can't continue on like this. She's running on empty and she's going to suffer an emotional breakdown if she doesn't rest better and heal."

Caleb closed his eyes. He should be there, damn it. But Tori had Beau and Quinn. Who did Ramie have? All of his research into her background when he'd turned the world over in his search for her told him she had no family. No close friends or even acquaintances. She had . . . nothing.

"I want to move on what we talked about," Caleb said. "I'm coming home and you and I are going to build this security firm from the ground up. Tori will never be a victim again if I have anything to say about it. And if we can help others in the process, so be it."

"I'll get to work on my end," Beau said. "I want to hire only the best."

"Agreed."

"So are you giving up on Ramie?" Beau asked.

Caleb hesitated before finally going with the truth. "No. She wanted to be left alone, in peace, and maybe that's what I should do. But I can't let it go. You didn't see her, Beau. I did. And she has no one. I have to find her and make sure she's okay. I won't rest until I do."

"I understand. We all owe her a huge debt so anything I can do to help find her I'll do."

"We start with the new company," Caleb said. "Then we'll work our way from there."

FIVE

NEVER let your guard down.

It had always been her mantra, but it was more pertinent than ever now. Fear was her constant companion. He'd found her. Somehow he'd found her and he was determined that she would be his next victim.

Obsession.

He was obsessed with Ramie. The one person who'd come close to bringing him down. But close hadn't been close enough. The killer had narrowly escaped capture, but Ramie had brought the authorities right to the location where he'd held his current victim.

He'd tortured the young woman for days. Endless days of pain and sorrow. He'd toyed with her, promising her death and then delaying it.

Before Ramie had dropped off the map, he'd *called* her. He was why she'd run. Because he knew who and what she was and that she was responsible for him losing his prey. In turn she had now become the hunted.

And he was close.

How could he continuously track her every movement?

He was toying with her. Fucking with her for the sake of fucking with her. It had gotten so bad that Ramie didn't dare sleep at night for fear he'd be there, waiting. She was on the move constantly, never staying in the same place for more than one night.

But she could sense he was closer than ever.

When would he tire of his cat-and-mouse game and make his move? And what would she do when he did?

Ramie pulled up to the roadside hotel and parked her small SUV outside number six, the room she'd rented before going out to get something to eat. And to scope her surroundings. Get a feel for what belonged and what didn't.

She forced her mind to go silent. Flush out the panic so her awareness of her surroundings could be sharper. With a killer tracking her every move, she had to remain calm and depend on her heightened senses to stay one step ahead of her pursuer.

Slowly she slipped her hand over the knob of the door to her hotel room but was careful to make no sound or to insert the key into the lock so she wouldn't alert anyone to her presence. She yanked her hand back as though she'd been burned. The sudden flood of evil, hatred and the mocking laugh of her tormenter made her unsteady on her feet. Her knees buckled and she turned desperately, prepared to flee when the door flew open and something dark and ominous grabbed her wrist, hauling her back even as she tried to run.

She struck out violently, fighting back, knowing that if he managed to get her into the room she'd be dead—if she were that fortunate. Because she knew her death wouldn't be easy, nor would it be quick. She'd seen inside his mind. Knew how he thought. All the sick, twisted fantasies he'd lived out through his victims, and hers would be the worst of all. She opened her mouth to scream, but he clamped his free hand over her lips in one bruising motion.

She sank her teeth into bitter-tasting, dirty flesh and was rewarded with instant withdrawal and a yelp of pain.

"You little bitch," he growled in a demonic, fury-laced voice that sent chills cascading down her spine. "You'll pay for that."

She turned, facing evil for the first time outside of her mind, and thrust her knee into his groin. He backhanded her in defense and her face exploded in pain. But he loosened his hold just enough that she could wrench her wrist free of his grasp. She took full advantage of her momentary respite, knowing she might not get another.

She didn't bother going for her vehicle. There was no way she'd be able to get in and drive away before he recaptured her.

So she ran.

Leaving everything she possessed behind, she sprinted toward the main avenue, her aching body protesting the overexertion.

She could hear him behind her, could almost *feel* his breath on her neck. Worse was the oppressive weight of his presence in her consciousness, spewing vile promises of retribution. She'd seen her long, painful death in his mind, knew it for the truth it was. That he would be relentless until he'd achieved his ultimate glory. Removing her existence.

It gave her the much-needed boost to run faster.

Warm blood trickled down her chin, quickly drying in the wind as she put more distance between her and her pursuer.

Where would she go? What would she do? She had nothing to her name, her purse and what little cash she had left behind.

A sob escaped her as she pushed herself even further. She was at her limit. Her reserves had dwindled down to nothing—she had nothing. She'd known that she'd have to stop in the next town. Take the horrible risk that he'd finally catch up to her because she had to stay somewhere long enough to get a job to build her cash back up. So she could run again. But by doing so she risked exactly what had just happened.

Discovery.

Chancing a glimpse over her shoulder, she saw that her attacker had given up. No, that wasn't right. He wouldn't ever simply *give up*. All he'd do is fall back, give her a false sense of security and then strike again when she least expected it. He had an uncanny knack for trailing her, which left her to wonder if he had psychic ability of his own. How else would he be able to anticipate her next move? Had he lived as a shadow in her mind since that horrible day she'd connected to him through his last victim? Had she somehow forged a connection with the very face of evil? God only knew that she hadn't been able to shake him from her dreams, from her every waking moment. Her only reprieve—though short—had been when Caleb Devereaux had shoved his sister's scarf into her hands so many months ago and for a few brief moments she'd experienced something other than the man who stalked her. She'd traded one hell for another.

That awful day on a Colorado mountain had

finally done what no one else had succeeded in doing. It had broken her. Though each time she'd used her abilities to track monsters had helped break her slowly over time, that had been her tipping point. Maybe she'd never heal. Some wounds cut too deep. Too much, too soon after her brush with blood and death from before. She'd felt something truly disconnect inside her when she'd been hurled into Tori Devereaux's mind, gone through every horror the other young woman had experienced.

Maybe it had simply been the last straw. Whatever the case, after Caleb Devereaux had left her to go find and help his younger sister, Ramie had never been the same. Maybe she never would be.

Would death be so bad? It felt to her as if she'd died each and every time she'd slid into the mind of a helpless victim. Most people only faced death once. She'd faced it repeatedly. Maybe in death, she would finally find peace. Except that she refused to allow the man hunting her victory. He would be unstoppable. Promoted to God in his sick and twisted mind. As long as he was focused on her then at least other women would be safe from his sadistic pleasures. That was reason enough to continue fighting.

It was reason enough to survive.

She halted, her legs refusing to take her another

step. A gas station loomed in front of her and she bent over, heaving for breath. Tears burned her eyes as a sense of fatalism enveloped her. It didn't matter that she refused to let the bastard win.

There was nowhere for her to go. No place for her to turn. No safe harbor.

Caleb Devereaux's face flickered in her mind, his parting words to her floating back to haunt her. The genuine regret in his eyes when he realized the consequences of what he'd forced her to endure.

I'm coming back, Ramie. Count on it. I'll make this up to you if it's the very last thing I do.

A year ago he'd torn her world apart and kept her on the endless cycle of running. Perhaps now he was her only salvation.

He owed her. She'd saved his sister. It was time to collect.

She hadn't wanted to go anywhere near him. Didn't *want* to remember what she'd suffered because of what he'd forced on her. But she didn't have any other option available. He was her last and *only* hope. No one else would understand. Who would believe her? Caleb had witnessed first-hand the price she'd paid for his sister's life. There was no way he could ever deny her abilities.

She didn't hate him for what he'd done. Perhaps she should. But in his shoes, could she say she would have done anything differently when the outcome was a saved life? No, she didn't hate him. She didn't feel anything at all except overwhelming weariness and the sense that she'd lost an essential piece of herself to the monsters she'd helped put away. They were a permanent part of her, engraved on her very soul. A stain that could never be removed.

No, she couldn't summon hatred or bitterness toward Caleb Devereaux. Even knowing that if he refused to help her, she was well and truly doomed. But she couldn't blame him if he did refuse. She represented everything she was certain he and his sister wanted to forget. If he helped her, then he reopened a door that had been closed a year ago.

She closed her eyes and took in several steadying breaths. He *had* to help her. She wouldn't entertain any other possibility. She just had to get in touch with him.

First, she needed a safe place to make a phone call. She didn't even know *how* to contact him. She'd done enough research on him to know he was extremely wealthy, his family name old and revered in wealthier circles. But that *hindered* not helped her because it meant she would have a much harder time gaining access to him. She'd be lucky if she even managed to connect with him at all. People like him didn't just answer the phone. There were layers to go through. And after what happened with his sister, he'd be even more guarded than ever.

Contacting him would likely be like trying to phone the president.

All she could do was try to hope for the best. She had to find somewhere to make a phone call. And before she would be able to place a call, she needed Internet access.

Her head pounded and she rubbed her hand over her blood-smeared face.

Think, Ramie, think! Use your mind for something other than touching evil.

The library. Of course.

Relieved to have a semblance of a plan of action, she walked into the gas station and asked for directions to the local library. When the attendant told her it was two miles away, her heart sank. It was a long walk and she'd be pushing it to get there before it closed. She couldn't call a cab because she didn't have a dime on her. And walking out in the open would prove to be a huge risk because *he* was still out there. Waiting. Watching. Not far away. And she might not get a second chance to escape his grasp. He'd be prepared for her to fight back this time.

Knowing she was only delaying the inevitable, she got the directions again and then started out at a brisk walk, watching her surroundings very carefully for any sign of her attacker.

It was minutes until the library closed when she

walked in, the wave of cool air welcome on her face. She shifted uncomfortably under the scrutiny of the librarian, but then remembered she had dried blood on her face and she likely sported a huge bruise as well. She probably looked like a domestic violence victim. That would explain the pity in the eyes of the older woman.

Maybe that would play to her advantage and the librarian would let her use the phone to make her call.

Ramie quickly accessed the Internet on one of the public computers and did a search for Caleb Devereaux. He now owned a security firm, formed in the year after his sister's kidnapping. She had no way of knowing whether he could be reached through it or not but all she could do was try. At the very least maybe she could get a message to him. But how would he contact her back? She had no number, no lodging, no way for him to return a call.

She closed her eyes as despair swept over her. It was all or nothing. One shot. If she couldn't reach him, she had no idea what she'd do. If she couldn't reach him, her death was inevitable.

Quickly committing the phone number to memory, she sucked up her courage and hesitantly walked toward the desk where the librarian stood.

"Ma'am," Ramie said quietly. "Would you be

willing to let me make a phone call? I have nothing. My purse and everything in it was stolen."

"Oh, you poor dear! Is that what happened to your face? Were you mugged?"

Ramie nodded, not feeling one ounce of remorse for the lie.

The librarian pulled out her personal cell phone and extended it over the counter.

"Why don't you go right over there in the corner where there's a place to sit and make your call," the librarian said kindly. "We close in just a few minutes, but I'll stay open until you're finished."

"Thank you so much," Ramie said fervently. "You're very kind. I appreciate this."

The woman smiled and then motioned for Ramie to go.

Ramie punched in the number as she walked toward the chair in the corner. Her entire body ached and she was so tired from all the sleepless nights that she could barely remain upright.

A somber-sounding male voice answered on the second ring.

"Devereaux Security," he clipped out.

"I need to speak with Caleb Devereaux," Ramie said. "It's a matter of life or death."

She flinched, thinking how cliché that sounded. Everyone who wanted to get a call through would say the exact same thing. And well, this was a security firm she was calling. Every call they received was likely a matter of life or death.

"Your name?"

The man sounded bored, as if he did indeed field such calls every day. Fear gripped Ramie's throat. God, don't let this man blow her off.

"Ramie St. Claire," she said, shaking so hard her teeth were chattering, making her words nearly unintelligible. Now of all times she needed absolute clarity. She clamped her jaw shut and spoke through tightly gritted teeth. "As I said it's imperative that I speak to him. If you tell him my name, he'll take my call."

"Hold please."

Boring elevator music flooded the line and Ramie sat there, waiting, hoping. Praying. Dying a little more with each passing second.

The wait went on for several minutes. She glanced nervously up at the desk where the librarian was obviously waiting for her to finish. She was staring expectantly at Ramie, which only served to make Ramie *more* anxious. Despair crept over her shoulders, weighing her down as she realized no one was going to answer. She started to pull the phone down to quietly end the call when a different male voice came over the line.

"Ramie? Is that you? Where are you? Are you all right?"

She'd know his voice anywhere. Could often hear it in her dreams, mixed with the voices of others. Only for some odd reason, she found comfort in his voice and she had no reason to. He'd pushed her those final inches over the brink of insanity. And yet . . .

She squeezed her eyes shut, relief making her weak and shaky. So much so that she felt faint. If she hadn't already been sitting, she would have collapsed on the spot.

"Yes," she said hoarsely. "I need your help, Caleb. You owe me."

She didn't flinch over the demand. He did owe her. There was no excuse for pride when it came to her life.

"Tell me where you are," he demanded. "I'll come to you at once."

She leaned her forehead against her free hand, trying to collect her jumbled thoughts. Her stomach churned, partly in fear, partly in gut-wrenching relief. He'd said he'd come. No questions. No excuses. Just . . . I'll come.

Was she dreaming? Was all of this yet another dream where there was a mixture of Caleb Devereaux and the demons of her past? Was she doomed to forever be haunted by so many faces of evil? But Caleb stood apart, the one good thing in a sea of fear and pain.

"I'm in Shadow, Oklahoma," she finally managed to choke out. "There's someone . . . I'm in trouble. I'm *scared*."

The words came out as scrambled as her thoughts were. She wasn't making any sense but she couldn't seem to get her tongue to cooperate.

"Okay, slow down, Ramie. Calm down and collect your thoughts. Then tell me exactly where you are and what's going on."

The soothing note of his voice was like a warm blanket surrounding her. The safety implied in his words was the sweetest thing she'd ever heard in her life. What if he got to her too late?

"Someone's trying to kill me," she whispered, not wanting the librarian to overhear. "I barely managed to escape him. He was in my hotel room waiting for me, but I touched the knob and I knew he was there. I had to leave my car, my purse, *everything*. I just ran. I have no place to stay, no money. I'm *terrified*."

"Everything will be all right," he said with calm she sure as hell didn't feel. "I'll get you someplace safe to stay tonight and I'll be there as soon as I can."

"But I have no ID," she said, panic fluttering deep in her stomach. "I can't just check into a hotel with no ID and no credit card. And I'm afraid to go anywhere because he's out there waiting for me."

"Ramie, listen to me. I *will* take care of it. I'm looking up the city now to see what I can do. Where are you right now?"

"I'm at the public library, but they're about to close," Ramie said, glancing up at the librarian again.

"Okay, here's what I'm going to do. I'm going to send a car for you and the driver is going to take you out of town to a hotel in a neighboring city. The driver's name is Antonio. Do *not* get in the vehicle with anyone but him. He'll take care of checking you into a hotel and you stay put until I get there."

Relief nearly flattened her.

"Do you understand, Ramie?"

"Yes," she whispered. "How long before he gets here?"

"Ten minutes tops."

"How on earth did you arrange something like that?" she asked in bewilderment.

"It's what I do," he said shortly. "My network is extensive. Now let me get off so I can call my pilot. I'll be there as soon as possible."

She ended the call and slowly walked up to the desk to return the phone.

"Are you all right, dear? Is everything worked out?"

Ramie nodded numbly. "Someone is coming to get me."

"Would you like me to wait with you until they get here?"

Ramie didn't even bother to do the whole pretend I don't want to be a bother thing. She nodded fervently. "Thank you so much. You've been so sweet to me. And yes, I'd feel so much better if you waited with me. I was told it would be ten minutes or less."

The librarian patted her on the hand and smiled reassuringly. "We'll just stay inside until someone comes for you. Then I'll lock up on my way out."

SIX

CALEB'S entire body was tense as the plane touched down in the small municipal airport just twenty minutes from Shadow, Oklahoma. Just as Ramie had disappeared off the face of the earth, she'd reappeared just as suddenly. And she was in trouble.

He'd never given up hope of locating her, of somehow, someway, making up for what he'd done, but as more time had gone by, he'd resigned himself to the fact that he might never find her. But still he kept feelers out and spared no expense in his quest to track her down. At times, in order to assuage his own sense of guilt, he'd told himself that she didn't *want* to be found and that he should just leave her in peace as a way of making amends.

But in the end, she'd come to him.

Maybe he would be able to repay his debt after all. The desperation in her voice kept replaying through his mind. Her fear had been broadcast as loudly as if she sat in front of him. Someone was trying to kill her. Who? He was frustrated by the lack of information he had, but he could hardly risk her life by making her be out in the open answering questions he'd soon have the answers to anyway. He would get to the bottom of things and assess the danger to her, but first he had to get to her and then do whatever it took to ensure her safety. He wouldn't fail her like he'd failed Tori.

His protective instincts were at a full roar. All he could picture was her fragile body huddled on the floor of her mountain cabin, experiencing the unthinkable. Her silent weeping had torn at his gut until his heart lay bleeding on the floor with her.

He would go to any lengths to keep her safe. There wasn't a price too high to pay to the woman who'd gone through hell to save his baby sister.

In the year he'd searched for her, he felt as though he'd gotten to know her, as well as anyone seemed to know a woman whose life had been by all accounts lonely and isolated, even though information was sketchy at best on her. But the image of this vulnerable yet unbelievably strong woman had lived with him every single day until she'd become an obsession. While she might appear fragile, and perhaps she was—now—no woman who'd suffered countless times in her aid of victims of horrific crimes could ever be considered anything but strong and resilient.

It had gutted him when he'd gone through the case files of the others she'd helped. This time with a completely new perspective than when he'd studied up on her to assess how much help she would be in finding Tori. Because now he knew what each of those cases had cost her. He had no idea how the hell, when she endured so much pain, she could continue to offer her assistance. It certainly explained why she'd reached her breaking point.

She had nearly a one hundred percent success record in bringing sick bastards to justice. There were only two instances when the monsters had escaped. One a mere six months before she disappeared and went off the grid, prompting his desperate search for her. The other? Tori's kidnapper was still free. Out there victimizing other women. Was the case six months before what had caused her breakdown? Did she suffer guilt for not having brought the man to justice?

A car was waiting for him and he hurried inside with terse directions to get him to the hotel he'd arranged for Ramie. What Ramie didn't know was that he didn't simply dump her at the hotel with no protection. Antonio plus two other men were strategically placed outside her room and in the lobby so that if anyone tried to get in her room they'd meet with immediate resistance. Until he heard from Ramie exactly what they were dealing with, he was taking *no* chances with her life.

Twenty minutes later, the car carrying him rolled up underneath the hotel awning and Caleb got out, striding into the entrance. He was met by Antonio, who reported that it was quiet and nothing had happened in the time since Ramie had checked in.

Caleb checked his watch, seeing that it was just past two in the morning. He hated to wake her up but then he doubted she was sleeping anyway. She'd sounded too panicked, too frightened on the phone. He didn't imagine she'd slept in days, if not weeks.

"Maintain your post and direct the other two men to do the same," Caleb said as they headed toward the elevator. "I want her under constant watch until I take her out of here."

"Yes, sir," Antonio said crisply. "We won't stand down until you give us the order."

"I appreciate you moving so quickly on this," Caleb said.

Antonio's face darkened. "Whoever the son of a bitch is, I'd say he got his hands on her at least for a few minutes. Her face is a mess. I'm surprised she was able to escape such a close call."

Caleb's thoughts immediately went black. Ramie had briefly mentioned that she'd had a run-in with the asshole, but he didn't realize she didn't escape unscathed. He shook his head, still mystified by a man roughing up a woman so small and delicate.

When he'd seen her the first and only time they'd met face-to-face, she'd looked hollow. Almost as if she'd been dealing with an extended illness. Only now he knew it was far worse and far more draining emotionally and physically than a period of sickness.

The fact that he'd added to her already overwhelming burden, things she had to live with every day, her sleep tortured by the taint of evil she'd confronted time and time again . . . his guilt—and genuine regret—ate at him with every passing day he'd been unable to locate her.

On his darkest days, he'd wondered if she was even still alive. Such desperation and despair as he'd seen in her eyes and then the resignation and fatalism in her features could well drive her to the ultimate act of finding rest at last.

Her death.

If she became reckless—careless—if she simply didn't care any longer whether she lived or died it would make her bolder. Death may well represent her final escape from the hell of her day-to-day reality.

What the hell could he do to help her heal? If she could even ever *be* healed. He saw the toll the events of a year ago had taken—and still was taking—on his sister and she'd only suffered once. Once was enough. But Ramie? She'd undergone the same kind of horror not once or twice. But dozens of times. He had no idea how she coped with it all without shattering into a million pieces.

Maybe she already had. Maybe she'd never be able to pick up the pieces. Maybe there was simply nothing he could do but helplessly stand by while she lost another sliver of her soul, until there was simply nothing left of her but a mere shell of the woman she once was.

She was only twenty-five. Not even to the peak of her life. And yet when he saw her dull, lifeless eyes, she'd seemed far older than her age. More weary. The weight of ten lifetimes, more than most people would ever endure in *a hundred* lifetimes all pressing down on her, suffocating the life right out of her.

But then she'd been helping victims since she was a young girl, when the extent of worry for a child her age usually amounted to making good grades, hanging out with friends and having a boyfriend. Certainly not the oppressive responsibility of having the lives of kidnap victims hanging in the balance, their fate in the hands of someone so young and vulnerable.

It was obvious to him that she'd had no childhood at all and that she'd been forced to grow up and bear adult responsibility far too young.

His heart ached for the girl she once was and for the woman he may have irrevocably damaged in his desperation to save *his* loved one. Had Ramie ever been anyone's loved one? It appeared from everything he'd read that she'd never had a stable family, never enjoyed the unconditional love of family and certainly had no comprehension of a life without the suffocating responsibility she'd been forced to take on at such a tender age.

Weariness and guilt assailed him because he knew in his heart that if he had to do it all over again, he wouldn't have chosen differently. If he hadn't found Ramie precisely when he did, his sister would have died the very next day. But knowing that didn't make the bitter pill any easier to swallow. And it didn't stop him from his determination to ensure she didn't suffer any longer.

"Do you have the key to her room?" Caleb demanded, his impatience rearing its head. He was in a hurry to see for himself just how much damage had been done to her.

Antonio grimaced and shook his head. "She wouldn't allow it. She was scared out of her mind and it was obvious she didn't trust me. I can't say I blame her. She's holed up in her room and I'd be surprised if she answers her door at all. I would have carried her to her room because she looked completely dead on her feet, but she was very careful not to let me touch her. She maintained several feet of space between us, and she locked herself in the minute she got inside the room."

"Fuck," Caleb muttered. "The room is registered to her but also to me. I'll get a key from the desk."

"Won't do you a damn bit of good if she's deadbolted the lock, and in her shoes I'd have done exactly that. When you're scared shitless someone is going to find you and subject you to God only knows what, you don't do something stupid like leave entry into a hotel room to chance. The only way you're getting in there is if she lets you."

SEVEN

RAMIE roused violently, bolting upright in the bed, fear surging, adrenaline racing through her veins. She heard the firm knock at her door. For a long moment she sat in bed, covers pulled tightly to her chin, staring at the door as if expecting it to burst in at any moment. What if *he* had found her?

Her mouth went dry and she couldn't swallow the burgeoning knot in her throat.

It took her another moment to gain her bearings, to remember where she was and that Caleb had said he'd be here as soon as possible. Was it him? Or was it the man she'd narrowly escaped just hours before?

Her hands shook, causing the covers to tremble like rolling ocean waves. She couldn't think for the roar in her ears. She did *not* want to answer the door not knowing what awaited her on the outside.

A peephole. She didn't have to unbolt her door to check the peephole.

She scrambled out of bed just as another knock sounded. And then she heard his voice through the door.

"Ramie? Ramie, it's me, Caleb Devereaux. You can open the door. You're safe now."

Logically she registered who it was, that she recognized his voice, but his assurance that she was safe now didn't provide any comfort because she *knew* she wasn't safe. Maybe she'd never be safe. Even though she'd recognized his voice she still approached the door with caution and rose up on tiptoe to check the peephole.

In the hallway she saw Caleb, his expression grim, his hair looking unkempt as though he'd been dragged out of bed to fly hundreds of miles to where she was. She glanced at the bedside clock and realized that he hadn't slept at all. It was in the early A.M. hours and she'd called him just hours before. He truly must have flown out the instant they'd rung off.

She frowned, her brow furrowing. Why would he have dropped everything to come to her? Yes, she'd said he owed her. She would have said anything at all to get him to help her. But that didn't mean he'd actually do as she'd asked. Or rather begged in her desperation.

And yet here he was. Standing outside her door. Waiting for her to open it. If only she could make herself get rid of the one thing that gave her the illusion of safety. A dead-bolted solid door. One that would be extremely difficult for one man to break down if he wanted inside.

For a moment she simply couldn't get her hands to cooperate. They trembled as she lifted one to unlock the dead bolt. She fumbled with it for several long seconds, unable to get it to work properly for her.

Her palms were sweaty. Even her knees shook. She recognized the signs for what they were. Panic attacks certainly weren't alien to her, even if they'd only begun eighteen long months ago when a killer had escaped the grasp of the police and then single-mindedly began his hunt for her.

By the time she managed to finally free the door, her breaths were coming in rapid bursts. Her chest constricted painfully as she tried to suck in air, but it was as though there were a solid barrier preventing oxygen from reaching her lungs.

She hastily took a step back when Caleb filled the open doorway. She kept backing away, her vision growing hazy, her hands fluttering wildly in her panic.

Caleb took one look at her and swore long and hard. He reached back only long enough to once again secure the door but when he turned his attention back to her, she felt her legs give way and she sank like a deflated balloon to her knees.

Her hands flew out in front of her, slapping noiselessly against the carpeted floor in an effort to prevent her fall. Caleb was beside her in an instant, his strong hands hooking underneath her armpits. He lifted her effortlessly and before she could muster any panic over her proximity to him he plopped her gently down on the edge of the bed but was careful to keep one hand on her shoulder to steady her.

"Breathe, Ramie," he said in a soothing, even tone. "Breathe before you pass out."

She closed her eyes, tears stinging the lids. She hated the helplessness that seemed to grip her with growing frequency. Control was something she valued, was something she *needed* in an effort to maintain her sanity. But over the past months she had been anything but in control. She could feel herself gradually sliding away with each passing day. When would it end? Would it ever truly end for her? Peace was an elusive, taunting desire. Just one night where she slept free of the monsters she'd helped imprison and the torment they caused—still caused in her shattered mind.

"Ramie, look at me."

Startled by the firmness of his command and his terse tone, her eyelids fluttered open and her gaze lifted falteringly to his. Then he lowered himself to one knee in front of her so she didn't have to crane her neck to look up at him. He gathered her hands in his, ignoring her visible flinch at his touch.

She braced herself for the tide of emotion to swamp her. To be filled with whatever darkness he hid from the rest of the world. Her gift was a sick twist of fate. As though fate was playing a cruel joke and laughing at her expense. Because she could only sense the *bad* in people. Underlying evil. Malevolence or bad intentions. She was never able to share the *good*. People's happiness, their joy, their celebration of life. Only what they tried to hide, what they never wanted others to know about them.

She could ferret out people's deepest, darkest secrets as though she were somehow responsible for being the judge and jury over their conscience. It wasn't a gift she wanted. Certainly wasn't something she'd ever asked for. She wasn't qualified to cast judgment. She only wanted to survive, to *live*. To enjoy something as simple as an ordinary day without the oppressive weight of so much evil bearing down on her. Was that so much to ask? At times she felt as though Ramie St. Claire no longer existed, that she'd *become* the very evil she tried so hard to extinguish.

But as Caleb's hands tightened around hers, all

she could feel was unwavering resolve. No blackness, no evil taint on his soul. And it wasn't as though she picked up on his resolve because her mind had touched his. It was clear in his eyes, his expression. Any idiot could see that he was determined, but then she'd never thought him anything else. After all, he'd tracked her down, ruthlessly forcing her to help find and save his sister.

She should be furious. She should be screaming at him for the ultimate betrayal. He'd sent her back to *hell*. And yet she couldn't summon anything but the yawning numbness overtaking her with every passing day that her *own* death approached. Because the man hunting her *would* find her. It wasn't a matter of if but when. She was only delaying the inevitable. Fighting for each new day and hoping it wasn't her last. And it was no way to live. So much fear. And . . . resignation. It should fill her with self-loathing that she'd accepted the inevitability of her death. It made her weak. Like she'd given up. But if she'd truly given up all hope, she wouldn't have called Caleb in her desperation. She wouldn't have reached out for help and protection.

What if . . . What if he truly could keep her safe? What if he could prevent her agonizing death at the hands of a madman? She was afraid to hope, to let herself be lulled into a false sense of security. And yet she couldn't quite prevent the fledgling glimmer of hope from unfurling in the deepest part of her soul.

"Look at me. Watch me. Breathe deep. In through your nose and out your mouth. You can do this."

Her pulse was a rapid staccato against her skin. She stared helplessly back at him, a single tear trailing warmly down her cheek, a contradiction to the icy chill that held her in its grip.

"Don't cry, Ramie," he said in a gentle voice. "You're safe now, I swear it. But you have to breathe for me. Like this."

She watched as he demonstrated sucking in deep breaths, his nostrils flaring, and then expelling the air, the warmth of his breath on her chin. Some of the terrible panic began to ease. Slowly, her lungs opened up and allowed a shaky intake. She shuddered violently, shaking off the chokehold anxiety had on her.

"Nice and easy," he soothed. "You need to slow it down." He glanced down at one of the hands he still held, his fingers circled gently around her wrist. "Your pulse is way too fast."

She had yet to say a word to him. He'd done all the talking. And now that her panic attack was abating, she had no idea what to say at all. He was here. He'd come. He'd responded to her plea for help. What could she tell him? Would he even believe her?

His expression grew dark, his eyes flaring with anger. It was instinctive for her to recoil when he lifted a hand toward her face. He frowned even harder at her reaction.

"I'm not going to hurt you, Ramie," he murmured.

He touched the corner of her mouth where the bruise and dried blood she still hadn't washed away were on her skin. His touch was infinitely gentle and once more she marveled at the fact that her mind wasn't thrown into the instant turmoil that was usually the result when people touched her.

Oh, she sensed anger. Deep, seething rage. But she knew it was directed at the man who'd struck her. The man who wanted to kill her. She could sense nothing from him, which meant he had no dark secrets. No violent tendencies. All she could feel was hatred toward the man who'd struck her.

"Now, tell me what you can," Caleb said, no hint of impatience in his voice. "You said someone was trying to kill you. I need to know every single detail if I'm going to be able to protect you."

It was the way in which he said *protect you* that struck a chord inside her. He hadn't said *help her.* He'd said *protect* in a possessive tone, one she found comforting. The first time in over a year she'd enjoyed one brief moment of comfort and . . . peace. The peace she was so desperate to achieve.

They sat there in silence, Caleb's fingers still a gentle caress on her face, when she realized he was waiting for her response. For her to say something instead of numbly staring at him like a brainless idiot.

God, where to start?

Weariness assailed her. Fatigue crashed into her like the surf against a rocky coast. She felt more battered and bruised in her heart and soul than she did from her stalker's physical attack hours before.

"I don't know where to start," she whispered. "It all sounds so . . . crazy. I wouldn't even believe my story coming from someone else."

His fingers fell from her face and back to her hand, rubbing over the top in a circular pattern meant to soothe and calm. Then he simply laced his fingers with hers and gave them a gentle squeeze.

"Start wherever you like. I'll listen. And I'll damn sure believe you."

She sucked in a steadying breath and then let it out, her shoulders sagging with the effort.

"A year and a half ago I helped locate a kidnapping victim. What that poor girl went through was horrifying."

She shivered just saying the words. No matter how hard she tried to block it from her mind it was there, image after image of blood, pain and impending death thick in her memory. It was as fresh as if it had happened yesterday and not eighteen months ago.

"And what *you* went through as well," he murmured.

Regret was stark in his eyes. Sincere remorse was etched into his features.

"Yes," she whispered. "What I endured as well."

"Go on," Caleb encouraged.

"The killer was never apprehended. And I say killer because though he didn't kill the victim I located, there were others. So many others. I was only able to save the one."

She squeezed her eyes shut as grief welled to the surface, threatening to completely consume her. Then she reopened her eyes and focused her gaze on Caleb.

"He's the one trying to kill me. He's been hunting me for months. He's why I tried to hide where no one could find me. And yet he somehow manages to find me no matter where I go. He's always there. I think . . ."

She broke off and lowered her gaze because this is where it got crazy. Caleb may well think she'd lost what remaining sanity she possessed.

"You think what?" he asked softly.

"I think he has psychic abilities himself. I think

it's why he's obsessed with me. It has to be why he keeps finding me. Why I'm constantly having to look over my shoulder. I swear at times I can feel his breath on my neck. He was waiting inside my hotel room today. I knew when I touched the knob that he'd been there but before I could run, he yanked the door open and grabbed me."

Caleb's eyes grew murderous, murky like a thundercloud.

"So, you've been running for a year and a half?" he demanded.

She shook her head slowly. "No. He waited. Just when I thought I had moved on and somewhat made peace with the ordeal of locating his victim he contacted me. He called me. And I don't know how he got my number. At the time I had a stable residence but no landline. Just a cell phone. And he began taunting me. Telling me what he would do to me and how my death wouldn't be fast and that in the end I'd beg him to kill me and end my pain and misery."

"Son of a bitch!" Caleb swore.

He pushed to his feet and began pacing back and forth at the foot of her bed. He paused briefly and turned, facing her again. He ran a hand raggedly through his hair and then gripped his nape in a gesture of frustration.

"I forced you out of hiding," he said in a grim

voice. "You left because of me. Because you were afraid if I found you then others could too."

Ramie wouldn't lie, even to make him feel better. Her tone had no anger or resentment. Just matter-of-factness. "It was the longest I'd ever remained in one place. I think it was the only time he didn't find me or at least he didn't make his presence known. But if I'm right and he's psychic then he would have known. He enjoys the thrill of the hunt. It's a high for him. He's a trophy hunter. You know, like hunters or fishermen have their own record books and when someone breaks the old record, there's this sense of glory, an adrenaline rush that is nothing compared to before then. He lives to taunt me. He'd like to lull me into believing I've escaped him and when I don't expect him there he is. He wants me to suffer. I'm his trophy kill," she whispered. "The kind hunters have preserved and mounted on their walls, the one that gets the special place above the fireplace mantel."

He knelt back in front of her. He took both of her hands, drawing them together in his clasp. Then he stared her directly in the eyes, remorse brimming in his gaze.

"I'm sorry," he said hoarsely. "God, I'm sorry, Ramie. I didn't know. I couldn't have known what it does to you. Or that I'd lead you back into the hands of a killer."

"Can you honestly say you wouldn't have done the exact same thing even if you *had* known?"

Her voice reminded him of cracking ice after a winter storm, though rare this far south, and the sound of the tree branches splintering away, their burden too great to bear any longer. He refused to allow her to slide away from him, like water through his fingers. He curled those fingers into tight fists as if to prevent that very thing from happening.

He closed his eyes and lowered his head. "No. God forgive me, but no, I would have done anything to save my sister. I know you hate me. You have every right to. But as you said, I owe you, and I fully intend to repay my debt to you."

"I don't hate you," she said in a low voice. "I don't even blame you. In your shoes I would have done the same for a loved one."

"How can you not hate me when I damn near caused your death? When I forced you to endure being brutalized by a psychopath? You may not hate me, Ramie, but I damn sure hate myself for what I did."

She reached out her hand and slid it gently down his cheekbone before cupping his jaw. He visibly flinched and his breath caught. He went so still that she couldn't even detect his breaths.

Warmth spread through her hand and up her

arm before spreading through her chest like a wild-fire. She yanked her hand away, appalled by the familiar way she'd touched him. But he caught her hand and carefully put it back to his cheek, keeping his hand over hers so it was trapped.

"Desperation makes us do the unthinkable. How can you hate yourself for being able to save your sister? How does it help your sister that you hate yourself? Never let her sense you regret your actions because those actions saved her from certain death. I'm sure she's very grateful to you for her life."

"She's grateful to *you*," Caleb said gruffly. "You are the one she owes her life to."

"You providing me sanctuary is payment enough if you feel you're in my debt."

"Count on it," he vowed. "You're coming home with me, Ramie. I formed a security firm with my brothers after Tori's abduction. I swore never to be without the right tools to ensure the safety of my family. We hire only the best."

"I need the best," she said in a low voice filled with conviction. "Because he's always only a foot-step behind me. No matter where I go. No matter what I do. And until he's taken down, all the women he kills will be my fault. I can't live with that guilt any longer."

Caleb emitted a soft curse as he slid his hand

underneath her chin, framing it between his thumb and the rest of his fingers. His gaze bored into her unwaveringly.

"I *will* protect you, Ramie. I don't make promises I can't keep."

EIGHT

CALEB watched a myriad of emotions flicker and swirl in Ramie's smoky gray eyes. The pupils were slightly dilated, making her eyes appear enormous in the delicate bone structure of her face. She was thin. Perhaps too thin because there was no spare flesh at her cheeks or eyes and her shoulders were narrow, her collarbone pronounced, making hollows between it and her neck.

He could circle her wrists with a thumb and one finger and she *felt* delicate. As though she would simply break if someone handled her with anything but the utmost care. And yet she was hauntingly beautiful. Not the sort of woman he was normally attracted to but he realized he was indeed attracted to her. The idea of another man causing her harm infuriated him beyond the fact that no woman should ever be brutalized by a man. It felt personal to him. As though she were *his* woman and another man had put his hands on her.

The idea that she would somehow blame herself for him still being at large, out there hunting new victims—God only knew how many there were that no one ever knew about or discovered. If he had anything to do with it, he was going to make sure she absolved herself of any ridiculous blame over the fact that one out of dozens had escaped the grasp of the authorities.

He paused a moment, his brows furrowing as he considered his sudden vow. Yes, he owed her a great deal, and yes, he would ensure she was safe, that nothing would ever touch her again. But to take on the monumental task of absolving her guilt?

It was an arrogant assumption on his part to think he would bring her anything but more pain, more regret. But if he could even bring her a small measure of peace, anything but the hell she must endure on a daily basis, then he would move damn mountains to make it so.

He frowned again when he took in the dried blood and the bruise that had already formed on her chin and mouth area. He released her hands, carefully placing them back in her lap before he pushed upward to his feet. He held up one finger to her.

"Don't move. I'll be right back."

The instant fear that sparked in her eyes made

him angry all over again at the bastard who'd made her life a living hell for the last year and a half.

"I'm not leaving the room," he said gently. "I'm just going to the bathroom to get a warm washcloth so I can wipe the blood and see how badly you're bruised."

Her hand shot upward, a faintly puzzled look in her eyes as though she'd forgotten all about her injury. She winced when she pressed too hard on the bruise and he reached out to tug her hand back downward in a silent command for her not to touch it and cause herself more pain.

He strode into the bathroom and turned the faucet on, letting the water grow hot before dampening and then wringing out a washcloth. Ramie looked relieved when he reappeared from the bathroom as if she truly had believed he'd somehow disappear. He hated the fear in her eyes. Wished he could wipe it away like the blood he planned to wipe from her face. But he knew no matter how much reassurance he gave her that it would take time for her to trust him. And it had suddenly become all-important that she *did* trust him. Why? He wasn't sure exactly.

It could be that he absolutely believed that all debts should be repaid, no matter the price. And Ramie had certainly suffered enormously because of his actions a year ago. There was no way to ever fully repay her, but he'd do anything he could to at least partially remove the burden of his and his family's debt to her.

But that wasn't his sole reason for being here, hundreds of miles from his family. Away from his sister who still so desperately needed his emotional support. Tori was still infinitely fragile, a shadow of her former self. Vibrant. Confident. Full of zest for life. That bastard had taken those qualities away from her and Caleb feared she'd never get them back. Caleb could kill him for that alone, never mind that *two* women had suffered at his hands.

As was the case in his search for Ramie, he wouldn't give up until his sister's kidnapper was found and brought to justice. Caleb would prefer to kill the bastard with his own hands. He'd feel no remorse whatsoever for doing so. But death was far too easy for him. Caleb wanted him to live in hell every day and for him to live a long life. Behind bars.

Caleb knelt once more in front of Ramie, who hadn't moved so much as an inch during the time he was in the bathroom. Gently, he began to wipe away the crusted, dried blood, and he cursed softly when she visibly winced.

"I'm sorry. I didn't mean to hurt you."

She shook her head in refusal. "It's okay. You didn't hurt me."

He didn't argue over the lie. He'd seen pain flicker in her eyes a brief moment. He just made sure he was gentler with her when he removed the last of the blood.

When he was finished, he leaned back and cupped her chin, tilting her bruised chin to the light so he could further inspect the damage.

"It's not too bad," he said. "If your jaw was broken there would be a lot more swelling. Still, you need to be careful and let me know if you continue to have pain so we can take you in for X-rays."

Her cheeks flushed with color and she glanced away, embarrassment crowding her eyes.

"I can't afford to have X-rays," she said in a low voice. "I have no medical insurance and I haven't worked since . . . since *him*. He took everything from me. My home, my job. Peace. I've not experienced a single day of well-being since I established an irrevocable link to him. He took . . . everything," she whispered. "I was down to my last few dollars but I don't even have that now. I had to leave my purse, my identification, everything when I ran from the hotel. And now I have nothing. Without ID I don't exist. It's as though he's already gotten what he wants most. My death."

Caleb's mood blackened. He was seized with murderous rage. Not only for what was being done to her now—stalked, hunted like an animal and taunted with her own death—but also for what had been done to her before.

"You will not *ever* have to worry about money— or health insurance—again."

He was surprised he could even get the words out through his tightly clenched teeth or that his rage wasn't reflected in his statement.

She lifted startled eyes and then her cheeks turned a dull red. "I don't need your charity, Caleb. You don't owe me anything. I'll make it. I always have."

His temper spiked before he could control it. "You are not some kind of goddamn charity case. Do you even realize the prices you could command for what you do? That victims' families would pay *any* amount to get back a lost loved one?"

Her eyes widened in horror. "I could never do that! What it would boil down to is *blackmail*. Hey, I'll find your kid, wife, mother, loved one but, oh, by the way, my abilities don't come cheap. Do you realize how . . . *mercenary* . . . that would make me? I couldn't live with myself having money stained with violence and death. The mere idea is repulsive!"

"And so you suffer in silence. Alone. No one to comfort *you* while the victims are surrounded by family and loved ones. But who do you have,

Ramie? Who picks up the pieces for you when you shatter and fall apart? I realize money isn't a cure-all but it can damn well make living a little easier, and anything is better than you having to scrape by, going without, and being constantly on the run from some deranged lunatic who wants to break you down, piece by piece until there's nothing left. No escape."

She stared bleakly at him, telling him without words that he'd struck a chord within her, and he was kicking himself for being so blunt. His words had to hurt her. It brought back with startling clarity just how dire her situation was. And he saw something in her eyes that made him want to put his fist through the wall.

Defeat.

Her giving up and accepting the hopelessness of her situation. Damn it, but that had not been his intention. He simply wanted to let her know that she was no longer alone. No longer without someone to turn to. Defeat was simply the absence of hope and she needed that more now than ever before. He wanted to provide her a safe harbor.

What was it she had said? She needed sanctuary. He'd make damn sure he provided her with *anything* she needed. And as far as her not accepting "charity"? She was just going to have to deal with it, because there was no way in hell he was leaving to chance any aspect of her protection, well-being and the financial support she needed so badly. Whether she liked it or not she was now fully under his care and protection and that meant in all areas. Not just her physical well-being.

And he wanted her to trust him. To believe that he would follow through with his promise, because once he made a commitment he *always* followed through. It would take her time to fully trust in his motives, to believe that he wouldn't betray her. He knew it wouldn't happen today. Or even the next day. But he was determined to slowly but surely win something so precious as her faith and trust in him.

He wanted to be someone she could depend on, perhaps the one person who hadn't failed her in her young life. He'd be damned if he became just another statistic in the list of people who'd let her down, draining her *capability* to put her faith in another living soul.

That was all going to change. Starting now.

He had his pilot on standby because he had no intention of keeping Ramie here and vulnerable to attack even a second after they decided on a course of action. But just because he was determined to take over didn't mean that he wouldn't keep her fully apprised of his plans. True, he had no intention of taking no for an answer, but he'd at least offer her the respect he owed her and not keep her in the dark.

Because she feared the unknown, and he knew she was still grappling with whether or not she could believe in his ability to protect her. She had no way of knowing that he intended to utilize every resource at his disposal—no matter the cost—in his effort to ensure her absolute safety.

"Do you have anything at all?" he asked carefully, mindful of her pride and her potential embarrassment over her circumstances.

And yet color still stained her cheeks and once more shame darkened her gray eyes to the color of a storm.

"No," she whispered. "Everything I own was in that hotel room and I dropped my purse when I fled because I didn't want anything to interfere in my getting away."

"Smart," he said sincerely. "You did the right thing absolutely. Nothing is more important than your life."

She blinked with obvious surprise over his statement and a string of obscenities burned his lips but he held them in check. She acted as though someone placing such importance on her life was an original concept.

Had the people she'd helped before expressed any gratitude? Did they, like him, have no idea what it cost her each time she delved into the twisted mind of a killer? How could the idea have been planted in her mind that her life wasn't worth anything?

"Since you have nothing to pack, it will make our departure much faster," he said matter-of-factly.

Again she looked confused. "Where are we going?"

"Home, Ramie. I'm taking you home."

Sadness and resignation pooled in her eyes. "I don't have a home."

"You do now. I'm taking you to my home—*your* home now. I maintain very tight security since Tori was abducted. I thought I maintained high security measures before her kidnapping but it's obvious I utterly failed in that area. My firm employs the very best money can buy. They don't come cheap but they're worth every penny if they keep my family—and you—safe."

She stared at him, a stunned look on her face. "When I called you to ask for help I didn't expect this, Caleb. I certainly don't expect you to move me into your home. I just thought you could offer some kind of peripheral protection."

"And that's precisely what I intend to do," he said calmly. "You staying in my home ensures your safety. It's the safest place for you to be. My house likely has more security than Fort Knox."

He smiled at the end, hoping to lighten the mood

and make some of the seemingly permanent sadness in her eyes ease with his exaggeration. Well, except that it was only a slight exaggeration because to a normal person his security measures *would* be deemed extreme and over-the-top, but he'd be damned if anyone accessed his home or were able to get to his family. Never again.

He was rewarded by a tiny smile and he was fascinated by the dimple that appeared in one cheek. He'd never seen her smile. Even the slight smile transformed her entire face. It brushed away some of the fatigue that seemed permanently etched in her features and she suddenly looked as young as he knew her to be.

But then what had given her cause to smile over the last year and a half? And even before then since she'd been immersing herself in evil since she was sixteen years old. Had she been as somber as a teenager as she was as an adult? It was damn hard to be lighthearted enough to smile when every second of every day she wondered if she would die at any time.

He added that to his growing list of things he vowed to do for Ramie. He wanted to make her smile again. To be able to laugh and take joy in living instead of merely surviving. Life was supposed to be filled with both highs and lows, but hers had been a study in lows with none of the highs to balance it out. Not many people could survive such an existence, but in his limited exposure to her, he'd learned that if nothing else, she was a survivor. Far tougher than she gave herself credit for. A normal person would have crumbled under the pressures she faced years ago. Or they would have simply given up and made it easy for a killer to find them, accepting the inevitability of their death. No matter what Ramie said or even thought, Caleb knew she simply wasn't capable of giving up.

But then her smile slipped and a troubled look took its place. "I can't stay with you forever. I can't hide forever. I won't live my life like that. Death would be preferable to waking up every morning and wondering if it's your last sunrise. It's no way to live."

Sorrow soaked her every word. Her emotional pain was as evident as if she had a sign plastered to her chest advertising that fact. It made him want to pull her into his arms and hold her. Offer her some measure of comfort. But she seemed extremely wary of being touched and he didn't want to do anything that made her uncomfortable around him.

But he did want to know if she feared him. It would gut him if she were afraid *he* would hurt her in any way.

"Ramie, why are you afraid to let me touch you?" he asked gently.

He purposely kept his tone measured and more inquisitive rather than defensive or that he was angry she was afraid of him. God only knew she had sufficient reason to fear men. She'd lived in the minds of the worst the male sex had to offer.

She shrugged one small shoulder. "I don't like being touched by anyone. It's just my automatic response to shun contact with others. Because when someone touches me I see their worst secrets. I see and feel the evil in them. Never the *good*. Only the worst. If I could feel joy, love or even genuine happiness or just *something* positive then at least that would balance the scales and maybe I could deal more with the darkness that stains people's souls. But my gift is the worst sort of curse because I'm only capable of knowing the *evil* people try to hide."

Caleb's brow furrowed and an uneasy sensation prickled his nape. "And when I touched you? What did you feel?"

He knew he sounded defensive now, despite his earlier determination that he not sound so, but knowing someone could read things no one else could possibly know about him unsettled him. He didn't want her having access to his thoughts. He was ruthless when it came to the protection of his family. He was ruthless when it came to business. Both traits could very well damn him in Ramie's eyes.

"I'm not a mind reader," she said wearily, as if she had indeed read his thoughts despite her denial. "It's hard to explain. It's not that I pick out exact thought patterns. It's more of a tangible thing that I *feel*, not *know*. I see things. Events. Actions. But I don't actually read people's thoughts. I sense emotions—negative ones—not good ones. Maybe I could handle it better if I ever got to feel goodness in people. Maybe I wouldn't be so cynical about human nature and the capacity in us all to be bad or at the very least gray. If it makes you feel any better, or at least not judged by me, I didn't sense anything evil. Or bad. Just . . . determination. And that's not a bad quality. At least not in my estimation. But then my opinion of you should hardly matter. I'm no one to you and what I think shouldn't even give you pause."

Caleb's lips tightened, because her opinion did matter to him. And maybe it shouldn't. But it had suddenly become all-important to him that she think him a good man, despite his thoughts. That she would eventually be able to trust him.

"Your gift isn't infallible then. I'm not a good man, Ramie. In fact I am *quite* capable of killing and of hurting someone without hesitation if I deem them a threat to someone I love."

"But don't you see?" she asked in a soft voice. "Protecting someone from evil *isn't* evil itself. It doesn't make you bad that you want to punish those who truly are a threat to your family. All I sensed from you was unwavering resolve and I didn't need to be in your head to see that. It's written all over your face and in your eyes. No one needs to have my gift—or rather curse—to determine how resolved you are."

"But you said you could pick up violence. And my thoughts most assuredly *are* violent."

She smiled, only the second smile he'd been gifted with and it took his breath away because he caught a glimpse of what the real Ramie must have been like before her curse took her down a path she couldn't return from.

"What I pick up on are people's true natures. While you may *entertain* violent thoughts—revenge, retribution, even murder—that isn't the true essence of who and what you are. I guess you could say my gift reveals the true heart of a person. Some people are inherently evil. Others are inherently good no matter if they deviate from their true nature in certain circumstances. But I have a way of seeing through a façade to the very soul of people and while our actions and words may speak differently, the soul is unchangeable. It remains constant. Some people are able to fight their true nature while others give in more readily to the darkness inside them. Even embrace it."

Listening to her calmly explain away such an unbelievable gift as casually as someone might discuss the weather was mind-boggling to him. It wasn't as if he didn't believe or have faith in her gift. He just hadn't realized the true *extent* of her abilities. He'd ignorantly assumed that it was a simple black-and-white matter where she touched something belonging to the victim and was able to trace the path back to them. He'd never once considered that her capabilities went so much deeper and were so profound—almost *spiritual* in a sense. Because only God was supposed to know the true heart and soul of a person. Only God could judge intent.

Caleb could well understand now why she'd led such a solitary existence. A reclusive who didn't surround herself with people. How would she ever be able to protect herself from anyone? If people knew the extent of her gift she would be in constant danger. People would kill to silence the truth about themselves. It was no wonder what little he'd been able to discover about her was sketchy at best.

He'd once thought her selfish, back when he was frantically trying to locate her in order to save Tori. He'd deemed her selfish for purposely disappearing from the public eye and refusing to help others desperate to recover a loved one.

God, what an ass he'd been. Now that he *knew* what it cost her each time she traced a line back to the victim, he couldn't imagine why she'd done it for as long as she had.

But now that he was assured that his touch wasn't harmful to her, he carefully pulled her into his arms, watching for any sign that this wasn't something she wanted. But he met with no resistance. She melted into his embrace and even buried her face in his chest, her head tucked snugly under his chin.

Her breaths were coming in ragged spurts and her chest heaved against him. He yanked her back in a hurry, worried he'd caused her yet another anxiety attack, but what he saw filled him with more dismay than if she had been suffering one.

She was crying. Heaving, heart-wrenching, completely silent sobs. Tears rolled down her cheeks, leaving damp trails in their wake. It was as if the final barrier had come down and something so simple as him offering a comforting hug had completely unraveled her.

"I'm not even sure I'm sane anymore. I feel . . . broken," she said around the tears that seemed to be streaming faster the more she spoke. "I'm not sure anyone can help me or if they even *should*. The person stalking me is a complete sociopath. He thinks nothing of killing anyone he feels is an obstacle to his end goal. Anyone I'm around is in danger. And I can't let your sister go through hell again. Not because of me."

"Do you forget she escaped hell *because* of you?" he asked softly.

She went silent, allowing his question to go unanswered, but she could hardly refute his statement of truth.

"And what is his end goal, Ramie? You said that he would kill anyone posing an obstacle to it." Even though Caleb had a very good idea, he wanted confirmation from Ramie. Even though he *knew*. And it was a stupid question.

"Me," she whispered. "His end goal is me. And until he gets to me, countless other women will suffer horrifically *because* of me. How can I save myself knowing that other women have to die in order for me to stay out of his grasp? How can I live with that on my conscience? That he won't stop torturing and killing other innocent victims until he finally achieves his ultimate goal? *Me*."

NINE

CALEB stared at her in a mixture of *what the fuck* and absolute disbelief. "You can't possibly think that the deaths of his past victims and any future victims he tortures are your fault. You're not a stupid woman, Ramie. Even you have to recognize the idiocy of such an assumption."

She looked angered by his statement. Her cheeks flushed with color and impatience flared in her eyes as though he simply wasn't getting the point. Oh, he got it all right. And it didn't make a goddamn bit of sense to him.

Her fingers curled into tight balls and she pressed one fist down on top of her thigh, repeating the motions as she spoke.

"Were he not so focused on me, and were I not so hard to pin down, then he wouldn't be so hungry for his next victim. The longer I keep him at bay, the more frustrated he'll become and he'll utilize substitutes for me. Because I'm the only woman who manages to evade him at every turn. Not because I'm smarter than he is or that I somehow am able to outwit him. I've just been *lucky*. But my luck won't hold out forever. And part of me wishes he *would* catch me because I know exactly what I'm dealing with and if I died I'd damn sure make sure he goes to hell with me."

"That makes no goddamn *sense*," he said, voicing his earlier thoughts. "I swear I want to shake you. That's the dumbest thing I have ever heard. You are not responsible for the decisions a maniac makes. You are not responsible for him torturing, degrading and ultimately killing his victims. Do you honestly think he would just quit after you? Hell, he'd think himself invincible if he managed to bring down the one woman who's proven to be his biggest challenge. And I'd be willing to lay odds that's why he's so obsessed with you. Because other victims are easy. They offer him no challenge. He enjoys the chase and the fact it *has* proven so difficult. It will only make him that much more egotistical if he *does* succeed in killing you. He's going to believe he's invincible. God of his own twisted universe. Because after you, how *could* he fail to bring down his next target? He's become obsessed with you because you're his Holy Grail."

He knew he'd scored a point with his logic. Ramie frowned, her gaze thoughtful. Her hand went still, her fist pressing hard into her thigh. She chewed on her bottom lip and then let out a long sigh, closing her eyes as fatigue and stress marred her forehead.

"I guess I never imagined beyond him being able to capture me."

She nodded slowly as she said the next, opening her eyes and fixing her gaze at some distant point beyond him.

"But no, you're right. I think he would only get worse, grow bolder and more confident once he managed to do away with me for good. I'm a thorn in his side. No one has ever come as close as I did to capturing him, or even figuring out who he is, and there seems to be no connection between his victims. No similarities, personality traits. Nothing. Just a thirst for torture and degradation that has his victims *wishing* for death."

"Do you know his name? *Any* identifying information?"

She threw him an impatient look. "Don't you think if I knew how to find him that I would have already done so? I'd kill him myself and damn the consequences if it meant eradicating his presence on earth. I'd willingly spend the rest of my life in prison if it meant no more women had to suffer the torture he so loves to heap on his victims."

He frowned. Not only at the utter conviction in her voice, but because he didn't understand.

"But you were so specific when you gave me the information on how to locate my sister even though he too slipped from our grasp. It was a case of misfortunate timing, because the police burst in when her kidnapper had left for a short period of time, and with so many police surrounding the house, he would have been alerted to their presence if he tried to return."

"He's not like the others," she said wearily. "I told you earlier that I think he may have psychic abilities of his own, but you probably think I'm crazy."

Caleb held up a hand. "I don't think you're crazy at all. I believed in your abilities before I ever met you." He hesitated before saying the rest, because his sister's own psychic ability was a very closely guarded secret within his family. But he also felt it would go a long way in helping Ramie trust him. If he first offered her *his* trust.

"Tori has psychic gifts. It's why I had no problem believing in yours. Though, even if I hadn't been a confirmed believer you've been one hundred percent accurate in all of the cases you've assisted on."

Ramie's eyebrow shot upward. "Your sister is *psychic*?"

"In a manner of speaking, yes. But let's go back to why you think the guy stalking you is psychic."

Ramie rose from the bed as if she couldn't remain still a second longer. She mimicked his earlier actions, pacing back and forth, concentration marring her features.

"There's no other logical explanation." She laughed a dry, brittle sound that in no way reflected amusement. "What you don't understand about my abilities—one of the many things you didn't or don't understand—is that my connection to the victim and their attacker doesn't go away immediately."

Caleb felt himself pale as blood leached from his face. "What does that mean exactly?"

"It means that I maintain a connection to both killer and victim. Sometimes for hours. Sometimes for *days*. Or in the case of the man stalking me, the connection has never truly been severed."

"Dear God," he whispered, "so your torment goes long beyond what you initially experience. How in God's name do you survive it?"

She shrugged as though it was no big deal, but Caleb knew better. He knew how long it had taken Tori to regain a semblance of her old self and she was *still* dealing with the aftermath an entire year later. And Ramie didn't endure it once, like the victims she helped did. She went through it time and time again and now she was telling him that her link wasn't severed when she rid herself of whatever article she touched in order to pinpoint a victim's location?

It didn't bear thinking about. How the hell had she survived this long without having a complete breakdown? But by all appearances she'd done just that eighteen months ago. And then so close on the heels of that, Caleb had appeared, dragging her right back into the hell she was so desperately trying to escape.

And then he understood what she *wasn't* telling him or perhaps what he hadn't understood until now. His eyebrows lifted, registering his shock.

"You still have an established link to him."

She closed her eyes and slowly nodded. "I should say *he* has the link since obviously I can't get a bead on his location. God only knows I've tried. But he's tapped into my mind somehow. It's why I think he's psychic or has some extrasensory abilities. How else can you explain his uncanny knack for tracking my every movement? And the dreams . . ."

She shook her head, her lips tightening as she went silent.

"What dreams?" he prompted.

"He's there in my dreams. But I don't think they're actual dreams. I think they're reality. *His* reality. It's his way of taunting me. Of never making it possible for me to forget, heal and move on. I wake up at night sweating and my pulse racing well over a hundred beats per minute. It's why I suffer frequent panic attacks. He's doing it to me. I'm *certain*."

She grimaced as she checked for his reaction. Did she think he was going to discount her intuition? Or that he had doubts about her sanity? Neither was true. He believed her absolutely.

"He lives as a shadow in my mind. There, but not there. His presence isn't overwhelming all the time. Only when he locates a new victim and he wants me to see what he's doing to her. It's his way of gloating. Telling me that he's unstoppable and that I don't have the power to shut him down. He wants me to suffer. He's succeeded there," she said in a painful tone that made Caleb want to weep for all she'd suffered—was still suffering.

That the bastard was continuing to hunt and kill, all the while hot on Ramie's trail. That he shared with her his victims' pain and suffering, knowing it would become Ramie's own. The more Caleb discovered about her abilities and the demented, twisted mind of the man stalking her, the more it sickened him. And the more it made him fear for her and his ability to fulfill his promise to keep her safe.

"How then did you know he was in your hotel room?" he asked curiously. "If you don't have a link to him but he has a link to you, wouldn't he be able to get near you undetected? Can't he control what you see about him?"

She nodded. "For the most part, yes. Today is the closest I believe he's come. Or maybe he's merely been watching me all this time. Toying with me. And then today . . . when I touched the handle of the door to my hotel room, his imprint was all over it. I felt a black wave of such hatred and violence that it staggered me. I was so shaken, so terrified that, before I could flee, he threw open the door and grabbed me. I was able to fight him off and escape but not before he gave me this," she said, rubbing absently over her bruised jaw.

Caleb's scowl grew even bigger, but he tried to temper his reaction so she'd continue talking. He needed to know exactly what they were up against without him going off his hinges and scaring the hell out of her.

"You don't think I'm crazy for saying he speaks to me in my dreams and that it's not just my worst fears manifesting themselves in my subconscious?" she asked in a disbelieving tone.

"Ramie. For the hundredth time I don't think you're crazy. It would be the height of hypocrisy to discount anything, considering my own sister has psychic abilities and you certainly possess them yourself. So it certainly wouldn't be a stretch to say that it's entirely likely—even probable—that there are others out there who also have special abilities."

She hesitated a brief moment, licking her lips as

if readying herself for what she was about to say. "What ability does your sister have?"

He could hardly refuse to tell her—to trust her—when he demanded her trust and for her to tell him everything about her situation. Even if he was breaking a sacred vow between him and his brothers and Tori.

"She has visions. Of the future. Of what is yet to come. They aren't always clear in their meaning. Sometimes she doesn't *know* their meaning until what she sees comes to pass. It's deeply upsetting to her because she believes she could prevent bad things from happening."

"That must be terribly frustrating," she said, sympathy brimming in her voice. Sorrow was an ache in her eyes, making the smoky gray darker, as though shadows of the past were flickering through her mind.

"At least she doesn't have to endure the pain and tragedy of others. In that regard she's fortunate. Unlike you, who suffers right along with every victim that you're helping. You see everything. *Feel* everything."

She let out a sigh and then sank back onto the edge of the bed, defeat evident in her posture. "What are we going to do?" she whispered. "I should have never asked for your help. I'm putting you and your family in unimaginable danger. Because he'll stop at nothing in his effort to capture me. Life means nothing to him. He'd take out any obstacle to his ultimate goal as if it were only a simple annoyance, like killing flies."

"Yes, you should most certainly have asked for my help," he argued. "And I'm going to help you, Ramie. I *will* protect you. This goes beyond the debt that I and my family owe you. I will not allow an innocent woman—I don't care *who* she is—to suffer a fate worse than death."

A flicker of hope lightened the stormy gray of her eyes. She stared at him as if afraid to believe the unbelievable.

"You can trust me," he said. "You touched me, gauged my intent. You know I'm not . . . evil. So you have to know I'd never hurt you."

"I do know," she whispered.

"Then I suggest we move and move quickly. He's not far from here and if he does truly have a psychic link to you, he'll know you're still close. The longer we stay here, the more opportunity we provide him to find you."

Fear and panic made her tremble, her shoulders and hands shaking. Then she simply nodded her agreement.

Caleb picked up his cell phone and made a series of calls, one to ensure his pilot had fueled the plane and was ready to go at a moment's notice. Then he

KEEP ME SAFE   95

called Antonio and told him to meet him outside Ramie's room so they could provide a solid barrier around her the short distance from the hotel room to the car waiting downstairs.

When he was finished, he simply held out his hand to Ramie, a signal that it was time to leave. Heaving a deep breath, she slid her fingers over his palm and allowed him to help her to her feet.

"You ready?" he asked.

She squared her shoulders resolutely and then nodded. "I'm ready."

"Then let's do this," he said.

TEN

RAMIE studied Caleb from her position in the plane. He seemed tense and ill at ease. But then wasn't she a stark reminder of what had happened to tear his family apart a year ago? She felt horrible for bringing that all back. But she was truly scared. She knew she'd run out of time and that her stalker was tiring of the game. That he was ready for the final chapter in his morbid fantasy of killing her.

No, she couldn't get a solid read on him, but when he slipped into her mind, she sensed frustration. Impatience. It was why she knew he'd established a link to her, one that she couldn't control. He remained there, a dark shadow in the deepest recesses of her consciousness. He lived to make her life hell. For her to be afraid every minute of the day, both awake and in her dreams.

Never before had she come up against something

like this. She tracked evil, could feel it—and the victims' pain. But no one had ever held such a hold on her mind. Never before had she experienced the kind of helplessness—and resignation—that she was feeling now.

He was controlling her. Not physically. *Mentally.*

The day she'd helped locate his victim, when she'd slipped into his mind and the mind of his victim, he'd gotten a lock on her. A reversal of roles because usually she was the one creeping into someone's mind. Not the other way around.

What was the extent of his psychic abilities? Was it how he'd controlled his victims in the past? How he'd been able to lure them by controlling their minds? And was that why he was so frustrated by her, because she wasn't as easily controlled as his other victims? Was it why he viewed her as the ultimate challenge? His ultimate victory?

And then a horrifying thought occurred to her. He had been able to track her as surely as she tracked others. What if he went after Caleb's sister, who'd already endured unimaginable horror? What if he went after Caleb or his brothers? Was she putting them all in terrible danger by association?

"What the hell are you thinking?" Caleb demanded.

She lifted her startled gaze to his to see he was staring intently at her, a frown marring his features.

"You look scared to death."

"What if I'm bringing pain and death to *your* doorstep, to your family and the people you love?" she whispered. "You're risking your sister, your brothers, *yourself*, by helping me. I'm a reminder of all your sister endured. Is she mentally prepared for that? Isn't there somewhere safe I can go that's away from you and your family?"

It was apparent he had no liking for what she'd said, but one of them had to face reality. She appreciated that he'd responded so quickly, and that he'd taken steps to protect her. But helping her didn't mean he had to become personally involved.

She sat forward, her expression earnest. "Think about it, Caleb. You have no idea what he's capable of. You didn't see or feel what he did to his victims. I did. I live with that reminder every single day and know that he's planned a lot worse for me. I could never live with myself if you or your family became collateral damage in his quest for me. Or that he knew by hurting you, he hurt me."

Caleb reached across to fold his hand over hers. Warmth traveled up her arm, filling her with undeniable heat. She snatched her hand back, shocked that what she was feeling was . . . *desire*. She'd felt the same reaction in the hotel room earlier, but hadn't recognized it for what it was. Now that she was somewhat removed from the hysteria of that moment, she could see that there had been something from the very moment he'd walked through her door.

Judging by his own reaction, he was just as aware as she had been that something had sparked between them. He frowned over her withdrawal but retreated, moving his hand back to his lap.

"I need you to trust me, Ramie. And I understand in your position that it's hard for you to trust anyone. Because you see the bad in people. But you've touched me, felt no sign of evil. So I hope that means you *can* trust me. The very best place for you to be is in my home, where I can be sure of your safety. I have security measures most government facilities don't have."

At her doubtful look he sighed. "Besides, I want you with me. There hasn't been a day in the last year that I haven't thought about you. And it's not just guilt. Or remorse for what I did to you. There's something between us, something beyond a passing acquaintance. You felt it. I felt it. And I'd like very much for you to trust me and to see what develops between us."

Her mouth rounded in shock. He was talking about a possible *relationship*? He couldn't possibly mean what she thought he was saying. For one, she didn't *do* relationships. It was impossible when she sensed the worst in others, never the best.

And then there was the fact that they didn't even know each other. Their only connection was one steeped in blood, violence, a bond she hadn't wanted but had been forced to endure. It certainly wasn't the basis for any relationship, much less one that involved her.

And yet he was right about one thing at least. She had touched him. Had felt the very heart of him and he wasn't evil. But did that mean she could trust him? That she could ever let her guard down enough to let him truly see *her*? Could she allow him past her carefully erected barriers to the very heart and soul of her?

At times she felt as though she'd lost herself years ago. Or perhaps she never truly existed. She wasn't capable of having relationships. She was too fucked up, and who would ever possibly care about her or love her with all the baggage that accompanied her? Someone would have to be a masochist to sign up for that kind of clusterfuck.

"I'm not capable of having a relationship," she said in a low, embarrassed voice. "I have too many issues. Issues that most men aren't exactly lining up to take on."

He gave her an impatient look, mild exasperation in his eyes.

"I'm not most men, Ramie. And hell, I don't know exactly where this is headed either. I sure as hell don't have all the answers. All I know is that when I look at you, when I touch you, something happens to me. I get all twisted up on the inside and it suddenly becomes imperative that I be near you. I have no explanation for it. You have no idea what it did to me when I realized what I'd forced you to do, made you experience every single thing my sister went through. God. That has weighed on my mind for the last *year*. Knowing that by saving my sister, I hurt an innocent. The very last person who deserved what I did to you."

She glanced away, the sting of tears burning her lids. Why couldn't she just be normal like everyone else? She'd never asked for her gift—or rather curse. At times she wished that each case would be her last, that somehow she'd have a mental overload and burn herself out, effectively ending the ability to track evil.

It made her selfish. Isn't that what Caleb had accused her of in the beginning? Of being selfish for not being willing to help him find his sister? But she couldn't continue doing this forever. Not when every single victim still burned brightly in her mind with no way to rid herself of the terrible memories.

And her dreams. God, the dreams. Not only did she have a maniac taunting her in her sleep, but there were also all the others, a litany of blood, pain and death. When would it end? Would it *ever* end?

She glanced helplessly back at Caleb, not even knowing what to say to him, how to respond to his impassioned statement. Did he merely need absolution for what he considered his sin against her? Was it guilt driving him?

"I won't push you, Ramie," Caleb said in a low tone. "I just want the chance to prove to you that we may well have something worth exploring. We weren't brought together by the best of circumstances, but it doesn't mean that the future isn't what we make it."

"I'm broken," she choked out. "On the inside. I'm broken where it counts. I'm not even sure I'm capable of love or even *like*. I have no concept of what lovers do. How they're supposed to act. All I've ever known is violence and death. Those are things I understand. Everything else? A normal life, a normal relationship? I can't give you those things. And it's not that I don't want to. God, I'd give anything to be able to enjoy what everyone else takes for granted. Happiness, love, relationships, *dating*, for God's sake. I don't know how to act in social or intimate situations. Why the hell would you sign up for that?"

He moved from his seat and knelt down in front of her so they were eye level. Then he simply curled his hand around her nape and pulled her toward him, his lips pressing against hers.

It was an electric shock to her system. She was assailed by desire, lust, all the things she'd never before experienced. It was overwhelming. She had no idea what she was supposed to do in return.

It turned out she didn't need to know. Caleb took over, brushing his tongue over her lips, coaxing them to open. When they did, his tongue flitted inside, sliding erotically over hers.

He fed hungrily at her mouth, deepening the kiss until she couldn't breathe. She put her hands on his chest, intending to push him away, but instead they remained there, her palms against the muscled wall.

Heat scorched her hands, the very hands she used to tap into the minds of others. But all she felt was answering desire—and determination—that she not push him away. Her fingers flexed, pressing into the solid wall of flesh. Never had she been able to enjoy something as simple as touching another person.

She found herself caressing him in light flutters with her fingertips. He tightened beneath her fingers, telling her without words that he was enjoying her touch every bit as much as she was enjoying touching him.

She should push him away. He was dangerous to her. She knew it instantly. That he had the power to connect to her in a way no one had ever been able to before. The question was, did she want him to? Did she want a chance at normalcy? Things that she'd always been denied? Desire. Sex. Flirting. Intimacy. *Fun*.

But no matter what her mind told her, her heart was saying something else entirely. Instead of pushing him away and severing the ever growing bond between them, she leaned farther into him and tentatively responded to the brush of his tongue with her own.

When he finally pulled away, his eyes were halflidded and glowing with desire. She immediately felt bereft of his touch, the warmth that had held her in its embrace disappearing, replaced by the chill of loneliness. Something that to now had never bothered her. She'd lived and survived in isolation her entire life. And now Caleb had her wondering for the first time what other alternatives were possible.

He gently cupped her chin, forcing her gaze to his. His eyes burned with sincerity, truth a warm light in them.

"Why don't you let me worry about what I'm signing up for," he said, determination etched in his every feature. "I'm a big boy. I can take a hell of a lot when it's something I want."

She studied him, not responding to his impassioned statement. She felt as though she were balancing on a high wire and one wrong step and she'd plummet thousands of feet to the ground. Dizziness assailed her and she sucked in her breath, knowing that she had to tread very carefully.

"And what exactly do you want?" she whispered.

"You, Ramie. I want you."

ELEVEN

RAMIE still wasn't used to warmer climates. It baffled her that it was still so hot in Oklahoma in October. She'd always chosen cooler, dryer areas. Colorado had been nice even if she'd known she couldn't have sustained the winter in the ramshackle cabin she'd stayed in when Caleb had unearthed her.

So she was unprepared for the humidity when Caleb ushered her from the plane just outside of Houston. It hit her like a freight train, oppressive, and made it difficult for her to breathe.

When she paused, just trying to suck in a more steadying breath, Caleb also stopped, his hand firmly curled around her arm. He looked at her in concern.

"What's wrong?" he demanded.

She gave him a weak smile. "It's October."

His expression grew puzzled and then more concern entered his blue eyes. He likely thought her last link to sanity had finally snapped.

"It should be cooler," she continued, still a little dizzy from the humidity. "It's hard to breathe here."

"We should get into the car," he said, ignoring her pithy comments on the weather. "You're too exposed here."

He urged her forward and thankfully as soon as she slid into the car, much cooler, dryer air washed over her. The air-conditioning was on full blast and she sighed audibly in relief.

Caleb landed beside her, giving the order to his driver as soon as his door was shut. She stared out the window as they pulled away, looking at her surroundings but not really seeing them. She listened as Caleb made several calls, one obviously to one of his brothers, but she tuned even that out.

She wouldn't have thought it possible, but she must have fallen asleep because suddenly Caleb was gently shaking her awake.

"Ramie, we're home," he said.

She roused sleepily, blinking away the fuzz as she took in their surroundings. She wasn't sure what she'd been expecting but it all looked so . . . normal.

They stepped into the sun and Caleb herded her toward the front door. They'd parked in a circular driveway that took them right up to the front entrance to the palatial home. It was a large house, two stories, and it sprawled over the land like a giant invader.

There was nothing but woods around them. No other homes. It was private and secluded, but all Ramie could think was that there were too many places for intruders to hide. How would anyone ever know if someone got close?

Unease gripped her and she wondered if she'd been a fool to place her trust in Caleb Devereaux. She'd acted in a moment of panic. There'd been nothing else she could have done. But now that the preliminary panic had passed, she feared she'd made a huge mistake.

"Ramie?"

She realized she'd halted, resisting his effort to get her into his house. She dug in her heels, tugging her arm free of his hold. Panic gripped her and she recognized the signs of an impending anxiety attack.

"It's not safe here," she managed to get out in a garbled tone. "It's too secluded. *Too* private. How would you ever know if someone was in the woods?"

Her vision blurred and she swore violently under her breath, what little breath she could take. Enough with the damn crying. She wasn't a crier. And yet she'd done little else since Caleb had stormed back into her life. Emotional upheaval was the very last thing she needed. It was all she could do to manage what little sanity she had left.

To her absolute shock, Caleb didn't argue. He didn't try to talk her down. He simply swung her into his arms and strode resolutely the remaining distance to the door. It opened just as they approached and Caleb swept by a man she could only assume was one of his brothers.

"Caleb, stop," she gasped out. "Put me down. *Please*."

He ignored her, carrying her into a spacious living room that housed two large couches, a smaller love seat and two armchairs. He set her down on the love seat and then grasped her shoulders firmly, forcing her to look him in the face.

"Breathe, Ramie."

He wasn't as gentle as he'd been before. Not as understanding. He looked . . . pissed. Impatient. Haggard from lack of sleep. Shame crowded into her mind. She knew she sounded ungrateful. And mistrustful.

"Pull it together," he ordered tersely. "You can't fall apart now. You're safe. Breathe, damn it."

His words were like a whip, snapping over her and bringing her sharply into focus. Calm descended and the loud buzz in her ears abated. He shoved a cool washcloth into her shaking hands and she buried her face in it, breathing deeply.

When she finally pulled the cloth away she saw two men standing just beyond Caleb, their expressions indecipherable.

Great. Her first face-to-face meeting with his family and she was a complete basket case.

"Okay now?" Caleb asked, his tone gentler than before.

She nodded, closing her eyes in embarrassment.

"Ramie, stop," he said in a low voice. "You have nothing to be ashamed of."

"What is she doing here?"

Ramie yanked her gaze to the doorway where the stricken, female voice had come from to see a young woman standing there, staring in horror at Ramie. Her words were shrill, almost to the point of hysteria.

Ramie didn't need an introduction to know who she was. Ramie knew her on sight. Tori Devereaux. Caleb's sister. A woman whose mind Ramie had been in. A woman Ramie had suffered with.

"You said you were helping her, not that you were bringing her *here*," Tori said, her voice rising. "What is she doing here? She can't be here. You have to make her leave."

Tears ran in rivulets down Tori's face as she stared at Ramie, shame burning brightly in her eyes. Ramie closed her eyes, unable to bear looking at Tori a moment longer.

It was obvious that Tori's brothers had been completely unprepared for their sister's outburst. And before they could react further, Tori turned and ran from the room.

Caleb looked as though he'd been punched in the stomach. His two brothers were equally stunned.

"I'll go after her," one of his brothers said in a low voice.

He departed the room leaving Ramie alone with Caleb and the other brother. Ramie knew the names of the family, just not who was who. Caleb was the oldest and Beau and Quinn were younger while Tori was the baby.

Her guess was that Quinn had been the one to go after Tori and that Beau, the second oldest Devereaux, had remained behind. The moment Tori's outburst had registered, Beau's expression had become unwelcoming. He stared at Ramie as though she were an unwanted intruder. She could hardly blame him.

"I'm sorry," Caleb said in obvious bewilderment.

Ramie shook her head. "Don't apologize. Her reaction isn't surprising."

Beau's brow furrowed. "Why do you say that? You sound as though you expected such a response."

Ramie stared directly back at him, her voice calm. "Because I know. Because I saw everything. Because I'm the one person apart from her and her kidnapper who knows exactly what she went through. You and your brothers didn't see. You know only what she's told you or chosen to share. She's embarrassed and ashamed because I saw her at her worst and I experienced it with her. You can hardly expect her to roll out the welcome mat for me. Because as long as I'm here, I'm a constant reminder of everything she's tried so hard to forget. And she doesn't get to console herself with the fact that I don't know *everything* as is the case with you and her other brothers."

"Jesus," Caleb said, running a hand through his hair. "I never even considered . . ."

"I should go," Ramie said, rising abruptly from her perch on the couch. "It's obvious I don't need to be here. I'm doing her harm. I should have never called you. I'm sorry."

"I disagree," Beau said bluntly, surprising her with his response. From the way he'd been looking at her ever since Tori's outburst, Ramie would have thought he couldn't get rid of her quickly enough. "I think you being here is *exactly* what Tori needs. You're right. We don't know what all she went through. We can't possibly understand. But you can and do. And no, she won't like it, but we've babied and coddled her for the last year and I think we've done her a huge disservice even though our instincts are to do just that. Protect and coddle her. Maybe it's time that the gloves come off."

"This family has used Ramie enough," Caleb said icily. "I won't have her used anymore. Not as a crutch for Tori. Not for anything. I promised her protection and safety, so yes, she *will* remain here. But not because we're going to use her as some kind of healing measure for Tori."

Beau looked surprised by the vehemence in Caleb's voice. His gaze narrowed as he glanced back and forth between Ramie and Caleb.

"She'll hate me," Ramie said softly. "She won't be able to bear being in the same room with me. Because every time she looks at me, she's going to know that I know. That I know things she's tried to forget. Things she didn't share with you—or anyone. And she'll resent me with every breath."

"Good," Beau said savagely. "At least then she resembles something of a human. Right now I'd take *any* emotion from her. Even hatred or anger. Anything but this lifeless apathy that has taken over my sister's soul for the last year. You don't deserve her anger, Ramie. But this is the first time I've seen so much as a glimmer of life from her. She's lived in a fog for the last year and me and my brothers have been helpless to do anything but watch her die a little more each day. If having you here makes her feel anything at all then I don't want you going anywhere."

Caleb shook his head, his frustration—and grief—palpable in the tension-filled room. "That's not why I brought her here. We owe her. We all owe her. There's some maniac out there who's been stalking her for a year and a half. He almost got to her yesterday. She's not here to be some punching bag for Tori, goddamn it. We owe her better than that. So you and Quinn keep Tori away from Ramie."

Beau went silent, his lips stretched into a thin line. Caleb put his hand on Ramie's shoulder and gently pushed her back down onto the couch. Then he turned back to Beau.

"Ramie doesn't think it's safe here. The seclusion worries her. The woods. She thinks we'd never know if someone was out there."

Ramie could tell Beau was startled by Caleb's words and then he glanced toward Ramie as if seeking confirmation of Caleb's assessment.

"So before we show Ramie to her room, where she can get some much-needed rest," Caleb continued, "you and I are going to show her why she has nothing to worry about."

TWELVE

RAMIE'S head floated effortlessly down onto the pillow, her eyelids fluttering closed. She felt swallowed up by the bed, wrapped in its comforting embrace, and she purposely shut out everything but the sensation of safety and well-being.

Because if she allowed herself to think of anything else, she'd lose her tenuous grip on her sanity.

Caleb and Beau had taken her into a room on the main floor that housed all kinds of electronics and television monitors. Every angle of the house was displayed in real time. Remote sensors dotted the entire landscape and would sound a warning if anyone ventured near the house. For that matter if anyone entered the wooded area surrounding the house, alarms would be triggered.

There was a safe room on the main floor of the house. Fireproof, impenetrable, stocked with enough food and water to withstand a natural disaster. Or the zombie apocalypse.

She suppressed the sudden burst of laughter that bubbled up from her chest. There was certainly nothing amusing about her situation, nor having absurd thoughts like withstanding a zombie apocalypse. Even if it was appropriate.

The important thing was that this house was bulletproof. Or crazed, homicidal maniac proof. No one could as much as fart in the woods without Caleb and his brothers knowing. That should ease her worry, and yet here she was, lying on one of the most comfortable beds she'd ever lain in, exhausted, and yet unable to relax enough to go to sleep. She simply couldn't shut off the fear, no matter how much her heart told her she was safe.

Heart and mind were not in accord, which only added to the sensation of her sanity slipping further and further from her reach.

Worse, on the way to the room Caleb had installed her in, they'd passed Tori's room and the sound of her weeping filled Ramie with sorrow and her chest ached for the emotional upheaval she was causing with her presence. She couldn't fault Tori's reaction to coming face-to-face with the unerring truth of what had happened to her. There was nothing wrong with denial. Everyone had their own way of coping. God only knew how Ramie had learned to cope over the years. It may not be the healthiest way to absorb tragedy after tragedy, but being able to compartmentalize each nightmare had been the only way she survived.

At some point the walls would likely crumble and everything she'd been stuffing down would come spewing out like a geyser erupting, but until that day she just . . . coped. Just like Tori was coping—or not coping. It wasn't her job—her responsibility—to heal Caleb's sister. She wouldn't even know how to begin even if she wanted such a task.

She cupped her hand over her forehead, eyes still closed, and she rubbed tiredly in an attempt to ease the awful tension and the painful ache in her temples. When would she stop running? Would she *ever* stop fleeing, and would she ever be able to lead a normal, boring life, something she craved with desperation?

If you think you're safe—that you'll ever be safe—from me, you're a very stupid woman. There is nowhere, no place you can hide that I won't find you. And when I do, you will suffer. You will beg me for death, and maybe, if you're a good girl, I'll be merciful and kill you quickly.

Ramie bolted upright in bed, her scream shattering the silence that had blanketed the room. Her gaze bounced wildly around the darkened room, pupils quickly adapting as she blinked, expecting to see him standing by her bed. Within touching distance.

She should run, but she was paralyzed, unable to move—to breathe. Terror gripped her until she felt bruised, as if an actual hand had wrapped itself around her throat.

When the door burst in, she screamed again and scrambled wildly for the other side of the bed. She landed with a harsh thump, pain lancing through her head. She planted both palms on the floor, pushing herself upward, prepared to fight for her life.

She'd known she wasn't safe here. Stupid, stupid, stupid!

Like a wild animal she reared her head, nostrils flaring as she evaluated her escape options. He filled the doorway and then suddenly light flooded the room, momentarily blinding her.

From a distance she heard her name and she jerked her gaze around the vividly lit room, desperately seeking the source. Strong hands wrapped around her upper arms, and she lashed out, self-preservation kicking in. She wasn't ready to die.

"Caleb, what the hell is going on?"

Ramie stared at the open doorway to see Beau Devereaux standing there in a pair of boxer shorts and nothing else. He was quickly shoved aside when Quinn appeared looking worried and frazzled.

"Jesus, this is not going to help Tori," Quinn bit out.

Ramie glanced upward, the haze of terror slowly releasing its grip on her. Caleb was on his knees just a foot from her, his hair mussed, his eyes bloodshot. Like Beau, he was wearing only boxers and it was equally evident that he'd been roused from sleep by her scream.

She closed her eyes, mortification taking over the fear.

"Go back to bed," Caleb ordered his brothers. "I'll handle this. Make sure Tori's okay."

Ramie held her breath as Caleb's brothers slowly withdrew, identical frowns on their faces. There was no hiding the looks of annoyance and welcome was the furthest thing from their expressions. No matter what Beau had said earlier, he was obviously regretting his words now.

The door closed gently, Caleb's brothers disappearing from sight. She became aware of her fingernails digging into her palms, marking her skin. She forced her hands to relax and closed her eyes, not wanting to look at Caleb and see the same thing she'd seen in Beau's and Quinn's faces.

"I'm not crazy," she whispered. "I'm not."

She wasn't even cognizant of her fist pounding on the top of her thigh. Nor of the tears that streaked down her face in silence. A low sob finally welled out and it was a horrible sound, one she never wanted to repeat. Because it sounded too much like defeat. As though the asshole had already won.

"I'm *not* crazy," she said again, fiercely, daring Caleb to argue with her, to judge her.

Caleb rose quietly from his position on the floor. He reached down and simply plucked her up and carefully placed her back on the bed. Then he simply climbed in next to her and enfolded her in his arms.

She inhaled and his scent was imprinted on her. She breathed . . . him. It was as though one by one, pieces of a puzzle were slowly being put together. Sliding into position all around her.

"I don't think you're crazy," Caleb murmured against her ear. "But I would like to know what happened. You don't scare easily, Ramie. So for you to have screamed that loudly something had to have scared the ever-loving fuck out of you."

Her eyes widened and her mouth drooped open as she stared at him like he'd lost his damn mind.

"I don't scare easily? Is that something you made up on the fly to placate me, pat me on the head and tell me what a good girl I've been?"

"Uh . . . I'm not sure what the right answer to this kind of question is so I'm just going to express my earlier opinion that you don't scare easily."

Ramie snorted and then wiped her damp cheeks against the fluffy pillows that her head should still be resting on were it not for the psycho stalking and terrorizing her.

"I'm terrified," Ramie said with no theatrics. She stated it as baldly as she would any other truth. Like the sky is blue except some days it's gray and sometimes black and also puffy white.

His tone was exasperated even though he kept her anchored tightly to his body. She was tucked up against him, his body cupping hers entirely, giving her safe harbor. She recognized it for what it was. Sweet relief. Because for however long Caleb was holding her in just this way nothing or no one could hurt her.

"*What* are you terrified of, Ramie?" he asked gently. "We showed you the surveillance system. We stole quite a few of the brightest military minds from Uncle Sam. These are men who'd make the average guy out there on the streets, just like the punk stalking you, look like freaking kindergartners and, well, I bet the kindergarten girls could kick the shit out of him. Have you ever seen kindergarten girls? They're freaking scary, let me tell you. My hat is off to anyone who can last an entire day with that many five- and six-year-old girls *and* boys."

He asked a question but then gave her no opportunity to answer it. He kept talking, drawing her thoughts from the scare she'd just been delivered and filling the gap with teasing stories of kinder-gartners.

He was giving her time. To tell him in her own way instead of demanding it and pulling it out of her teeth. He'd likely just recently had to learn that kind of patience. With Tori. It would have frustrated her brothers for her to be uncommunicative because they'd want answers. To everything. And who knows what would have happened had they been able to pull any identifying information from Tori's fractured dreams.

Ramie yawned and suddenly Caleb was closer, mounding pillows between their backs and the headboard of the bed. Then he pulled her into his arms so she was cradled by his body, his warmth soothing her.

She'd felt the chill the moment Caleb had opened the door to the "guest room," which was all the way down the hall from the Devereaux siblings and had its own guest bathroom to boot. But she didn't like the room. It was . . . cold. Sterile. Quite frankly it freaked her out.

Caleb brushed his lips over the top of her hair. "What happened, Ramie? Did you have a bad dream?"

"You're just going to think—*know*—that I'm crazy. You'll know it like I'm starting to know," she whispered.

Even as she was dancing around Caleb's target, the chill in the room grew even colder. Ramie shivered, her teeth chattering in a not so very attractive manner, but at the moment she didn't give a shit what she looked like. She just wanted to be warm.

"You're freezing to death," Caleb said in disbelief. "Are you sick? Why the hell didn't you say something? I could have had a doctor come out to see you."

Ramie threw up her hand. "I'm not sick. I'm not crazy. Those are the only two things I know for sure in my life right now."

"What was the dream about?" he asked, pinpointing the topic so there'd be no sidestepping.

"It wasn't a dream," she whispered. "I wasn't even asleep yet. I was tired and I was thinking that I was lying on the best bed I'd slept on in months. Lots and lots of months. I was lying on the bed staring up at the ceiling and trying to make my brain shut down. My head was aching a bit around my temples so I was just rubbing my head and trying to relax. And then . . ."

"Then what, Ramie?"

She hesitated, wondering just how far she should take things with Caleb. How much she could trust him with. What if he turned on her? What if he'd worked some sort of sick trade where he handed Ramie over, gift-wrapped and in a bow in exchange for Tori and her continued safety? Maybe they were just throwing her under the bus so that none of their family would be remotely involved— or responsible for a man being brought to justice.

He stared her down with those ice-blue eyes that could at times seem glacial. Like he could freeze someone at a glance. Her skin prickled. As if she weren't cold enough already.

As if sensing her chill, or perhaps clued in by the fact that the entire bed was shaking with her, he pulled the blankets over them both and tugged Ramie back into his arms so there was no space between.

Heat scorched over her skin, warming her from the inside out. She hated that her T-shirt was a barrier between his bare skin and her own. She slipped her hands, palms down on his chest, between them, ignoring his flinch over the coldness of her touch. Gradually they both relaxed as more of his warmth seeped into her body.

His lips were tantalizingly close to hers. Their breaths mingled and it was so silent she could hear his heartbeat. Could feel it beneath her fingertips.

"Kiss me," she pleaded softly. "Make me forget."

Their lips touched tenderly, just a gentle brush that trailed warmth all the way to her heart.

"Forget what, Ramie? You have to talk to me.

If I'm going to keep you safe, you can't keep me in the dark."

The spell was broken and the cold returned. A shiver stole up her spine and she gathered the covers, rolling onto her back and pulling them to her chin. She stared blindly up at the ceiling as Caleb lay beside her, his strong body touching her side.

"He spoke to me," she said quietly. "I'm not crazy. It's not my subconscious or me projecting my fear nor is it the manifestation of my fears or paranoia. He has a link to me. It's how he always manages to find me. It's how he knows where I am now."

Caleb went rigid next to her. She chanced a glance out of the corner of her eye and saw that his face was every bit as tense as the rest of him. What she didn't see, however, was disbelief.

Relief coursed through her veins, making her heady, dizzy almost, as though she'd just had an IV injection of alcohol or a potent drug.

"You believe me," she said in wonder. "You *believe* me."

He slid his large hand over her belly, splaying his fingers outward and then he continued upward until his fingers gently touched her chin and he pushed it in his direction so her gaze met his.

His stare was serious, intense. The blue was more vivid, darker, not as glacial as it normally was. His eyes looked . . . warm. Tender. It wasn't the look he'd give a stranger. Or someone he considered a threat or even a casual acquaintance. It was an intimate look, and sincerity was evident in every facet of his face.

"I believe you, Ramie."

She closed her eyes, this time not fighting the tears as they gathered and burned a trail down her cheeks. He believed her.

"What did he say to you?" Caleb asked in a terse voice.

The fury in his voice shook her from her emotional response. She hastily wiped away the tears with her hand and then turned slowly onto her side so she once more faced him.

"He knows where I am. Or at least he knows what it looks like. He told me that if I believed all these security measures would prevent him from getting to me that I was a very stupid woman. He said there was nowhere I could hide that he wouldn't find me and that my death wouldn't be quick or merciful unless I was a very g-good g-girl and then he'd consider k-killing me quickly."

She was barely able to choke the words out. It felt as though a ton of cement were pressing down on her chest.

"I'm not ready to die, Caleb," she whispered. "I thought I was. I gave up. I'm ashamed to admit this, but I have to be honest with you. I resigned myself to my own death. I even thought it was what I wanted, that maybe I'd finally find peace. But then when confronted with my death, when he caught me outside my hotel room, I found myself fighting back. I ran. I didn't give up. And I called you. Because I knew you were my only hope. I have no one else. No family. No one who cares. I realized that I wasn't ready to die. No matter what I may have thought. Or how wimpy I've become. And that it doesn't matter that I don't have anything or anyone to live *for*. I'm not ready to die."

Caleb's hand slid over her cheek and then delved into her hair as he pulled her to meet his lips. Their noses bumped and nudged as he figured out the best angle and then his tongue glided over hers, tasting, savoring.

Their breaths were noisy in the silence. The only sounds were the rapid puffs of air, the sound of their mouths as they molded hotly to one another and the harsh sounds of their breathing as they sucked in breath after breath through distended nostrils.

His hand slipped from the strands of her hair and gently slid down her neck and over her shoulder and then glided underneath her arm, his fingers spreading out over her rib cage. His thumb brushed the under swell of her breast and then his fingers gathered the thin material of her T-shirt and inched it upward until the hem was in his grasp.

When he touched her bare skin, a soft moan escaped her, breaking the silence. She tensed for a moment, afraid that once again she'd shattered the spell, but his grip only grew tighter, more possessive.

His open palm traveled around her waist and to the center of her back. He rolled her underneath him, their mouths never separating. His weight bore down on her, hot, hard, his body undulating in perfect rhythm with her heart. She closed her eyes, surrendering to the magnetic pull between them, a different kind of link that had been present from the start.

Her hands explored the muscled wall of his back, his shoulders and then slipped downward where his waist narrowed. The muscles rippled in reaction and his breathing hitched, stuttering over her lips.

His erection bulged against the apex of her thighs, rubbing erotically over the thin layer of her panties exerting just enough pressure on her clit to bring her to orgasm.

He pulled her hands away from him, lacing their fingertips before lowering them to the bed

KEEP ME SAFE   129

just above her head. Hands twined, his mouth sliding from her mouth down her jaw and then to her neck, he whispered against her ear.

"You do have someone to live for, Ramie. You have me."

THIRTEEN

WHEN Ramie awoke the next morning, she immediately reached behind her, searching for Caleb, needing that reassurance. When she was met by emptiness, she frowned and turned her head to look over her shoulder.

He was gone, and by the looks of it, he'd been gone for quite some time. There was no indentation on the pillow or the bed. Had he returned to his own room the moment she'd fallen asleep?

She flinched when she turned just enough to catch the full force of the sun shining through one of the slats of the blinds. The sun was high enough to signal that it was rather late in the morning and when her gaze drifted to the clock by the bed she got confirmation that it was in fact late.

Still she lay there contemplating the events of the night before. Caleb in her bed. His arms around her, anchoring her and offering comfort. Intimacy had cloaked them, making her restless and edgy. Unfulfilled in a way she'd never experienced.

She had no idea what was happening between her and Caleb and whether or not she wanted it to happen. Being so close to another human being—especially a man—was a new experience for her. One she discovered she liked. A lot.

She threw off the covers and swung her legs over the side of the bed but then caught herself. Where was she going? She didn't have to be anywhere and she couldn't very well just barge through Caleb's house like she owned the place.

Did she simply stay in her room? Or was she supposed to come out at some point?

The growling in her stomach decided the dilemma for her. She was starving.

She shuffled toward the bathroom and turned the shower on, making sure the water was cool enough to wake her more fully. She gasped when she ducked under the spray. The temperature jolted her senses and as she'd hoped, some of the fuzz and haze clouding her mind and dulling her senses evaporated under the chilly water.

She hastily washed her hair and body, not lingering under the coldness of the shower. Throwing one towel over her hair, she wrapped another around her body and stepped back into the bedroom.

Instant cold assailed her. Even colder than the shower had been. Why was it so damn cold in this bedroom? It wasn't that cold in the rest of the house.

I'm here.

She stopped breathing. Went utterly still as goose bumps popped out over her flesh and raced along the surface until every hair on her body was on its end. She shook her head. No. She wouldn't allow him to unnerve her.

Still, she hurriedly pulled her clothing on and scrubbed at her damp hair. Tossing the towel to the floor, she all but fled from the room.

The moment she stepped into the hallway, warmth embraced her. She inhaled sharply, sucking in the much warmer air. She quickly put as much distance between her and that awful room as possible. She slowed halfway down the stairs and forced herself to at least appear calm even if her insides were a seething mass of nerves.

She hadn't paid much attention to the downstairs tour yesterday. The only thing she could remember with any clarity was the room where all the security monitors were housed. That one she remembered down to the smallest detail.

Knowing the living room was on her right, she veered left at the bottom of the stairs and took the hallway past the security room, the safe room and finally arrived at the kitchen. When she hesitantly entered the doorway, Tori looked up from where she was sitting at the island and anger burned in her gaze.

Without a word, Tori shot upward, knocking over her glass, and she stalked away, leaving Caleb standing there, his features drawn, his eyes haunted.

"She doesn't want me here," Ramie said unnecessarily.

Caleb turned, his gaze not quite meeting hers. "No," he said quietly. "She doesn't."

"You argued over me. My being here."

Again her words were completely unnecessary. But still, she spoke them aloud if only to get Caleb to realize the ramifications of her presence. She couldn't stay here. He couldn't choose a promise to her over his family. No one should ever have to make such a choice.

He simply nodded, confirming her assessment.

"I'll go then," Ramie said simply.

"No!" Caleb barked out, his expression growing black. "You are *not* going anywhere. It's not even an option."

She blinked at his vehemence. "I was hungry," she said in a low voice, her attempt at changing the focus of the conversation.

"Of course you are. I'm sorry. I should have had

something sent up to you. You shouldn't have to come downstairs to . . . this," he said, gesturing in the direction his sister had departed.

The grief in his eyes was too much for her to bear. She closed the distance between them and took his hands in hers, looking into his eyes.

"It isn't your fault, Caleb. You can't blame yourself for this. For her. For me. Any of it. And you shouldn't have to choose between a stranger and your sister."

His eyes suddenly blazed, his fury bursting through her mind. It was so scorching that she instantly dropped his hands to break the connection between them.

"You are not a stranger," he said savagely. "You aren't nobody, Ramie. You're somebody. You're important. To *me*. You're important. So stop telling me what I can and can't choose. Stop telling me what to feel."

"I'm not . . . I'm sorry," she said quietly.

She turned away, her heart beating so rapidly in her chest that it was a dull roar in her ears, her pulse. She had no idea what to say, how to respond to what he'd said.

"That's it?" he demanded. "You apologize . . . for what, Ramie? What exactly are you sorry for? Sorry that I care? Sorry that you aren't dead? What are you apologizing for, or do you even know?"

She turned back, going still, her hand resting on the back of the bar stool. "I don't know," she said honestly. "I don't know the answers to any of it. I'm not trying to make you angry, Caleb. God knows I'm grateful—"

He lifted his hand and pushed it outward as if outright rejecting her words. "I don't want your fucking gratitude. Just save it. Nor do I want you to keep offering goddamn apologies left and right."

"Then what *do* you want?" she burst out. "What do you *want*? Because I don't know and I'm not good at playing mind games or guessing games for that matter."

He was suddenly right in front of her again, heat radiating from him in waves. His jaw was tightly clenched, his features as hard as stone. And he was pissed.

"You don't get it, do you?"

"What? What don't I get?" she yelled at him. "What is it that I'm supposed to be *getting*? Because I don't know! All I know is that I'm bringing more pain and suffering to a family who has already experienced way too much."

She broke off as a sob welled up in her chest, constricting her throat before spilling out, ugly and guttural. Her shoulders heaved and she covered her face with her hands.

Caleb sighed and then suddenly she was in his

arms. She buried her face in his chest and wrapped her arms around his waist, holding on as if he were the only anchor in a vicious storm.

"What don't I get?" she whispered against his shirt. "Because it seems to me I get exactly what the situation is."

He grasped her shoulders and pulled her away so they were looking each other in the eyes.

"That I want *you*."

She stared soundlessly at him as his words penetrated the thick curtain of despair and isolation. She went so still that she realized she was holding her breath and finally let it escape in one long exhale.

"What you don't get is that I want you," Caleb repeated. "What you don't get is that the idea of you in the hands of a monster terrifies me. What you don't get is that you are important to me. And what you don't get is that no matter how much my sister hates you being here, I'm not letting you walk out of my life and that has nothing to do with any debt I or my family owes you. Or any obligation I may have felt a year ago. It has absolutely nothing to do with you saving Tori. I won't let you go because I want you to stay. I realize you've never had anyone fight for you, Ramie. But you do now. You have *me*."

"No one has ever wanted me," she whispered.

"They've wanted what I can do, what my abilities can do, but never *me*. Do you know what that feels like?"

Caleb's expression softened and his eyes darkened, not with pity, because that truly would have driven her over the edge. But with understanding.

"We aren't as different as you think," he said quietly. "I'm a Devereaux. And people—women—want what that name brings. Money, power, prestige. But they don't want me. Caleb. They want Caleb *Devereaux*."

Sharp understanding hit her and shame burned her cheeks. She was so self-absorbed, so ensconced in her own pity party that she failed to see beyond her own issues. Caleb had considered her selfish, before, when he hadn't known how her abilities worked. He wasn't wrong. She *was* selfish. And it wasn't a pleasant revelation.

She'd gone through her whole life expecting the worst, settling for the worst. Never fighting for more. Never expecting more. How could she hope to gain more if she didn't demand it?

She'd spent so much time railing at the injustice of it all and poor little unloved Ramie. She'd allowed herself to be stripped of her soul. No one had done that to her. She'd done it to herself. Because she wasn't strong. Because it never occurred to her to want more than what she'd been dealt. Or to go

after happiness instead of waiting for it to be magi-
cally bestowed on her. Instead she'd wallowed in
her own misery for a decade.

Right here, right now, right in front of her stood
someone who professed to care about her. Not her
abilities. He wasn't asking her for anything. She'd
be a fool to walk away even though it meant endangering him—his entire family. Maybe together,
they could fight.

"I want you," she said softly. "Me, Caleb. *I* want
you. No matter what your last name is."

FOURTEEN

CALEB stared back at Ramie, at the fear and vulnerability in her eyes, and marveled at what it must have taken for her to open herself up to him. There was doubt and her expression was troubled, not exactly the kind of reaction a man wanted to see on the face of the woman he planned to get intimate with, but Ramie wasn't most women. Most women hadn't seen the world through Ramie's eyes.

He reached for the hands that had dropped his just moments before, and he knew why she'd severed the link between them. But he was calmer now, and he wanted her to see—to know—that she had nothing to fear from him.

She shivered when he tugged her back into his arms and her body went soft and pliant against his frame. There was still a hint of dampness in her hair. Hair that smelled like honeysuckle.

He wanted to take her to bed. Right now. He wanted to spend the entire day making love to her. Showing her without inept words the ever-strengthening bond between them.

Instead he smoothed his hand over the top of her curly hair and stroked reassuringly, getting her used to being touched by someone. A man. A man who had no intention of hurting her. It occurred to him that her sole experience with sex might be the degrading crimes that had been committed against so many women Ramie had helped.

And if that was the case, then he had to handle her with extreme caution. No rushing her into physical and emotional intimacy before she was ready. Yes, he wanted her to be able to depend on him. Willing to depend on him and trust him. But he didn't want to be her crutch. For him to merely be a coping mechanism when he wanted so much more.

He dropped a kiss on top of her head as he continued to caress her back and nape, tangling his fingers periodically in the unruly strands of hair. And he simply enjoyed the feeling of her in his arms. Of her standing in his home and him knowing that she was safe. Not out there alone and vulnerable. Afraid that each breath would be her last. It was no way to live. And certainly no way to die.

Thank God she'd called him. Else he'd still be

searching for her. Or worse, she could be in her stalker's hands suffering indescribable torture.

He closed his eyes against that image and inhaled through his nose so he wouldn't flood her with rage all over again.

There was too much anger and animosity in this house as it was. Caleb had never given thought to whether Tori would object so strenuously to Ramie's presence. It wasn't until Ramie's explanation that he understood.

He hated feeling so goddamn helpless. If he gave in to his sister then Ramie suffered. She could die. She *would* die. If he dug in his heels, as he'd already done, he'd cause a rift between him and Tori that might never be mended.

"I want you to fight for your right to be here," he murmured.

She stiffened and pulled away, glancing up at him with those troubled gray eyes that seemed too enormous for her face. Eyes that had several lifetimes of violence and pain behind them.

"I know what I'm asking isn't easy," he continued. "You don't deserve Tori's hostility and you don't deserve for my brothers to look at you without welcome in their eyes. But I'm asking you to stay. For me. And you owe me nothing. God only knows how much I owe *you*. I'm still asking, though."

"What exactly are you asking me to be?" she asked hoarsely. "Friend? Lover?"

"Yes and yes," he responded quietly. "More. A lot more. But we'll get to that in time. For now, yes. Friends. Eventually lovers. After that? It's whatever you want. What you need. I hope to God I'm able to give you what you need."

"And what about what you need?"

He stared back at her, momentarily off balance by her question. Need? He needed a lot of things. Things he had no control over. For a man used to being in control of every aspect of his life, suddenly not being in control was daunting. It made him feel weak at a time when his family needed his strength more than ever.

"I need . . . you," he finally said. "I need for Tori to be able to sleep at night. For my brothers to quit blaming themselves for what happened to her. I need for the animals who have terrorized both you and Tori to be captured and punished. I need a lot of things, but the only thing I have any control over whatsoever is you and your presence in my life. So give me that, at least. If nothing else, give me that."

"Okay," she said in a near whisper. "I'll stay. I'll try. I've been running for so long that I don't know any other way, Caleb. I don't know how to be normal. Don't let me run this time. I need you to believe in me even if I don't believe in myself."

He squeezed her hand and then slid his other hand up her arm to clasp her shoulder, balancing her, infusing her with his will and determination. Then he leaned down and pressed his lips to her forehead, inhaling her scent.

"I won't let you run, Ramie. Never again. I want you here with me and if you try to run, I'll just come after you. Always."

He watched the slow realization of his words sink in and the shocked look in her eyes but also unfettered hope. Maybe he was finally getting to her. God, he hoped so.

"Now, let's get you something to eat," he said. "After you've had a decent meal, we'll sit down with my team of investigators so we can get an idea of what we're dealing with here."

FIFTEEN

IT was a frightening concept for the hunted to become the hunter. Ramie had spent all her time running, trying to avoid being captured, and yet now she was suddenly on offense. Going after the man who wanted nothing more than her death. Was she insane for agreeing to stay in one place for any length of time? Shouldn't she be constantly on the move, remaining one step ahead of her stalker?

She rubbed her hands repeatedly over the tops of her thighs, the denim of her jeans worn and faded. Holes had formed, a look people paid good money for on perfectly new pants. For Ramie it was just the result of having no way to buy new clothing.

"Ramie?"

Caleb's voice drifted through her consciousness and she guiltily turned her head in his direction. She could feel the tightening pressure of an impending panic attack, but she was determined not to give in and not to freak out in front of the people Caleb had hired to bring down the man hunting her.

"I'm sorry. Can you repeat the question?"

Caleb sighed but at least he didn't look angry. He wore a look of understanding. And then, as if realizing how perilously close to the edge she was, he sat down beside her on the couch and slid his fingers through hers. Perhaps it was so she could share in his resolve and determination. She could certainly use a transfusion of those qualities.

"Can you describe the man who attacked you?" Caleb asked.

She drew a complete blank. Her forehead wrinkled and her skin tightened around her eyes as she focused her absolute attention on trying to grab an image of her stalker from the fragments of her mind.

"It will be helpful if we can get a sketch of him," the woman who'd introduced herself as Eliza said gently. "If we plaster his face in enough places, sooner or later we'll ferret him out."

Ramie swallowed, her mouth going dry. Was he out there even now looking into her mind, seeing what she was seeing, hearing what she was hearing? Did it do any good for them to plan traps for him if he knew about them because he was a constant presence in her mind?

Which was why *she* didn't need to know.

She bolted off the couch as the realization hit her. She spun to explain to Caleb just as he grabbed her arm, a confused look on his face.

"I can't know," she babbled out. "Because if I know, *he* knows. So you have to leave me out of it. I can't see or know any of it."

"Whoa, slow down," Dane Elliot, one of Caleb's security specialists, said, holding his hands up in a placating manner.

He wanted her to calm down. He thought she was being hysterical. A nitwit. No, she was finally being smart.

"He's there," she said, including each of the people in the room in her sweeping gaze. "He has a psychic link to me. It's like having someone sit on your shoulder all the time. He has an unobscured line of vision, a pathway into everything I see or do. So you see, it does us little good to plot and plan because he'll know exactly what we're doing."

Caleb swore and murmurs arose from the occupants of the room. They likely all thought she'd lost her mind. She had no idea what if anything Caleb had told them about her. If they even knew psychic abilities were involved.

"I can't be in here. Sorry," she whispered.

She turned and fled from the room. There was an invisible hand clutching at her neck, choking her, preventing her from getting oxygen into her lungs. The oppressive weight of evil was so heavy on her chest that it felt like she was being crushed.

She stumbled into the downstairs bathroom and hastily turned on the cold water in the sink. She splashed water on her cheeks and then leaned on the countertop with her elbows, hands covering her face as the water still ran full blast.

Her hand clutched her neck in an effort to remove the invisible grip. But it was as bruising as if she were really being choked.

"Ramie? Are you all right? What the hell is going on?" Caleb demanded.

He reached around her and turned off the water and then he grasped her by the shoulders and gave her a gentle shake. She held up her hand to halt him, straining to find the words around the strangling sensation in her neck.

"I have to learn to beat him," she bit out. "I have to close myself off to him. I have to be better about knowing when he's there and I have to be able to shut him out. Or maybe he's simply there all the time. I don't know. Why don't I know?"

"Is he . . . there . . . right now?" Caleb asked as he stared holes through her.

It was as if he were looking for her stalker in her. Her eyes, or expression or like she'd developed a split personality and one half of her thought she was a sick monster who preyed on women. Or maybe he thought she was demonically possessed. It wasn't as though she'd given him any other explanation.

She couldn't bear the disgust—or the worry—in his eyes.

"You do think I'm crazy," she whispered. "Maybe I am crazy."

"Goddamn it, no, I don't think you're crazy," Caleb said in a frustrated voice. "I just want to know who the hell I'm talking to and if it's you or the asshole who's trying to kill you."

"He's just a passive observer," Ramie explained. Or rather she tried to explain. Because how did one explain the inexplicable? "It's like he has a porthole into my brain. He can see what I see, hear what I hear. Be aware of what I'm aware of. It's why he told me last night that I wasn't safe here. That all your security wouldn't keep him from me. He knows everything."

"How does this happen?" Caleb asked. "Has it ever happened before? Can you block him?"

"Oh God, don't you think I've tried? That I don't want him in my mind all the time? That I'm vulnerable every hour of every day because he sees everything that I see?"

"Of course," Caleb soothed. "But there has to be a way of blocking him. We need to work on you schooling your thoughts. Of making your mind go completely blank. It's a therapy that Tori used when she was younger. One of the many things we tried in an effort to make the visions go away. But somehow I think it's more applicable to your situation than it ever was to Tori's."

Her pulse beat painfully at her temples. It felt as though her head would explode at any minute. Her blood pressure had to be sky-high.

She rubbed absently at her forehead as she tried to collect her scattered thoughts. His explanation was logical. But how to put it into practice? She wasn't prepared to fight off a mental invasion. She'd never thought herself susceptible to such a thing. She was always the one intruding, thrown into others' minds. But she still had no control over how long the connection stayed intact.

Perhaps that's what her stalker was merely doing. It wasn't that he could slip in and out of her mind at will. He'd found a way to prevent the link from being severed. Whereas before, after a period of hours or sometimes days, her connection to victim and attacker was broken and mental silence ensued, this one hadn't been cut. It had remained. It was like the story of Hansel and Gretel and their trail of breadcrumbs. She'd left a proverbial trail behind her everywhere she'd gone since first establishing the link a year and a half ago.

"Ramie?"

Startled, Ramie's head came up to see Eliza standing in the door.

Eliza glanced up at Caleb. "Can I have a moment with Ramie?"

Caleb frowned and sent a questioning stare in Ramie's direction. Ramie nodded and Caleb backed from the room.

"I'll be right outside," Caleb said quietly.

Ramie swallowed hard when Caleb disappeared from view. She hated how dependent she already was on him. And the fact that she felt safe only when he was in her sight.

"You have to help us bring this guy down," Eliza said firmly.

Ramie shook her head. "You don't understand. I'm endangering you. All of you. Caleb, his family. Tori."

Eliza pinned her with her steady gaze. "What I understand is that there is a monster out there preying on women and you are the only person who can take him down."

Ramie closed her eyes, shutting Eliza out. Shutting everything out while she tried to blanket her mind to nothing. A big yawning black hole. That was what she had to become.

"He's taken another woman," Eliza said quietly.

Ramie's eyes flew open. "What?"

"We think he has," Eliza amended. "Evidence points to that. Either that or an eerily good copy-cat."

Ramie's pulse pounded, a deafening roar in her ears. No. God, no.

She hadn't realized she'd spoken aloud until the sound of her tortured voice filled her ears. She lifted her gaze to Eliza's, knowing she had only one choice.

Resolve edged out the fear and despair. She wouldn't let him win. Wouldn't let him control every aspect of her life.

Eliza was right. Ramie was the only one who could bring him down. The only one who could end the pain and suffering of too many women to count. It was time to stop being that victim and fight back.

There was nothing she could do to remove the memories, the pain that she and the other women had suffered. But she could make certain that no more women had to endure what others had.

Calm descended. Peace, sweet and aching, filled her. Her jaw firm, she stared Eliza in the eyes, watching as Eliza's own eyes widened in realization of what Ramie was about to do.

"Can you get me something the victim owned?" Ramie asked.

SIXTEEN

RAMIE'S words reached Caleb where he stood in the hallway and fear slammed into him, rocking him back on his heels.

"No!"

His reaction was explosive. He pushed his way back into the bathroom where Ramie and Eliza stood, shaking his head fiercely as he pinned Ramie with the full force of his stare.

"No way in hell," Caleb bit out. "Don't even *think* about it, Eliza. If you even try it, you're fired. Your job is to *protect* Ramie, not expose her to more hurt."

Eliza's lips thinned but she remained silent. Instead she turned her head to Ramie, looking pointedly at her as if she expected Ramie to make Caleb stand down.

Ramie's eyes were haunted. Her lips quivered

and her nostrils flared. She had the look of prey being stalked by a predator. As though she knew she was about to be attacked.

"I have to, Caleb," Ramie said tonelessly, resignation clear in her weary gaze.

"No," Caleb said emphatically. "You *don't* have to. Why would you put yourself through that kind of torture again?"

A tear slipped soundlessly down her cheek. Her eyes were dull as she stared back at him.

"I have to do this," Ramie repeated. "You know I do, Caleb. There's no other way. Eliza is right. I'm the only one who can take this guy down."

Caleb exploded in fury, his anger directed at Eliza. "You weren't supposed to say any such thing to her! That is *not* the job you were hired for. You're off this case. You and Dane both. Get *out* of my house."

Ramie saw Eliza's lips thin even more and her cheek twitched in irritation. She bit her lips as though she desperately wanted to say something but held it in check. But there was something about Eliza that made Ramie pause. She didn't come across as a brassy, uncaring, ball-busting woman only wanting to do her job. That wasn't what Ramie had seen in Eliza at all.

"You may as well say it, Eliza," Ramie encouraged. "If he's firing you anyway, what have you got to lose by speaking your mind? And by all means, let Dane have his say so he doesn't sink with your ship."

Dane wasn't pleased with Ramie's statement of sinking on Eliza's ship but at the same time it was apparent he was backing Eliza completely. He stood behind her in a gesture of support. Both he and Eliza stared at Ramie but then Dane shook his head.

"It's not Ramie we have to convince, Lizzie," he said in a low, affectionate tone. "She's with us. It's Caleb who wants our heads."

One thing Ramie was fast learning about Eliza was that she was not the type of woman to simply bow out, take a more subservient route. Not when she knew her way of handling things was far more superior.

Eliza stomped right up to Caleb's face, Dane right behind, but Ramie got the impression he wasn't supporting Eliza so much as he was potentially protecting Caleb from the brunt of Eliza's fury.

Eliza put a finger in front of Caleb's nose, making him stumble backward until he was against the wall.

"Don't talk to us about not forcing people to do things against their will. Or do you forget we know all about your very unexpected visit with Ramie St.

Claire and that you wouldn't take no for an answer and then you pushed her right into hell. Tori's hell at that. So now you have two women suffering the same attack but only by one man and one instance.

"Sure, we can nail the bastard for what he did to Tori. We have evidence, DNA trace. He'll go down. It's just a matter of time. But we can't do a damn thing about what he did to *Ramie*," Eliza said in a black voice. "Not a single goddamn thing."

"It doesn't matter," Ramie quietly interjected. "As long as he's punished, it doesn't matter who and what he's punished for."

"And can you live with that, Ramie?" Dane asked gently. "Knowing that there is no justice for what was done to you? For what *you* suffered?"

"I lived with that all my life. Nothing has changed. No one really knows the extent of my abilities. They leave, excited that they have hope. They never see what they leave behind so they have no way of *knowing* that more than one woman suffers."

"*I* know," Caleb roared. "I know *exactly* what is done to her and I will *not* allow her to go through that again. It's demeaning. It's degrading. No woman should ever have to endure such sick, twisted fantasies acted on them without their will, their consent, or their knowledge!"

Ramie shook her head adamantly, life flaring

in her eyes for the first time. "But this time it *will* be with my will and consent, Caleb. I'm making a *choice* to fight back. It's what I should have been doing all these months I spent cowering around every corner, terrified that I'd walk right into his arms. That's no way to live. I *can't* live that life anymore."

Desperation bled into her every word. In that moment of unguardedness he saw straight through her defenses though they were pitiful at best. She was truly at her rope's end. Bringing her here, in her way of thinking, was only delaying the inevitable of what she'd already expected. Her death. And peace.

"There has to be another way," Caleb said stubbornly. "One that doesn't involve you going back into hell. Think of what it will do to you, Ramie. You would be weak, defenseless after undergoing unimaginable trauma. And that's when he'd strike. When you were at your lowest point. Vulnerable. Unable to fight back."

"What I can't and won't do is stand here with my hands over my ears and face so I don't know someone else out there is suffering horrifically because of . . . me. Maybe you could live with that on your conscience. But I can't. I'm not wired that way. I knew what I was getting into all those years before. When I began aiding police in locating victims when I was just a teenager trying desperately to find my place in this world.

"My only 'family' came through the foster system and believe me, they had little interest in a girl who could track killers. I terrified them. But they took me for the money. The stipend they received to take me into their home. They only got me the bare essentials. Two pairs of clothes. A coat for when it got cold. Flip-flops for warmer weather and boots with socks for when it was cold. None of it fit me because my foster parents shopped at Goodwill Stores for the things they bought me. But for their real children, they bought the moon. Nothing was too good for them. I'll never forget one of my foster sisters," she said painfully. "Becky. She was such a sweet kid. Several years younger than me, and she didn't understand that I didn't fit in, that I wasn't family. She was upset that I never got presents like the others. Why I wasn't getting those same gifts."

"Jesus," Caleb muttered. "I don't want to hear the rest of this. Stop it, baby. Don't do this to yourself. It doesn't matter."

"I want to hear," Eliza softly interjected, ignoring Caleb's look of fury.

Ramie spoke unemotionally, as though she were reciting a news story that had no personal connection.

"My foster mother made it succinctly clear that

I was not her real daughter. That I was not their real sister. My foster father didn't even bother to acknowledge the question because to him I simply didn't exist. The only time he spoke of me, not *to* me, mind you, was if a check from the state was late arriving and then he'd storm around the house complaining about what a burden having another mouth to feed was when it was their own children who needed things. Not some street kid who told lies to police officers so it got her sympathy."

"Goddamn it," Caleb cursed savagely. He glanced at Dane and Eliza, furious that they had pushed her to this. It was like ripping off a bandage and causing a wound to bleed fresh blood.

Ramie was in her past now, digging up old hurts and disappointments. Her eyes became distant, the light flickering and dying slowly in her gaze.

"Becky disappeared on the way home from school. She walked with me sometimes, even though she wasn't supposed to. She'd hold my hand and smile up at me. I was so many years older than her and yet she seemed determined to take care of me. It always astonished me that something so good could come from such evil. Becky was sweet. Nothing like my foster parents or her other siblings. It was cold that day so I was walking fast, even though I was in no hurry to get home. As soon as I walked through the door the dad grabbed my shoulders, bruising me with his strength. I was always small for my age."

Caleb's and Eliza's expression blackened and became stormy. Dane shook his head, muttering God only knew what under his breath. He looked as pissed as the people he worked with.

"I knew he was putting up a front, but I didn't comprehend at first just what he'd done or *why*. He made accusations. He told the police I had threatened Becky and they believed him. Of course they did."

She broke off and went silent a long moment, the retelling obviously one of the many demons in her past.

"He didn't believe in my abilities. If he did, he would have made an effort to mask his thoughts. It was repulsive. I was in shock. And then I was terrified. I knew that no matter what happened that I needed to run and get as far away from the evil inside that house as I could."

"Did he hurt you?" Caleb asked menacingly.

Ramie's gaze shot upward, surprise reflected all over her face. "It doesn't matter now, Caleb. That was ten years ago. I'm not that scared teenager anymore."

"No, you're just a very scared adult," Eliza said gently.

Ramie swallowed visibly, not refuting Eliza's

assertion. She looked frozen, her hands trembling violently.

"Ramie?" Caleb asked gently. "What happened next? What happened to Becky?"

"He touched me," Ramie choked out. "Not sexually. But he grabbed my shoulders, putting on a show for the police, playing the role of the frantic parent who feared his daughter had been harmed by the freak teenage foster child. And I could see what he wanted, every sick, demented fantasy he'd conjured. He had no idea that the minute he touched me I felt every single thing he wanted to do to me in full color. It was as if it really happened. I felt as violated as if it had happened."

"I'm going to kill him," Caleb said with such fury that it seemed to scorch the air around them.

"What happened to Becky?" Eliza persisted, steering Ramie back forcibly.

Her voice was whipcord strong, snapping over Ramie and making her compliant. Anger bristled Caleb, his nostrils quivering. He held up his hand to stop it all but Dane shook his head.

"Wait," Dane said quietly.

Ramie stood as still as a statue, her features frozen. Caleb reached for one of her hands, and she flinched at the contact. Her fingers were icy and goose bumps spread rapidly up her arm, every hair on end. She snatched her hand back as if he'd burned her, and she cupped the hand he'd touched with her other, rubbing absently as if he'd injured her.

"There was one police officer who at least looked as though he hadn't already judged me and found me guilty. He kept silent, watching the father. And me. I think he knew, or suspected. He separated me from my foster parents, telling them he needed to question me. When we were alone, he told me that he'd done research on me. And that he thought I could help find Becky. He said if I'd help find her that he would make sure I was placed with another family—a good one."

"He *blackmailed* you," Eliza said in an appalled voice.

"You agreed," Caleb said grimly.

His stomach turned over and he traded glances with Eliza and Dane, saw the same knowledge on their faces of where this was going. It sickened him. He'd do anything to protect Ramie from her past, but there was nothing he could do. The damage was already done. Maybe she'd never recover.

Ramie nodded slowly. "Yes. I agreed. Of course I agreed. I had to prove that I had nothing to do with her disappearance."

She closed her eyes, visible pain furrowing her brow. She swayed on her feet and Caleb wrapped his fingers around her arm just above her elbow to steady her. This time she didn't flinch away from him, but he was calmer now. He had to be more careful to control his thoughts and not hurt her with his emotions.

"Becky's father said he'd found her backpack on the roadway where she walked from school, that he found it when she didn't come home and he got worried. He truly didn't believe in my abilities or he would have never given me that backpack. He called me a scammer. An exploiter of parents frantic to find their children. Of people trying desperately to find a loved one. I didn't need to touch the bag to know he'd done something terrible. The police officer knew the same. And yet I wasn't prepared for what I saw. I picked up that backpack and then I immediately bent over and threw up. And I kept throwing up. I didn't think I'd ever stop."

Ramie went silent, her eyes haunted and her throat working up and down as if she were trying to prevent herself from throwing up *now*.

"What did you see?" Eliza prompted gently.

Ramie licked her lips. Her face was chalk white, and her shaking intensified. Eliza quickly ran cold water over a washcloth, wrung it out and then held it to Ramie's face. Eliza's hand was on Ramie's shoulder, her touch motherly even though there wasn't a large gap in age between the two women.

It took a few moments for Ramie to compose herself. She sucked in several steadying breaths, and her chest rose and fell harshly, as if she were swallowing away her nausea. Then she sank onto the closed commode seat and scrubbed both hands over her face.

"I was terrified to call him out. I was too afraid of what he might do. The police officer knew, though. He whispered to me where the father couldn't hear and all he asked me was 'Where?' "

"I told him where to find my foster sister, but I knew they'd be too late. He left her there to die, and I wasn't in time to save her. Sometimes I wonder if she only stayed alive long enough for someone to know what he'd done. She was so young, so good. How could she have come from such evil?"

Caleb slid his hand into Ramie's hair and then knelt in front of her. He pressed his lips to the top of her head, uncaring of Eliza's and Dane's presence.

"I'm so sorry, honey."

She twined her arms around his neck and clung to him. He leaned in, touching his forehead to hers, and then he wrapped his arms around her slight body.

"I have to do this, Caleb," she whispered. "Not only for myself, but for you. For Tori. For the woman who is suffering while we argue her fate. I have to do this. I'll never be able to live with myself if she dies and I did nothing to help her."

He closed his eyes, knowing she was right but hating it all the same. He turned his head to look up at Eliza and Dane, who still stood in the doorway.

"Make the call," he said shortly.

"I guess that means we're not fired," Eliza murmured as she brushed past Dane and disappeared down the hallway.

SEVENTEEN

RAMIE sat on the edge of the couch, her gaze focused forward. She rubbed her palms up and down her pants legs and then wrapped her arms around herself, her fingers pressing into her flesh.

She wasn't even aware of the fact that she rocked back and forth, distress radiating from her in waves. Caleb felt powerless, unable to shield her from what she was about to do.

Her lips thinned and her gaze flickered in question. Her gaze found Eliza.

"How could you possibly know there's another victim?"

Caleb frowned when he saw Eliza glance rapidly at Dane and they both frowned.

"That's a very good question," Caleb said softly. "I think you forget who signs your paychecks."

"He's taunting you," Eliza said bluntly. "He

called it in himself. He wanted you to know, to track him. The victim is his message to you."

Caleb's pulse leapt in alarm. "She's not doing this. Are you insane? He's setting her up. Ramie, you can't do this."

"When did he call it in?" Ramie asked. "How did he call it in? How do you know it's him?"

Dane grimaced. "This morning. He called the Houston police. Left a message for you."

Ramie stared back at Dane in shock.

"It's why I wanted to get a sketch artist to draw his face," Eliza said. "Leak it to the press. Post it on the Internet. Get people looking for him. Houston's a big city. We don't even know that he's here, only that he called the downtown precinct and told them to let Ramie St. Claire know that she couldn't hide from him forever and that he was waiting for her and until then he'd found someone else to entertain him."

"Detective Ramirez wanted to bring Ramie in," Dane said. "We told him we were sitting on you and that he was trying to draw you out."

"You have to beat him at his own game, Ramie," Eliza said, her gaze sharp and piercing.

Ramie slowly swiveled her head in Caleb's direction, question in her eyes. Not a question of whether she should do it or not. But the question of whether he was with her. Whether he'd be here for her.

He sat next to her and slid his hand over her leg to catch her fingers between her knees. He laced their fingers together and squeezed reassuringly, even though the last thing he felt was confident.

He hadn't felt so much fear since the day Tori had been abducted. Nor as helpless. He wasn't used to having so little power or control over his surroundings. He was always in command but over the last year, he'd been anything but.

"I'll be here, Ramie," he murmured. "I'm not going anywhere. But I need you to promise me something."

"What?" she asked, her eyes never leaving his face.

"I don't really know how to say what I'm thinking because I don't truly understand how your powers work, but if it gets bad, promise me you'll pull back. Don't stay there with him. Come back to *me*."

She sucked in a breath. "I'll try."

He didn't like how unconfident she sounded. How uncertain. And how afraid. Her voice trembled, her lips quivering slightly. She tucked her bottom lip between her teeth, chewing nervously at the tender flesh.

He thumbed her lip from her teeth and soothed the ravaged skin. Then he leaned in and brushed a kiss over her mouth.

"I'll be here the entire time."

Ramie closed her eyes, relief settling over her features. She leaned toward him, resting her forehead against his. He framed her face with his palms and then moved his lips up to press another kiss over her brow.

For several minutes, they sat that way, their breaths mingling and mixing. He stroked a hand down her hair, soothing her or perhaps himself.

"What the hell is going on?"

Caleb turned to see Quinn standing in the doorway to the living room, Beau right behind, coming to stand next to him. They were both wearing frowns and Beau's gaze darted between Caleb and Ramie. His frown deepened as though he sensed the heavy undercurrent in the room.

"Caleb?" Beau queried. "I just left Tori's room. She's upset. You should go up and talk to her."

Caleb felt Ramie stiffen next to him, and he cursed under his breath. Beau and Quinn both didn't want Ramie here. Not when it upset Tori so badly. But there was no way in hell he was leaving her to shoulder her burden alone. Especially not when she was going back into the mind of a victim and a killer.

Eliza stood, crossing her arms as she stepped between Ramie and Caleb's brothers as if shielding her from their disapproval.

"HPD is coming in," Dane interrupted as he

glanced down at his phone. "You'll need to let them past security."

Ramie seemed to make herself even smaller next to Caleb.

"What the hell is the Houston police doing here?" Quinn asked. "We aren't in the city limits here."

"Ramie is helping them," Caleb said evenly. "Let them through."

Beau's gaze narrowed and he studied Ramie in silence, finally allowing his gaze to drift back to Caleb. "If it's so damn hard on her, then why is she agreeing to do it again?"

Caleb could see Ramie's nostrils flare from the corner of his eye. Her fingers curled into tight fists and she stared down at the floor, so quiet he couldn't even hear her breathe.

Finally she raised her head up and Eliza stepped to the side as Ramie stared his brothers down.

"I guess you'll be the judge of how hard it is on me," she said evenly.

"I'll get the door," Quinn said, stepping back.

"You need to back off, Beau. You and Quinn both," Caleb said, anger bristling over him. "Tori isn't the only victim here."

"That's strange. I'm pretty sure Ramie was nowhere near the place where Tori was held captive. Maybe you've forgotten your priorities but Quinn and I haven't," Beau said in an equally angry tone.

"Stop it, both of you," Eliza snapped. "She's not a piece of raw meat for two dogs to fight over. And Beau, Tori isn't the only woman who's suffered. There are a hell of a lot of others out there, and Ramie is seeking justice for all of them. Your sister included."

Ramie sent Eliza a look of gratitude. Her jaw was clenched tightly, and she refused to even look at Caleb. Damn it. Before Caleb could respond or try to smooth things over with Ramie, Quinn returned to the living room, two men on his heels.

Ramie went pale, her eyes closing. Her hands trembled in her lap and Caleb slid his fingers down her wrist to curl around one fist.

"You aren't alone this time, Ramie," he assured her.

EIGHTEEN

RAMIE'S palms became damp, and sweat formed on her upper lip. She sucked air in like a guppy out of water, her chest tight, each breath like fire through her lungs.

She couldn't believe she was willingly putting herself through this again. When she'd sworn not to. She felt like a circus freak show, put on display and expected to perform.

At the very least, it would go down her way. No one else was going to call the shots.

Her jaw was clenched so tightly that her teeth ached. She barely managed to nod as the two detectives introduced themselves. Caleb was impatient and in no mood to prolong the matter. He swiped at his hair and gripped the back of his neck as he listened to the men explain the phone call they'd received from the man stalking Ramie.

She tuned out the voices. Sinister laughter echoed through her mind and she wasn't sure if she imagined it or if he was amusing himself at her expense.

When she realized that evidently everyone expected her to channel the killer right there in the living room while they watched, she shook her head. One of the detectives held out a small handbag, waiting for her to take it. She refused, staring at it like it was a snake. She knew the second she touched it, she'd be pulled into the abyss and this time she wasn't sure if she'd return.

"Ramie?" Eliza said softly. "Tell me how you want to do this. You're the one calling the shots."

Her mouth went dry and she swallowed painfully. She nodded her acceptance but made no move toward the detective holding the clutch. There was dirt on it.

And blood.

She stared at the purse, dread tightening her chest and stomach.

Caleb pulled her into his arms, turning his back to the rest of the room, shielding her from view. He pressed his lips to the top of her hair. His arms were strong around her. Implacable.

She stood silently, absorbing his strength, preparing for the onslaught ahead. Steeling herself, she stepped away from Caleb and then turned her focus on the two detectives.

"Not here," she said in a low voice. "Give it to Caleb. I'll do it upstairs."

Detective Ramirez exchanged looks with the other detective and then cleared his throat. "This is evidence. I'd prefer not to let it out of my sight."

"Do you want to find her?" Ramie interjected bluntly.

Beau and Quinn had identical looks of distaste on their faces, but she wouldn't let them shame her. She had to be strong. Ruthless. Or she'd never get through this.

"Everyone out," Caleb said tersely.

Eliza hesitated, glancing at Caleb. "Do you want me to stay?"

"No," Ramie said quietly. "Just Caleb. He's seen it before. He knows what it's like."

Caleb flinched, regret simmering in his dark eyes. "Go," he said in a low voice. "I'll take care of her."

"I'd like to tape her," Detective Briggs spoke up.

"Absolutely not," Caleb said before Ramie could launch her own protest. She was horrified and appalled. The very last thing she wanted was her vulnerability broadcast far and wide. All it would take is one leak to the media and the video would go viral all over YouTube and Facebook.

A chill descended, like it had upstairs in the bedroom she had no desire to go back to. She clenched her jaw to keep her teeth from chattering. They'd all think she was crazy or ill. It had to be ninety degrees outside. In October. How did anyone bear the heat for so long?

Caleb noticed though, his gaze sweeping up her arm where chill bumps dotted her skin. He frowned and gestured for the others to leave the room as he'd instructed.

"Are you all right?" Caleb murmured. "Perhaps you shouldn't do this."

"I just want to get it over with," she said through her clenched jaw.

Her head was starting to ache fiercely. Nausea welled in her stomach and she hadn't even established a link yet.

"Hurry, please," she whispered.

Caleb barked orders at the occupants of the room. Ramie broke away from him and sank onto the couch, bending over to stare at the floor. His hand slid over her shoulder and to her nape, gathering her hair between his fingers, tangling and then soothing.

She turned her gaze upward, seeing the small purse in his grasp. She stared at it, holding her breath, wondering what horrors it hid.

Caleb lowered himself to one knee in front of her, not extending the bag yet. She ran her hands up and down her legs, feeling the rasp of the worn denim beneath the pads of her fingers.

Sucking in a deep breath, she tentatively reached for the bag and blackness consumed her. Dizzyingly, she spiraled down, screams so loud in her ears that she was nearly deafened.

The scent of blood was overpowering. Metallic and acrid. It burned her nose, assaulted her senses. She knew with certainty that it was too late for this victim. She'd never had a chance.

There was a gasp of awareness in Ramie's mind. The victim thought she was already dead and that the sudden burst of warmth in her mind was an angel. Ramie didn't dissuade her. Instead she tried to comfort the dying woman the only way she could.

"I won't let him get away with this," she whispered to the victim. "Justice will be served."

"Thank you," the woman whispered.

Ramie's head exploded, darkness engulfing her. Evil so strong, so radiant it was like a black hole sucking her inward.

"I've been waiting for you," he murmured. "Amusing myself until you arrived. Now that you're here . . ."

"No!" Ramie screamed just as the woman's eyes went glassy with death.

His laughter echoed in her tormented mind. Where was she? Why hadn't she come back? The victim was dead, no longer holding the link alive through Ramie.

"I'll keep collecting them," he whispered silkily. "You can't stop me. But you can give yourself to me. You for them. You would keep me entertained, Ramie. They can't. They're too weak. They give up too easily."

"I'll kill you," she said in a savage whisper.

He laughed again and she felt the brush of his fingertips on her skin. Repulsed, she tried to withdraw, tried to sever the connection he was holding to her. Blood pumped through her head, pulsing violently at her neck as she fought back.

Pain assaulted her. She couldn't breathe. Blood, there was so much blood. Everywhere, covering her hands, her clothing. She glanced down at the woman, at all the blood seeping from the still-warm body.

"Ramie! Ramie! Goddamn it, come back to me!"

So far away. Someone calling her name. It was a jolt to her system and she realized that she'd quit fighting. That she was slowly being sucked away from Caleb, dying inexplicably.

She was being shaken. Caleb was shouting at her not to go. Cold. She was so very cold.

She floated, buoyant, so light. Her eyes fluttered open and she stared into the face of death. He was strangely beautiful, not at all like the demon she imagined. He looked benign, his features sculpted like art.

His teeth flashed. Perfectly straight, impossibly white. This was not a man who blended in. He would draw notice wherever he went. How could he have escaped capture for so long?

"People see what they want to see, Ramie," he murmured, his breath hot on her face. He tilted his head this way and that, sliding his finger gracefully down her jawline. His smile was gentle, a caress. Satisfaction . . . victory, shone back at her. She blinked and then closed her eyes, searching within herself for the power to fight back.

She opened her eyes, staring into his, mesmerized by the startling blue orbs.

"Fuck you," she said coldly.

Rage clouded his face as he stumbled back. She was suddenly free, the oppressive weight gone. It was as though she'd been sucked down into water and suddenly turned loose. She shot upward, swimming back to consciousness. And Caleb.

Her eyelids fluttered open and she saw Caleb nearly nose to nose with her, his hands framing her face as he shouted hoarsely for her to come back and not let that bastard win.

"Ramie?"

Her breath escaped her noisily. She sagged, slipping from his grasp, hitting the floor. She lay gasping, weak and vulnerable, huddled there in a ball, shaking convulsively.

The others pounded into the room, their heavy footsteps vibrating the floor as they rushed toward her. Caleb leaned down, his own eyes closed, relief pouring from him in waves.

"Oh God, Ramie. I thought I'd lost you," he whispered.

"Is this what you did to her before?"

The shocked exclamation yanked Ramie's gaze up, Tori's face going into and out of focus. She stood between her brothers, looking terrified and appalled, apology in her eyes.

"Did you do that to her when she told you where to find me?" Tori demanded.

Caleb slid shaking hands over Ramie's shoulders, pulling her from the floor, into his arms. He pressed her face into his chest, heaving in exertion. His fingers flexed in her hair and then smoothed the tangles as he kissed the strands.

"Yes, I did this to her," Caleb said wearily. "God help me, but I did."

Ramie lay limply against him. She lacked the strength to even sit up on her own. She couldn't force herself to open her eyes. Tears slipped endlessly down her cheeks. A sob welled in her throat and stuttered out against his chest.

"Do you know where she is?" Detective Briggs demanded. "Were you able to locate her?"

"Don't cry, Ramie," Caleb whispered. "Please don't cry. I've got you. You're safe."

"She's dead," Ramie choked out. "He killed her as soon as I established the link. It's what he was waiting for."

Detective Ramirez swore. Eliza knelt down beside Ramie and Caleb, her face drawn in sympathy.

"Where, Ramie? Can you tell us where she is? Don't let her die in vain. If you can tell us where to find her, they may catch him."

Dully, Ramie gave the location in a monotone, all the life sucked out as surely as the victim's life had been.

Beau's gaze flickered over Ramie, something that resembled remorse in his eyes. Quinn wrapped an arm around Tori, who was shaking, crying, as was Ramie, silently. The two women locked gazes, a moment of kinship before Tori glanced away, distress radiating from her. She ran from the room and Quinn swore violently.

"How could you have done this to her?" he said, raising his voice to Caleb. "The very last thing Tori needs is this, in her home."

Ramie dropped her head, looking away from Caleb's brothers. Exhaustion took hold and she drifted, uncaring, into the black void. There was peace in the silence. She reached for it, allowing it to suck her into its firm embrace. She was tired and there was too much pain for her in the present.

So she simply let go and let it swallow her whole.

Caleb felt Ramie go completely limp against him. Fear seized him, made him irrational.

"She deserves better from you," Caleb hissed. "No matter what you think she's done, she doesn't deserve your judgment. I sent her to hell to save Tori. That will always be between us. And now she's gone back because she's the only person who can stop a cold-blooded monster. What is *wrong* with you that you would treat a woman this poorly? What the hell has she done but try to survive with her sanity intact?"

Quinn's eyes widened at Caleb's vehemence. Beau frowned, guilt tugging at his implacable features.

"Is she . . . alive?" Beau asked uneasily.

The two detectives looked alarmed and immediately started toward Ramie. Caleb wrapped his arms around her, shielding her from everyone.

"What the hell happened in here?" Detective Briggs demanded.

"I damn near lost her. That's what happened," Caleb said fiercely. "Go. Find the victim. Call it in. Find him so she's safe. Don't let her have suffered this for nothing."

Detective Ramirez was already on his phone, barking out orders to dispatch.

"Let me look at her, Caleb," Dane said grimly. "Is she breathing?"

Caleb's hand twisted in her hair. He pressed his lips to her temple so he could feel the reassuring puff of her breath against his neck.

"She's alive," Caleb said tersely. "I'm taking her upstairs."

Caleb slowly got to his feet, mindful of jostling his precious burden. He scooped her into his arms and strode for the stairs, her pale face still buried against his chest. His heart thumped rapidly, fear still a living, breathing entity inside him.

He'd lived without fear for most of his life. Only in the last year had he been made vulnerable, realizing what it truly meant to be afraid every minute of every day. He hated fear. It was a paralyzing quality that he had no use for. And yet with allowing himself to care about someone came the knowledge that he'd live with fear the rest of his life because there were simply some things out of his control.

He carried Ramie into his bedroom, easing her down onto his mattress. Her hands and feet were blocks of ice, her skin so chilled she seemed tinged with blue. He pulled the covers back and then crawled into bed with her, pulling her body into his, offering his warmth to her.

She never even stirred, her breathing so light that he continually sought reassurance that she was breathing at all.

What the hell was he going to do? He'd never felt so goddamn helpless in his life. There was no amount of money he could throw at this problem to make it go away. Money had long since lost any intrinsic value to him. It was simply a tool like any other that made life more comfortable. It certainly didn't solve all of life's problems and it didn't make him immune to hardship and pain.

He inhaled the scent of her hair, closed his eyes and wondered what the hell he was going to do to make *her* pain go away.

She murmured something unintelligible and burrowed more firmly into his embrace. The small gesture gave him a measure of comfort. He relaxed, allowing the brief spurt of pleasure at having her molded against his body to surge hotly through his veins.

He would be here when she woke, so she didn't wake alone and frightened. No matter how long she slept, he'd be here, holding her when she came back.

NINETEEN

IT was nearly two in the morning before Ramie *finally* stirred. Caleb had lain tensely beside her all afternoon and evening, worrying over the fact she'd been out for so long. The moment he felt her move, he tensed and glanced at the clock beside his bed. He'd only just fallen into a light sleep.

A low whimper of distress escaped her lips. His hand immediately cupped her cheek and he tilted his head so his lips covered hers. She went utterly still against him. He could practically hear her working it all out in her mind. Remembering the torment she'd endured and her sudden awareness of where she was now.

Her body shook with silent sobs. It broke his heart to hear how defeated and hopeless she sounded.

"You aren't alone, Ramie," he whispered against her ear.

"He killed her. Oh God, Caleb, he *killed* her. He used her to bait me."

"Shhh, baby. It's not your fault."

Her fingers curled into his chest and her lips turned up against his neck. He felt the dampness on her cheeks and he kissed one of the tear trails away.

"Make me forget," she said brokenly. "Please. I can't bear it. She's all I can see. And all I know is that I failed her."

Caleb shook her a little, placing himself on eye level with her as he stared fiercely at her. "You did *not* fail her, Ramie. If you want to start assigning blame, then blame the right person. That sick bastard out there stalking you."

He rubbed his hand up and down her back, underneath the hem of her T-shirt, up her bare spine to her nape. He trailed his fingers around to her stomach and then up, molding her breast in his palm.

His lips stuttered over hers, sucking in her sob, her breath, and returning it in a heated rush. His thumb rasped over her nipple, teasing it to a puckered, rigid peak. Her arm slid around his waist, anchoring herself against him. Her hand splayed wide over his back just as he rolled her underneath him, pushing her shirt upward with his right hand.

His skin was on fire, wanting, needing to touch

her, to caress her. He'd never been so patient and gentle before. He wasn't sure she even knew what she'd asked him, and he'd never take advantage of her. He gave her time to tell him no, to change her mind, and then he wondered if he should say no for her, if she would hate him for making love to her.

"Ramie, baby."

Her lips whispered over his neck, up to his ear, where she nipped the lobe, sending a cascade of chills spilling over his skin.

"Tell me you want this," he rasped. "Be sure. I've already done enough to make you hate me."

"I don't hate you," she whispered back. "I understand. You don't have to keep explaining, Caleb. I'm so cold. Keep me warm."

His knee nudged her legs apart, rubbing over the thin material of her underwear. She shivered when his fingers dipped below the band and into her plush folds. She was damp, but not wet enough to take him yet.

He pulled her shirt up over her head then wrestled with his own as her hands tangled, trying to take it off him. There was a sense of urgency even as he tried to slow the pace down. He didn't want to overwhelm her. He didn't want her to do something she'd regret. But at the same time he wanted her with a desperation he'd never felt for a woman before.

It was hard to temper his urges. He wasn't used to denying himself anything. He'd never had to.

But Ramie was special. So fragile. He touched her like she was precious and breakable, his mouth glancing over her satiny skin. Her taste was sweet on his tongue. His tongue swirled around her nipples, his mouth sucking them to hard points. She gasped frantically, bucking upward, pushing herself farther into his mouth.

"Please, Caleb," she pleaded.

The hell she'd ever have to beg him for anything he could provide.

"Be sure, Ramie. Before I get inside you. Be very sure this is what you want. I'll stop now. All you have to do is tell me no."

She put her fingers to his lips, suddenly going still beneath him.

"I need you."

The simple elegance of her statement unraveled him. There was stark vulnerability in her words. He was achingly hard and yet he'd deny himself for her, to protect her. In order not to hurt her. He'd hurt her already. Enough for two lifetimes. He could never forget that even if she could.

He kissed a line down the center of her chest, his hands skating down her sides to pull at her panties. She arched, bowing up off the bed to allow him to slide her underwear down her legs. Her thighs fell open. He inhaled her scent, his body throbbing with heavy need.

Dying to taste her, he licked from her opening to her clit, his body tightening when she gasped in pleasure. Her fingers dove into his hair, flexing into his scalp. She held him in place as he sucked and licked, tasting her from inside out.

He had to have her. He was perilously close to coming and he wasn't even inside her yet. His cock was slick already, the head coated with precum. He wedged inside her opening, stretching her to accommodate his width.

He should give her more time. Prepare her more fully, and yet he still found himself pushing inward, sucking her surprised gasp into his mouth.

The sound of discovery she made, the sudden burst of moisture that coated his dick nearly made him come on the spot. Gritting his teeth, he forced himself back, holding himself rigidly just inside her opening.

"Now," she choked out. "Now, Caleb. Please."

He surged forward, planting himself hard and deep. She cried out and he fused his mouth to hers, remaining still inside her as she spasmed softly around him. Slick and hot she gripped him like a velvet fist. She clutched greedily at him, pulling him deeper.

He surrendered to her pull, the roaring in his

ears growing louder. He closed his eyes as color burst around him, sharp, explosive, his entire body drawn tight. He began thrusting hard and fast, the friction almost unbearable. So intensely pleasurable that he made a sound of agony through clenched teeth.

She went soft around him, her body molding sweetly to his. She let out a small hiccup into his mouth and then gasped, her breath hitching. Her fingers dug into his shoulders and she bucked upward, her cry sharp in the silence.

He pulled at her hair, tipped her head back while he devoured her mouth, consuming her like an addict in need of a fix. There was a violent need that consumed him, ricocheting up his spine and through his veins like a potent drug.

He surged forward, planting himself deep, holding there, his hips pressed hard into hers, their pelvises locked and undulating wildly. He dimly registered that he wasn't wearing a condom. That he hadn't even considered wearing a condom, and it was too late. His orgasm was unleashed like a wildfire, a furious storm that held him powerless in its grip.

She buried her face in his neck and held on tightly, her body shuddering wildly as her release broke over them in waves.

He'd never felt anything so beautiful in his life.

Never held something so precious in his hands before. He whispered her name over and over, overcome by the power of their coming together.

His body slowed, riding hers like ocean waves. He couldn't get enough of her. He was still hard and aching even after his release and reveling in the aftershocks. He gathered her tightly in his arms, rolling and bringing her on top of him.

She lay sprawled over him, her hair spilling like a curtain over his chest. He cupped her face in his palms, held her still for his kiss. Their tongues mated just as their bodies had. Twisting, turning, hot and wet.

Slowly her head lowered, her forehead touching his chest, the top of her head brushing his chin. He was still buried deeply within her. She pulsed around him, tugging rhythmically, pulling the last drops of his semen inside her body.

He'd never felt so complete in his life, and he had no idea how *she* felt.

He bunched up her hair in his fist and then relaxed his grip, stroking the soft curls against her head. Her chest heaved up and down, her entire body draped across his like a limp towel. She was warm and soft, so very feminine and delicate. He couldn't resist touching her, gliding his fingers over her pale skin.

He raised goose bumps where he touched. They

pimpled over her skin, raising the tiny hairs in their wake. He pressed his mouth to her neck, nuzzling softly with his lips.

"Did I hurt you?" he murmured.

She made a low humming sound and then shook her head, bumping it gently against his chin. "I never knew it could be like that," she said in wonder. Her voice cracked and she lifted her head so she could look into his eyes.

He slid both hands down her slender back to cup her behind. She was astride him, still pulsing around his cock with little quivers that were like electric shocks to his system.

His hand went still on her rounded bottom. "I didn't use a condom. I'm sorry. I've never been so caught up in the moment that I didn't use protection."

She shivered but didn't immediately respond. Her vagina clenched wetly around him and he felt himself harden again. He hadn't worn a condom the first time but he'd be damned if he made that mistake again.

Gently he turned her so they rolled to their sides. She snuggled against his body, her eyes closing as he withdrew from her liquid heat. He was immediately bereft of her warmth. He felt hollow and empty.

"You must be hungry," he said. "You had nothing to eat since breakfast."

She shuddered delicately. "I don't think I could eat even if I was hungry."

"You can't afford to skip meals," he pointed out. "You have to take better care of yourself, Ramie. If you won't do it, I will."

"Did they find her?" Ramie asked softly. "Did they catch him?"

Caleb tensed, his arm tightening protectively around her. "They found her. And no, they didn't capture him."

Her exhale was sharp. Her breaths hitched and stuttered from her lips.

"He's going to keep killing," she said painfully. "He wants me. He'll trade me for future victims."

"No!" Caleb exclaimed, fear gripping him by the throat. "Don't even think it. There will be no trades. No deals. No negotiating with insanity. You're staying here with me. Where I can be sure you're safe and protected."

"I can't hide forever," she protested.

"Can't you?" he challenged. "I have resources you can't imagine. I can make sure he never reaches you."

"At what price? How many more women have to die because of his obsession with me? Maybe we should talk to the police about a trade. A setup. Give him what he wants."

Panic slammed into his chest. He couldn't force air into his lungs. He was holding her so tightly that he was likely bruising her. He forced himself to relax but rage burned through his gut, eating a hole in his stomach.

"There will be no trade," he said tersely.

"It's not your decision."

"The hell it's not! One of us has to play it smart and it sure as hell isn't you. You aren't in this alone, Ramie. And there's no way in hell I'm letting you offer yourself like a sacrificial lamb to a deranged psychopath who wants your death. It's not up for negotiation. If I have to tie you to the goddamn bed and sit on you I'll do it and suffer no remorse whatsoever."

"What do we do then?" she asked in frustration. "I can't live like this, Caleb. I can still smell blood, feel it on my hands and remember the instant he killed her. It's a game of chess to him. He's cold and calculating and he enjoys death. He's god of his own universe and is an unstoppable force."

He kissed her furrowed brow, trying to ease her fretting. "You being dead won't save anyone." She sucked in her breath as he continued ruthlessly. "Do you honest to God believe he'd stop with you? He'll always need the rush. A bigger challenge."

She made a frustrated sound of grief. "He's probably already hunting for his next target. He'll keep taunting me until he gets what he wants."

"I don't give a damn what he wants," Caleb

snapped, his arm tightening around her body. "I will not hand you over to him nor will I allow you to be drawn into a trap that may or may not result in his capture. We'll find another way."

"There is no other way," she said quietly. "You know it and I know it. Eliza and Dane know it. The police know it. How long do you think they're going to put up with a maniac killing off women before they throw me at him?"

"If I have to take you out of the country I will," Caleb said, his jaw clenched tightly. "This isn't open for debate, Ramie."

She sagged against him and then sighed wearily. "We can't do this, Caleb. It's insane."

He frowned, a growl of frustration welling in his throat. "We've already discussed this. I asked you to stay. To fight for your right to stay. With me. For me. If I'm willing to make sacrifices, shouldn't you be as well?"

Ramie pushed herself up on her elbow, tugging the sheet over her breasts. "Any other time I'd say yes. If we'd met . . . before. Maybe we would have had a chance. But this has no shot at working out the way it stands now. What kind of life will you have with me in hiding for the rest of my life, unwilling to confront a killer? A constant reminder to your family of what happened to Tori."

"Shut up," he said rudely. "I never said I had all

the answers. But I happen to think you're worth fighting for. I'm not giving you up."

"God, Caleb. It's not that I don't want you or that I don't want to fight for you—us—whatever. I'm just trying to get you to understand what kind of life it will be, not only for you but for your family. I can't hide for the next fifty years."

"I don't see why the hell not," Caleb bit out.

She let her head fall to his chest, pressing her forehead against his skin. He sighed and slid his hand into her hair, absently massaging her nape.

"I have feelings for you that I've never had for another woman. And I want to explore those feelings. See where it takes us. All I know is that I can't—won't—give you up. Not for Tori or my brothers and definitely not for a homicidal maniac. As I said, I don't have all the answers—yet. But that doesn't mean I'm just giving up and handing you over like some virgin sacrifice."

She stared at him in silence. He could see her processing his statement, obvious befuddlement in her features.

"Just accept it," Caleb said. "You aren't going to talk me out of it. You aren't going to tell me what I do or don't feel for you. And you may as well resign yourself to the fact that I'm digging my heels in whether you like it or not. Now, I'm going to go down and fix us something to eat and then we're going to go back to bed and in the morning we'll sit down with Dane and Eliza and brainstorm some more. And one more thing, Ramie," he said, tugging her hair so she was forced to look at him. "Get used to being in my bed because that's where you're going to sleep from now on."

TWENTY

TORI sat up in bed, coming awake with a gasp. Her heart pounded violently in her chest, her pulse so rapid she was weak. She scrambled out of bed, the images still vibrant and alive in her mind. She could still hear the gunshot, smell the blood and could see the face of her tormentor as he pointed a gun straight at her.

She went into her bathroom and splashed cool water on her flushed face. Then she lifted haunted eyes to her reflection in the mirror and winced at how pale and gaunt she looked.

It had been a year. It was time to move on. Time to stop being afraid of her shadow. Live.

Was the dream a vision or was it simply a nightmare? It was too real, too crisp and vivid to be a dream. Dreams didn't usually make sense and were jumbled images randomly thrown together.

She went still for a moment, her brow furrowing in concentration. She didn't recognize where the shooting took place. It definitely wasn't here or anywhere she was familiar with.

It should be easy enough to avoid, if indeed it was a prophetic vision. She never left the house. She was too afraid to go out, either with someone or alone. Especially alone.

What had her life become? Who had she become? She no longer recognized the girl in the mirror. She was dull and lifeless. Scared and timid. A far cry from the woman she'd been a year ago before she'd gone to hell.

How did Ramie do it? How could she bear to endure that over and over? Tori flinched at how angry and rude she'd been with Ramie. The idea that someone had seen her shame was more than she could bear, though. Great injustice had been wrought against Ramie St. Claire, but Tori couldn't find the empathy to soften against this fragile woman.

She stood in the bathroom a long moment before finally going back into her bedroom. She crawled under the covers, pulling them to her chin. She lay there shaking, her stomach churning endlessly.

An hour later, she gave up. A trip to the kitchen would be a welcome—and necessary—nightly patrol. One she didn't confide in her brothers. But between the times they or their men scouted the house, inside and out, Tori had her own route she followed, moving her markers so that she would notice a difference if someone touched them. Her brothers would think she was crazy, clinically insane if they knew how obsessed she was with the fear of someone coming into her home and taking her again. She hid a lot from her brothers. This was just another thing in a long list they didn't need to know about because they'd only worry more than they already did.

Sleep wouldn't happen tonight. Just like so many other nights in the past year, she'd be awake, staring up at the ceiling and trying to shut the door on things she'd rather forget.

At least if she had food and coffee, then the middle-of-the-night munchy run wasn't all that strange.

As much as she wanted to put her past behind her and cower in the corner of her choosing, she hated being alone. She just didn't want people always psychoanalyzing her. Always knowing what she needed or wanted. They had no idea.

She just wanted to be normal and focus on what all young women focused on. Their first job out of college. The knowledge that they're ready to take on the world, live in their own apartments, make their own choices.

Except Tori, who, at twenty-three, was focused on none of those things. Not that she didn't give them a passing thought every once in a while.

TWENTY-ONE

RAMIE lazily opened her eyes and sighed, stretching like a cat next to Caleb's body. Her mind was refreshingly blank. No fragments of violence and death. Just blissful calm. Maybe she had Caleb to thank for that. She'd told him to make her forget, but she hadn't really believed anyone could ease her torment.

"Morning," Caleb murmured as he pressed his lips to her forehead.

His arm tightened around her, pulling her into his side. She slid her hand over his taut abdomen and up the hard planes of his chest until her palm rested over his heart. The thud of his pulse against her skin was reassuring.

"Good morning," she returned.

"I have to leave for a few hours," he said, an

apology in his voice. "There are things I need to take care of. I have a meeting with my attorney to sign several business documents. I'll be back as soon as I can."

"Don't put your life on hold for me," she said firmly. "And don't jeopardize your business by babysitting me twenty-four/seven."

"Hate to break it to you, baby, but my life is already on hold for you."

Even as she felt dismay over his statement, warmth spread through her veins at the conviction in his voice. She closed her eyes and allowed herself to daydream and ponder the what-ifs. She knew it was stupid—and dangerous—to pin her hopes on a normal life. Her life would never be normal. But it didn't make her want it any less.

"I'll work with the sketch artist while you're gone," Ramie said in a low voice.

It was ridiculous to fear putting his face down on paper, but it terrified her nonetheless.

Caleb squeezed her to him. "If you want to wait for me to get back I'll stay with you while you talk to the sketch artist."

She shook her head. "No. It needs to be done as soon as possible. It should have already been done. Perhaps if I hadn't been so hysterical we could have saved his last victim."

"Stop," Caleb said in a terse voice. "Don't go there again, Ramie. You are not to blame and I won't have you thinking it much less saying it."

No matter how convinced Caleb was, Ramie didn't feel the same way. She hated being so power-less. She hated that she was helpless to do anything to prevent him from targeting his next victim. God only knew how many women he'd already killed.

But she fell silent, not wanting to argue with Caleb when he was so determined not to place blame on her.

Caleb gathered her up with his arm and leaned down to kiss her. "I'm going to go shower so I can get gone and back as soon as possible. Eliza and Dane will be with you until I return. You won't have to worry about Tori or my brothers. Dane has been instructed to keep you away from them."

She bit her lip to stanch her reaction to his words. He didn't mean them to be hurtful, but how could they not be when the people most important to him wanted her gone and out of the way?

She brushed her mouth over his chest and hugged him tightly. "Hurry back," she said. "I miss you already."

It was the truth. Knowing he wouldn't be here, protecting her, fueled her anxiety. But she had to keep it together so she could help put a psychopath behind bars.

She rolled away, taking the top sheet with her. As she stood, the sheet unfurled and she wrapped it loosely around her body, suddenly conscious of her nudity—and his. He pushed himself out of bed, and she saw his erection that had nothing to do with it being morning.

She clutched the folds of the material over her breasts as he walked around the end of the bed to stand just in front of her. Then he reached forward, tugging at the sheet until finally she let go. It pooled at her feet and Caleb's avid gaze burned a trail over her skin.

He cupped her shoulders and pulled her into his embrace. His warmth was a shock against her chilled skin. His big hands roamed over her back and down to the curve of her behind, squeezing possessively.

"I thought you had to go," she whispered.

"I do. But we both happen to need a shower, so why not kill two birds with one stone?"

She shivered delicately, her pulse bounding. His lips found hers in a heated rush. His hands tangled in her hair, tugging lightly so her chin was angled upward and her mouth fit perfectly to his.

He began backing them toward the bathroom, his lips never leaving hers. When they got inside, he fumbled for the light switch and then he lifted her, hoisting her up his body before placing her on the counter between the two sinks.

His cock was rigid, straining upward toward his navel when he hurriedly turned on the shower. When he returned to her, his erection pressed hard against her belly as he gathered her in his arms once more.

She let out a sigh and let her head rest on his shoulder. He brushed his lips over her exposed neckline and then nibbled a path to her earlobe. Again she found herself lifted. She wrapped her legs around his waist to anchor herself more firmly. Holding her with one arm, Caleb stuck his free hand into the spray to test the temperature.

Evidently satisfied with the result, Caleb stepped into the shower and lowered Ramie to her feet. Even so, he still kept one arm firmly wrapped around her while reaching for the shampoo with his other hand.

He soaped her from head to toe, petting and caressing until she was nearly mindless with need. She was aroused to fever pitch, craving, wanting so badly. Steam rose, coating their skin with dewy moisture, and then he ducked her back under the spray to rinse her off.

Not five minutes later, Caleb tugged hard at the faucet to turn off the shower and then he was out of the stall in seconds, lifting her to the counter and fitting his erection between her thighs all in one smooth motion.

He plunged deep and hard. Ripple after ripple

of raw pleasure consumed her. She threw back her head, bumping the mirror behind her. Her hair clung wetly to her body as she arched her breasts forward for his mouth to find.

Her hands slapped the counter and her fingers curled around the edge to give her leverage as he continued to drive into her. And then with a muffled curse he swiftly withdrew, his face a wreath of strain. The veins at his temples were distended and he tugged in shaky breaths, his chest heaving with the effort.

"Don't stop!" she gasped. "God, Caleb, you can't stop now!"

"I forgot the goddamn condom *again*," he growled. "Give me just a minute."

It seemed an eternity before he yanked one of the drawers open and then ripped at one of the packets. He fumbled between her legs a moment and then spread her wide once more.

He pushed into her and they both moaned. She curled both arms around his neck, pulling him down to kiss her. Had there ever been a man like Caleb in her life? Never had she felt the tumultuous rush of raw, hedonistic desire.

"God, what you do to me, Ramie," he said through clenched teeth. "You make me forget everything until all I want is to be inside you and never leave."

She slid her mouth down his jaw and then nipped lightly at his throat, causing him to shudder violently against her. She inhaled deeply, the combination of powerful male and his soap swirling through her senses.

He slid his hands underneath her behind and lifted her upward, his fingers digging into her flesh, branding her irrevocably. Her body clamped down around his erection, holding it, sucking it deeper inside her.

"You make me forget too," she whispered.

Her nails scoured his back and he let out a growl of pleasure. He swelled within her, surging hard and fast until the only sound that could be heard was the slap of flesh against flesh.

The mirror was completely fogged from the hot shower and their rapid heavy breathing. She tilted back, allowing her head to rest against the glass once more. She gripped his forearms as her orgasm roared over her, tightening, clenching every muscle in her body.

Her release was so explosive that her vision went blurry and she seemed to float outside of her body. His name was a litany on her lips, whispered over and over as he claimed his own release.

He convulsed against her, his hold on her almost bruising, and yet it gave her comfort to know she was completely sheltered in his arms.

His breath stuttered over his lips, his entire body heaving as they both tried to catch up.

He smoothed wet hair from her forehead and then kissed the spot he exposed.

"I know you probably aren't ready to hear this, Ramie, but I'm not just falling in love with you. I *am* in love with you."

She froze, holding her breath as he pulled back just enough that he could look into her eyes. Panic struck and she couldn't get her tongue to cooperate. Would he be angry that she couldn't find the same words? That the idea of being loved and in love was terrifying to her?

She was marked for death. She couldn't afford emotional entanglements because it would only end in grief. She didn't want Caleb to love her because then it would hurt him if something happened to her.

"Caleb . . ."

His name was all she could muster. Tenderly, he pressed a finger to her lips.

"Don't," he said. "It's all right, Ramie. I can wait until you're ready. Just know that you are loved and you aren't alone. For now, it's enough."

TWENTY-TWO

FINALLY, his quarry was in his sights. He smiled a slow, satisfied smile as he watched Caleb Devereaux walk into the building that housed all of his businesses. He was especially amused by the newly formed security company. Did Devereaux honestly think his security experts were any match for his genius?

Chuckling to himself, he shook his head and then hunkered down to wait for Devereaux to exit the building. He was a patient man and patience was always rewarded. Always. Patience was a virtue according to the Bible.

"I'm coming for you, Ramie," he said in a sing-song, soft voice.

His mind was flooded with images of Ramie St. Claire being punished for interfering in his quests. It was his duty to rid the world of the weak and the sinners. But then Ramie had turned the investigators loose on him. She'd cost him valuable time. He'd had to fall back and regroup, lying low and lulling everyone into a false sense of security. They'd thought he'd stopped the cleansing, but in truth he only took a sabbatical.

He laughed again. A sabbatical from sin. It had a certain ring to it.

Ramie St. Claire didn't have his entire focus. He was capable of splitting his attention, especially when it came to new blood. Another waited for him. He licked his lips in anticipation and rubbed his hands back and forth together.

As soon as his job was done here, he'd take care of his latest conquest. Ramie would be pleased, no doubt, that he had another victim because it meant she wasn't his yet. But soon. Very soon all the pieces would fall into place and Ramie would be punished for her sins.

He came to attention, his nostrils flaring and eyes narrowing as he focused on Caleb Devereaux leaving the office building. He started forward, his stride hobbled, his clothing dirty and torn. There was nothing about his current appearance to hint at his identity. He was very careful and he knew he was smarter than the others. They wouldn't find him.

His pulse accelerated and a giddy thrill coursed through his veins as Caleb Devereaux approached.

Caleb didn't see him. Men like Caleb never saw the less fortunate. He looked past others as though they didn't exist in his privileged world. His short-sightedness would cost him dearly.

On cue, he stumbled, falling forward directly into Devereaux's path. His arm flailed upward as if he were trying to catch himself. His fingers curled tightly around Devereaux's arm as he went to one knee.

"Sir, are you all right?" Devereaux asked in a concerned voice.

Surprise prickled down his spine at Devereaux's reaction. He blinked and forced his attention back to the task at hand.

Devereaux helped him to his feet while he had his hand clamped around Devereaux's wrist.

"Do you need medical attention?" Devereaux asked, his brow furrowing.

He shook his head and rasped out, "No. Thank you, sir. You've been kind. But I'm all right. I just tripped. Sorry to have bothered you."

"You weren't a bother," Devereaux said kindly.

Then to his surprise, Devereaux reached into his billfold and pulled out several twenties. He held the money out to him, urging him to take it.

Even better. He now had something that had been in Devereaux's possession, which had his im-print all over it.

"Have a blessed day," he said to Devereaux in a gravelly voice that sounded as aged as he currently looked. And then he turned and shuffled away, careful to keep the guise of an old, homeless man. A smile hovered on his lips and adrenaline pumped through his veins, giving him a euphoric high that could only be topped when he had Ramie St. Claire at his mercy.

TWENTY-THREE

"THE eyes aren't right," Ramie said, frustration beating at her temples.

She scrubbed a hand over her face and closed her own eyes momentarily. She tried to force herself to relax and allow her mind to hone in on her stalker's features. But every time she pulled up his face it was all a giant blur.

Her head pounded viciously. The harder she tried to bring the image into focus, the more her head hurt. It felt as though she could burst a blood vessel in her brain at any moment.

"Do you need to take a break?" Dane asked.

His concern was evident as his gaze swept over her. Judging by his reaction, she must look pretty terrible. If she looked even half as bad as she felt then the expression *death warmed over* applied.

"We can stop for a few moments," Eliza said

gently. "Maybe get some fresh air. Would you like something to drink?"

"My head," she moaned, pain assaulting her over the two words she verbalized. She sandwiched her head between her hands, pressing her palms to her throbbing temples.

"Are you all right?" Dane demanded. "What about your head?"

"Migraine." It was all she could or wanted to get out. Her voice was so loud in her ears that even the three words she'd uttered felt as though she'd screamed them.

Eliza cast a worried glance in Dane's direction.

"Do you have meds?" Dane asked. "Or do we need to call a doctor to come see you?"

Ramie's brow wrinkled. One eyelid twitched spasmodically, one of the many side effects of her migraines. Any direct exposure to the sun or bright lights made the twitch more pronounced.

"Doctors don't make house calls, and if we leave to go to the ER, I'll be waiting for hours and it will be that much longer before we get a likeness of his face distributed. For his next victim, every minute counts."

Dane shrugged. "Doctors make house calls when you're Caleb Devereaux."

"Of course," Ramie muttered, pushing her fingertips in a tight circular motion at her temples.

"And I did have medication but I used it sparingly because I don't have a regular doctor anymore and I can't just walk into the ER or an urgent care center and demand migraine meds. I lost it, and everything else I owned, escaping my stalker in Oklahoma."

"I'll ask Tori for a pill for you," Dane said, his gaze gentle and his tone matching.

She wondered just how awful she looked and sounded for Dane and Eliza to be on virtual tiptoe around her. Then, as she took in what he'd said, she frowned and shook her head. The very last thing she wanted was to involve Tori. It was better for everyone if Tori remained in blissful ignorance locked behind the walls of her bedroom.

"Her doctor prescribed the medication after what happened last year because she gets debilitating headaches when she has visions or dreams. It might make you a little drowsy, but that wouldn't be a bad thing," Dane said pointedly. "I imagine you could do with some actual rest rather than running on fumes like you are now."

As he spoke the last, he rose from his seat on the couch and made a gesture to the artist, who'd patiently tweaked and rearranged each time Ramie got it wrong.

"Take a five-minute break. I'll get her something for her headache. There's no sense in pressuring her more right now. A few more minutes won't make a difference if he's already moved on to his next victim."

Mocking laughter echoed in Ramie's mind and she squeezed her eyes shut, her hands trembling violently in her lap. She wouldn't let him unbalance her. He wasn't *really* there.

The ache in her head intensified, the pressure building so much that it felt as though something inside her would shatter into a million pieces. It was as though someone was piercing her skull.

Too late . . .

The thought drifted through her mind leaving her to question whether it was her own manifestation of her deepest fear or if the killer had truly communicated with her through their link.

Of course she wasn't imagining it. She wasn't an idiot and it had been as plain as day the night before last when he'd told her there was nowhere she was safe from him. She wasn't a hysterical person by nature, though to anyone seeing her now it would appear she was a complete nutcase.

Dane didn't wait for confirmation or for her to refuse his offer. He simply left the room.

When he didn't reappear within a few minutes, Eliza frowned and checked her watch. Her foot tapped impatiently on the floor and then she glanced at Ramie, apology in her eyes.

"I know how hard this must be for you, Ramie. Or maybe I don't. I'll spare you any condescension by claiming I know what you're going through. I'm not trying to say I've experienced anything on the scale that you have. But I can *imagine* how scared you must be and I can also imagine me not having the courage to see it through like you have."

Ramie laughed, the sound jarring and abrasive, scratching like a steel wool scouring pad over her skin.

"Scared? Absolutely. Courageous? Not even *close*. If it weren't for Caleb, I'd still be out there hiding, trying to cover my trail and praying that each day wouldn't be my last. If I was brave—or whatever . . ." she said derisively.

She paused a moment and swallowed back the knot in her throat. Then she looked straight through Eliza.

"If I had courage, then all the women he killed in his efforts to get to me would still be alive. If I was brave, I would have taken a stand much sooner instead of acting like a frightened child and burying my head in the sand."

She held up her hand when Eliza launched an immediate protest.

"Save your breath," Ramie said, fatigue swamping her. "I didn't say that to earn your pity or to get you to argue and tell me it wasn't my fault. Nor do I expect or want validation. Rationally I know I can't be held accountable for the actions of others. But at the same time, if I had only tried to confront him instead of spending the last year running and constantly looking over my shoulder then maybe he'd be in prison right now. Or dead. And all those women who died would still be alive, enjoying their families, children . . ."

"Or maybe *you'd* be dead and he would still be out there stalking his next victim, still taking innocent lives because there was no one to bring him down. There are a lot of maybes, Ramie. A lot of what-ifs and second guesses. You forget that you *saved* a hell of a lot of victims. You saved Tori from certain death. They got to her mere hours before he planned to kill her. And the others you helped. They'd all be dead if you hadn't intervened. Focus on those lives you *saved*. Not the ones you didn't."

Dane returned just then, a bottle of water in one hand, his jaw tight. His eyes glinted with anger and Ramie saw Eliza's eyebrow go up. Evidently she saw the same thing Ramie had. Ramie didn't need to touch him to know he was pissed.

"What is it?" Ramie asked softly.

Dane ignored her and held out the medication. Ramie eyed it dubiously, knowing she likely wouldn't be sensible in an hour's time. She was sensitive to any medication that altered her level of consciousness in any way, no matter how weakly it might affect her.

She was at her most vulnerable when she took medication. She couldn't school her thoughts as well and didn't have protective barriers in place. From past experience she knew that memories and dreams of past victims would be unleashed, and she would be unable to control her thought patterns. She shuddered, her skin prickling, the hairs standing on end.

"Take it, Ramie," Dane urged.

Though he wasn't in the least bit threatening and he'd tempered his voice in deference to her sensitivity to sound, she could sense his steel resolve that she down the pill. With a sigh, she allowed him to drop it into her hand, but still she paused after he handed her the bottle of water.

Emotion swamped her. She jerked in surprise at the strength of the impressions from just a tiny pill. But Tori—and Dane—had touched it and so the remnants of their volatile encounter was transferred to Ramie.

Dane studied her, his eyes sharp as he took in her reaction. His lips thinned as if he realized what had happened and had little liking for it. She could barely hear the muttered curses under his breath.

"Before you get pissed, understand that it's high time someone quit coddling her and pulled her back into the real world where everything doesn't revolve around one individual," Dane said.

It was obvious that Tori and Dane had faced off about something. Her? Giving her relief from the mental strain of a migraine and the psychic weight of so many souls, pulling her left and right, all demanding justice for what was done to them?

That heaviness gave her much-needed impetus to face the task ahead. If everyone thought Tori unreasonable and recalcitrant then what must they think about her? Tori had more reason to be angry than Ramie. After all, no matter that Ramie shared the same fate, it still wasn't the same as being there, suffering it firsthand and being helpless to stop it. And there was the fact that Ramie had been so difficult to find. And unyielding, only giving Caleb the information he demanded after it was forced on her.

She swallowed the pill, grimacing as it went down. She'd never been able to swallow pills. Even as an adult, she often resorted to crushing tablets into a fine powder and mixing it with a tiny amount of liquid.

It took a few more sips to wash it completely down and then she leaned back, focusing her attention once more on the drawing. In an hour's time she wouldn't trust herself to remember details accurately so she needed to get this right. Every minute the killer walked free was another minute his victim had to endure the unimaginable.

Even the effort it took to get the pill down sent shards of pain through the base of her skull. Her stomach lurched and she inhaled sharply through her nose in an effort to stave off the nausea. She felt as though tiny little fractures formed a spider-web over her skull, cracking and splintering as they raced, weaving a crisscross pattern through her hair.

She reeled precariously, her stomach revolting once more. She swallowed furiously, forcing herself to keep the pill down and not promptly throw it up.

Dane swore colorfully. "That's enough for right now. She can't do this. This can't be good for her, and Caleb will have my ass if we allow her to continue as is."

The sketch artist looked mildly surprised but shrugged as though he didn't care one way or another and that angered Ramie. It was irrational. She knew that. But the unfortunate artist just happened to be an outlet for her anger, and she was at her boiling point.

Anger was a more acceptable emotion than fear. Anger didn't make her weak. Just careless and volatile as she unleashed her rage.

The artist's apathy infuriated her. Made her feel as though no one really cared about all the women who'd been victimized. Or cared that *she* had endured hell with each and every one of them. It made her feel negligible. Overlooked just as the other women had been forgotten about, just another sad statistic in a growing stack of them.

"Do you *really* want the next victim to be on your conscience?" she asked in a frigid tone, her gaze narrowing at the artist. She continued to coldly stare him down until he fidgeted under her scrutiny. He at least had the grace to look abashed but he refused to meet her challenging stare. With a sound of disgust, she glanced up at Dane. "We'll stop when we get it right and not a minute before."

Eliza reached for Ramie's hand, squeezing it in a silent show of support. Ramie immediately flinched and braced herself for the inevitable onslaught. Eliza's shocked gaze met hers and Eliza swiftly removed her hand, as though she'd forgotten all about Ramie's ability to read people through touch and she had secrets she wanted to remain hidden.

Ramie carefully schooled her features, forcing herself not to show any outward reaction to the flood of rigid anger buried beneath Eliza's cool façade. Rage. Billowing like a black thunderhead at the front of a huge storm.

It put Ramie into sensory overload. Her pupils constricted and then dilated in a few blinks. It was like being caught in the path of an avalanche and knowing there was no escape. Just waiting for the white wall of snow to envelop her.

"Don't touch her," Eliza said sharply.

Ramie assumed she was talking to Dane and that Dane had in some way reached for her, perhaps to steady her.

"No," Ramie whispered. "Don't touch me, please."

She curled inward on herself, pushing the dizzying rush of fragmented emotions as far from the epicenter of the storm as possible. She closed her eyes and pulled her knees to her chin, rocking back and forth in an effort to soothe the raw edges that had been seared through her mind.

For several long minutes she rocked, her forehead touching her knees, her arms hugged around her legs, a barrier to anyone in the room. It was a protective gesture, not that it ever did her any good because there was no defense for the mental onslaught she experienced.

She blew out steadying breaths, determined to get her thoughts back under control. The last thing she wanted was for Caleb to return to this. He couldn't pick up the pieces and put her back together forever. She had to learn to cope. Her old defense—denial—was no longer an option.

She knew too much. She understood far too well the consequences of her closing her eyes and shutting out reality. Her doing so had far-reaching ram-ifications. Women died. Families were destroyed. Children had a future with no mother.

"The eyes are wrong," Ramie finally whispered. "The bridge of the nose should be flatter and wider, the eyes set farther apart and more rounded at the corners."

Respect gleamed in Dane's eyes. She could feel his approval, broadcasting in waves as he stood silently by and watched. Eliza's expression eased as she turned her attention back to the artist.

Ramie's brow wrinkled in concentration when the artist presented the next draft. She studied the face, looking for signs of evil. But he looked . . . *normal*. Above average. As she'd done before when she'd stared him in the eyes, she was struck by how handsome and wholesome he appeared. There was nothing to outwardly indicate the demon behind the polished façade.

"That's him," she choked out.

TWENTY-FOUR

WHEN Caleb entered the living room he stopped dead in his tracks, his leather briefcase falling from his grasp and landing on the floor with a resounding thud. The only other sound was coming from Ramie. She was trying to gather herself and be stoic and that made it worse because she was fighting a losing battle. She made small noises, much like a wounded animal might make. And she had her arms wrapped tightly around her legs, her knees drawn up to hide her face. She rocked back and forth, her knuckles white from where she dug her fingers in where they rested on her arms. There would be marks, small bruises from her own grip.

Caleb surveyed the room, took in the grim mood of Dane and Eliza and confusion in the eyes of the artist. "What the hell happened?" he demanded.

Not waiting for an answer, he crossed the room

and went to his knees in front of where Ramie rocked herself on the sofa.

"Ramie?" he said in a gentle tone.

There was something about the way she held herself that suggested utter fragility. Her head never came up. Her face wasn't visible. Her hair was in disarray and her knees covered her eyes, the rest of her face hidden behind the tops of her thighs.

Caleb rounded ferociously on Dane and Eliza, both of whom were watching intently, worry marring their expressions.

He let out a low growl, the sound rumbling from his chest. "What did you do to her?"

"She identified the killer," Eliza said in a low voice. "The artist has his likeness, so we can distribute it through the proper channels and hopefully someone, somewhere, will recognize him."

Caleb's gaze drifted to the sketch lying on the coffee table in front of where the artist sat and his brow wrinkled, his gaze narrowing as he took in the killer's likeness.

He looked like the last person who'd ever commit such atrocities but then wasn't that the case with most serial killers? He recalled several famous cases where the criminal was the picture of bland mediocrity. Certainly nothing that indicated the viciousness of the crimes he committed.

"I gave her one of Tori's pain pills," Dane said.

"She had a horrific migraine and I was afraid she was going to stroke out on me. If she's not any better soon, she'll need to take another. She was in a lot of pain and she needs relief."

Caleb blew out his breath and turned his attention back on Ramie. He couldn't very well take her to the hospital or even a private clinic. No way would he expose her. As long as she remained here, behind the impenetrable fortress he and his brothers had created, then she was safe from harm.

"If she's not better soon I'll call a doctor to see her here."

Dane nodded. "I told her that. I don't think she believed me. You operate in a world completely alien to her. She's lived such a Spartan existence that she doesn't know any other way. Your kind of wealth and means, your connections and power mystify her. That is if she even comprehends the full scope of your world."

Caleb reached for one of Ramie's small hands, gently rubbing the fingers to restore circulation.

"It's your world too, Ramie. Maybe it wasn't but it is now."

She lifted her haunted gaze to his and he winced at the starkness of her features. She didn't refute his statement nor did she confirm it. She just stared blankly at him as if trying to comprehend the ramifications of his quiet vow.

Then to his utter amazement she wrapped her arms around his neck and slid from the couch to the floor in front of him. She pressed her face into his chest and he could feel her trembling uncontrollably against him.

He stroked his hand through her hair, not saying anything as he sensed she just needed quiet—and comforting.

"He was here," she whispered so only Caleb could hear her. In fact, he had to strain to catch what she was saying. When it sank in and he realized her meaning, his blood went cold.

He pulled her gently away from his chest and cupped her chin so he could see her eyes and her expression.

"What do you mean by that, Ramie?"

"I heard him."

Frustration was audible in her voice, impatience simmering. She knew her stalker would never give up. He'd displayed ultimate patience, drawing out the pursuit and making her dance to his tune like a puppet being manipulated by his puppet master.

He was simply waiting for the day when she made a fatal mistake.

"I can't go on this way. I don't want to live like this, always running. I want what everyone else wants. A family. Friends. I've been alone my entire life, but I don't want to be alone forever."

Caleb cupped her cheek and then pushed her hair back behind her ear. "You won't be alone again, baby. You have me. You have my family."

She winced at the mention of his family. His family would never be hers. There was too much pain and resentment. She would always be a reminder of what happened to Tori. There was no erasing it, no making it all better. Tori—and Ramie—would bear the emotional scars for life.

"Ramie, look at me," he said in a firm voice.

She instinctively obeyed before she could think better of it or shy away. Their gazes collided and his eyes were brimming with sincerity. There was pleading in his expression. A request for understanding. He was torn between two loyalties, one to his family and one he'd imposed on himself when he vowed to protect Ramie.

"My family is your family, warts and all. They aren't heartless people. We're all still reeling from Tori's abduction. And I'm still appalled by what I forced on you. They just need time, and while it isn't fair to you because you've done nothing to earn their censure, time will change their points of view. Right now my brothers are lashing out and guilt-riddled because they think they failed Tori. You aren't an acceptable outlet for their anger or mine. I'm precariously close to begging you for the chance to back up my words."

Her heart clenched painfully, her breaths suddenly rapid. Her pulse sped up as she stared into the intense blue gaze stroking over her skin like the softest paintbrush. Stroke after stroke, striving for perfection.

"And let me make one more thing clear," he continued, not waiting for or perhaps not *wanting* to hear her response. "I don't want you tracking him. It puts you at too much risk and I don't want to lose you."

She reached up to hush him with a finger. She let the tip rest on his lips and then traced a line around the edges.

"No matter what it may feel like, he can't reach me. Not telepathically. I just have to remind myself of that when panic overwhelms me. He's using the link between him and me to frighten and intimidate me. He wants me to slip up and make a fatal mistake. And I won't allow that to happen. It's taken me long enough to make sense of it all and actually *think* instead of reacting blindly, but if he could somehow harm me physically, he would have already done so. I've unwittingly aided him in his pursuit of me by my rash and frantic actions."

Caleb didn't look at all happy with her firm resolve. For once she sounded convincing, a halfway intelligent woman, instead of coming across as the hot mess she was. He dragged a hand through his short-clipped hair in agitation.

Before he could argue, she slid her fingers into his and squeezed, for the first time offering *him* the comfort she'd been provided time and time again. She marveled at the fact she *could* touch him when she was unable to touch anyone else without enduring unspeakable pain. She had to be strong and grow a spine instead of being a pathetic excuse for DNA. For whatever reason, God had given her a special . . . gift? She wouldn't go that far, but she'd been given this ability and it was time to use it to her advantage.

"He said *too late* when earlier today Dane made the comment, *a few more minutes won't make a difference if he's already moved on to his next victim.*"

Caleb's eyes widened in shock and then they darkened as he glanced between Dane and Eliza.

"He's already found his next victim," Ramie said softly. "Or at least he's actively acquired a new target. I suspect he's out there right now, stalking an unsuspecting woman; perhaps he's already put his plan into motion. If he holds true to his pattern then he'll call it in. He'll want me to know. And he's going to continue to punish me by accumulating victim after victim until I finally break."

Caleb shook his head, his lips pressed together in a thin line.

"You won't break," he said with conviction.

"That's where he's mistaken and hopefully that's where he'll make *his* mistake by coming after you."

A halfhearted smile tugged at the corners of her mouth.

"I wish I was as confident as you are about me not breaking."

"I won't *let* you break," he said softly, his hand clenching around hers with a reassuring squeeze. "You'll never have to worry that no one loves you. You'll never be alone again if I have anything to say about it."

The utter conviction in his tone, the love, warmth and worry in his eyes gave her a surge of confidence.

He fused his mouth to hers, utterly ignoring the other occupants of the room. It was exquisitely tender. So very precious and sweet as though she were utterly treasured. She sighed into his mouth and he swallowed her breath before she took it back. A discreet cough sounded and Caleb stiffened. He turned and slashed a withering stare in the artist's direction.

"You can leave now," Caleb said tersely. "If the sketch is done, Dane will show you out. We'll handle the rest."

The artist rose as if he couldn't wait to be out of Caleb's house. He shoved his sketchpad and pencils into his bag and then hurried for the door, not waiting for Dane to lead the way.

Caleb turned his attention back to her. He slid his thumb over her cheekbone, his touch warm, a balm to her frayed nerves.

"He'll call it in like he did the last one," Ramie said. "This time we're expecting it so our reaction time should be faster. Maybe that will give us an advantage in locating him before it's too late."

Caleb swore and her hand fell away from his as he paced the living room floor between her and where Eliza sat.

"He can't touch her here," Eliza said. "Here is the very *best* place for her to be if she's going to trace a link back to the killer." She hesitated a moment and then rested her gaze on Ramie. "I've been doing some research on psychic abilities. Most of it hypothesized, mind you, since there aren't any documented cases of mental telepathy or pathos, but one researcher theorized that it was possible for someone who taps into the mind of another to then establish a more permanent link. Which is, as I think you'll both agree, precisely what our killer has done with Ramie."

"What are you getting at?" Caleb asked.

Ramie remained silent, mulling over Eliza's words. She had a good idea where the other woman was going with this and it infuriated her that she *herself* had never thought of the possibility before. But to analyze her abilities meant embracing them in some small measure, and Ramie had never even come close to acceptance. She'd spent her life fighting the very demons that may well save her now.

"I'm suggesting that since he and Ramie share a mental pathway and that he's able to project inside her mind to glean information . . . that she can do the same to him." Eliza watched Caleb closely, no doubt concerned about his reaction. But instead of a volatile outburst, he turned, looking inquisitively at Ramie.

"Can you do that?" he asked, skepticism written all over his face.

"I don't know," she said honestly. "I've never tried. I've never *wanted* to try. I'm able to establish a mental pathway to the victim by touching something that belonged to her so it stands to reason that I'd be able to tap into him doing the same."

Caleb blew out his breath and shook his head. "And that's the catch. You can't very well track him when you have nothing he's touched."

"Not so fast," Eliza murmured.

Caleb's head shot up and his brow wrinkled as he stared back at Eliza.

Eliza fiddled with a pencil the artist had left and then she slid the drawing closer to her, studying it intently.

"I don't know how it would affect her," Eliza said after a moment's hesitation. "It's not like we have case histories or actual research to back us up. The conversations and speculation center on a what-if scenario and pose the question what if a person had a specific psychic gift, which of course we all know to be factual even in the absence of actual proof. But what if she visited the crime scene? If he keeps the same MO then he will have left an item belonging to the victim at the scene of the crime, his invitation or perhaps challenge to Ramie to come after him. Which also means he was there and touched *something* in the vicinity. No one can be that careful not to leave a single trace behind. And Ramie doesn't need a tangible object. She's able to collect information when she touches someone or touches something another person came in contact with."

"No way will I risk Ramie by taking her some-where the killer is likely close by," Caleb said, shaking his head vehemently. "Not only that but if she has a link to both killer *and* victim, think what that would do to her! She'd suffer everything the victim is subjected to but then she would also expe-rience torture, pain and death through the *killer's* eyes and it would be as if she murdered the victim herself. We can't put that kind of burden on her. It may well push her over the edge."

How calmly they discussed her sanity, or rather the lack of. She knew Caleb had her best interests—

her absolute protection—at heart, but she also knew that this could very well be their only real shot to take a monster down.

Instead of fear, anticipation—a sense of *excitement*—coursed through her veins.

Her voice, when she spoke, was strong and convincing, a spark for the first time she could remember in forever. She was suddenly imbued by hope that she'd refused to allow herself to even consider until now.

"Caleb, it could work."

Caleb jerked his head around in obvious surprise. She winced at just how shocked he was that she would entertain anything but avoidance or running away. An art she'd perfected over the last year and a half. It was a testament to just how much of a coward she was that he now stared at her in disbelief.

"No," he finally said. "Don't even think about it, Ramie. There are a million things that could go wrong in a scenario like this. I won't chance it. I won't risk your life or trade it for another."

"It's a good idea and you know it," she argued. "If it were anyone else but me, if your security firm had been hired to protect someone like me, you wouldn't hesitate because you'd know that you were providing top-notch protection. Ever hear the saying that the best defense is a good offense? It's time for me to stop running and start hunting him like he's hunted me all these months. He'd hardly expect it. He's certainly become well acquainted with *my* MO. As long as he sticks to his, we have the upper hand."

"This is insane," Caleb bit out.

"I think it's better that we don't bring up my mental status or lack thereof," she said dryly.

Caleb winced, apology reflected in his expression.

"She wouldn't be alone or unguarded," Dane interjected from the doorway to the living room. He walked toward where the others were seated and stood next to Caleb, his stare gauging Caleb's temperament. "The killer would be a fool to return to the crime scene. Besides that, he'll have no way of knowing that she'll be there."

Caleb shook his head, his eyes shooting sparks. "The hell he won't know. If he has an open line into Ramie's mind and can see her surroundings then he'll know *exactly* where she is and what she's doing. We may as well paint a bull's-eye on her forehead and tie her to a tree."

"And that's where we come in," Eliza said in a calm, placating voice. "We put our best team on this. Make sure we have all the bases covered. She goes in, sees if she can pick up on anything and then we get out and hope we nail the bastard before he murders another innocent woman."

"I agree," Ramie said firmly.

She rose from her perch on the couch but went still when she swayed precariously. She let out a frustrated curse because everything had shifted around her the moment she stood. The effects of the medication Dane had given her hadn't been pronounced until now. She was light-headed and the jackhammer in her head had subsided to a dull ache at the base of her skull.

"Are you okay?" Caleb asked anxiously.

"I'm fine, Caleb," she confirmed. "I think the medication is kicking in, that's all."

Caleb's expression was worried and grim. "I think you should go lie down for a while. God knows you're going to need all the rest you can get if we're even considering this fucked-up plan to let you go after a monster."

She locked gazes with him and then she closed the distance separating them, taking the few steps to where Caleb had ended his last pacing session. She laced her fingers through his and squeezed in an effort to give him some reassurance.

Tension radiated from him in waves. His mind was a jumbled mass of chaotic thoughts and fears. She could feel how terrified he was that something would go wrong and that she would pay the ultimate price.

"I have to do this, Caleb, and you know it. I don't

relish the idea of immersing myself in a myriad of fear, pain, blood and violence, but if I don't stop him, who will? Police always say eventually he'll mess up and make a mistake but this guy hasn't and won't make that mistake. He's too good. He's the most dangerous sort of killer. Cold, calculating, patient and methodical in *everything* he does. If it takes the next five years, or even *ten*, he'll wait for the time when I screw up and make a mistake or let my guard down. And I don't want to live the next five to ten years constantly looking over my shoulder and allowing fear to control me. I'm ashamed it took me this long to come to this conclusion. A lot of women had to die to get me to this point but that's something I'll have to live with for the rest of my life. Taking him down for good will go a long way in easing some of the burden I bear."

Caleb's expression softened, his eyes losing some of the harsh glint. "Baby, you can't save them all."

He smoothed her hair back, framing her face in his hands. His eyes were such a rich shade of blue that it felt as though she were drowning in an ocean. They were warm with love but there was also a trace of fear. For her. That he would lose her.

"I'm afraid of losing you too," she whispered. "Don't you see? You worry about me and what happens if I fall back into his hands, but I worry that you or Tori or one of your brothers and even

Dane and Eliza will pay the ultimate price for offering me protection. He's ruthless and unfeeling. Murder and death amuse him. He's convinced of his superiority and that's why I've become an obsession with him. Because he didn't best me, and I got too close to him. He considers that the ultimate insult."

"Unbelievable," Eliza said, incredulity in her voice. "You pegged him. You were word for word what his FBI profile came back with."

"We need to get this sketch to the police and media," Dane said. "The sooner we're able to warn the public and heighten awareness of the fact a serial killer has taken up temporary residence in the Houston metropolitan area the sooner we can bring him to justice. Maybe we'll get lucky and he's taken down before he chooses his next victim."

"Get on it then," Caleb said. "I'm taking Ramie up so she can rest until her headache is better."

TWENTY-FIVE

"IS this where I say *sorry, honey, I've got a head-ache*?" Ramie asked in a drowsy tone.

She yawned widely, her jaw popping with her effort before settling her cheek back onto Caleb's bare chest, nuzzling sleepily into his arms. He laughed softly, his hand roaming up and down the slender arch of her body.

Her skin was baby soft, like the finest silk. He was thoroughly enjoying the simple pleasure of touching her, of having her in his arms and in his bed. He turned his head just enough that his lips pressed against the hairline of her forehead.

"I'll let you get away with it. This time," he said in amusement.

It suddenly struck him that for the space of a few stolen moments all was quiet. Peaceful. No intrusions from the outside world. Intimacy surrounded them, enfolding them both in its gentle embrace.

"How is the head?" he asked as he trailed his fingers through the curls spilling over her shoulder. "Better yet?"

She yawned again and nodded, her cheek rubbing up and down his chest.

He liked her here in his arms all warm and sweet and contented. This was where she belonged whether she readily acknowledged it or not. He could be a patient man when the reward was worth it, and Ramie's heart and trust were absolutely worth any amount of patience he was forced to exert in his quest to seal their newly formed relationship.

"Are you sure you want to do this, Ramie?" he asked in a quiet tone.

She went absolutely still next to him. Not even a breath escaped her. He resumed his idle caress up and down her body in an effort to ease the sudden tension.

"Yes. No . . ." she trailed off and then expelled a long breath. "Yes, damn it. Well, that isn't exactly true. I'm not a complete idiot. I don't *want* to do it but I have no choice. I *have* to do it and there's the difference."

"You're a courageous, selfless woman," he said. And he meant every word.

She made a sound of disgust. "What's with calling me brave all of a sudden? Eliza said the same ridiculous thing earlier. Do I look like someone who is fearless? I'm *terrified*," she said, her voice rising an octave.

He attempted to soothe her agitation by stroking her with his hand, allowing it to glide over her slight curves, but she was already worked up over his words.

"There is nothing brave or courageous or even special about me," she said bluntly.

Her words weren't spoken with emotion in an obvious effort to get him to argue his point. It was a matter-of-fact statement, one that she truly believed of herself. He only wished she saw what he saw.

It wasn't desire, lust or even love that made him view her through rose-colored glasses. Regardless of their relationship or his feelings for her, nothing about her actions contradicted his assessment of her character.

"I've lived my entire life lonely and afraid," she said, pain evident in her voice. "Running. Hiding. From who I am and *what* I am. I'm done with that life, Caleb. And before you argue whether I should take this on or not, you need to consider that *you're* the reason I no longer want to be that frightened, weak shell of a woman I've been for so long. You're the reason I want . . . *better*. You deserve better than that. *I* deserve better. Whatever we have, wherever this is going between us doesn't have a chance in hell if I can't regain control over my own life. As nice as it sounds that you'll protect me and take care of me, how long do you think it would take before you realize that you got a shitty deal? And that we are in no way equals in a relationship but rather I'm a codependent leech sucking the life right out of you? You can't possibly think you'd be happy with a woman like I just described. You're too strong for that. Your personality is too strong for you to have a much weaker partner. You may as well be a parental figure for all the dependence I've demonstrated."

There was so much disgust and self-loathing aimed at herself that he flinched under the force and vehemence of her words. She simmered with rage, her entire body shaking. The hand that rested on his chest had curled into a tight, white-knuckled fist.

As much as he wanted to do exactly those things she described, he realized that it was grossly unfair to her. And it certainly didn't do justice to her intelligence or determination. It was his nature to charge in, take control and put her in a box where he knew she'd be safe. But it was no way for her to live. He was starting to understand her frustration, that she was reaching her boiling point. Maybe she was already there.

His protective instincts were strong. Not only

when it came to Ramie but when it came to his family as well. The idea of sitting back and loosening his tight hold on either of them went against who and what *he* was. But if he didn't learn to do just that, he would very likely lose Ramie.

Maybe not right away but eventually she'd tire of his authority and control.

"I understand," he murmured. "I get it, Ramie. I do. But we're going to just have to agree to disagree when it comes to your supposition that you aren't strong or courageous. This is one area I refuse to back down over. I don't know of anyone, man, woman or child, who could so stoically endure all you have for the last decade."

She lifted her head, raw emotion swirling in her smoky, storm-colored eyes.

"But that's just it, Caleb. I *haven't* stoically endured. God, I wish I had or that I *could*. The problem is I feel *too* much. I *absorb* too much. It's wrecked me more times than I can count. And just when I finally reach a point where I think things will return to some semblance of normalcy again I'm pulled right back into a world of pain and death and *misery*."

His hand threaded through her hair, and he stroked her scalp through the tresses in an effort to soothe her.

"Shhh, I understand, baby. Stop beating yourself up. It does no one any good. I'd rather talk about the fact that you just admitted that I was the reason you want more—better," he amended.

"I do. You are," she whispered. "But I'm afraid to dream. I never have good dreams, Caleb. Only bad. Just once I want something good and wonderful."

He wrapped his arm around her waist and then rolled her underneath him. His lips met hers in a heated rush, his tongue sliding over hers and tasting.

As he lifted his head, their lips parting, their gazes locked and held.

"I'll give you good dreams, Ramie. And I'll hold you during the bad. And we'll dream the good together."

Her gaze was intent, seeking and searching, testing the veracity of his vow.

And then her eyes softened, some of the darkness chased away, sunlight replacing summer storm clouds.

"Dream the good," she murmured. "I like that."

His head lowered to take possession of her mouth. Even as he kissed her, his hand slid underneath her shirt, his palm splayed over her belly and then slid upward to cup one breast. He brushed his thumb over her nipple, coaxing it to a rigid peak.

Gently he divested her of the rest of her clothing and then did the same to himself before covering her body with his own.

"Tonight I want you to only dream of me," he

murmured between kisses. "And for you to go to sleep feeling loved and protected. Because I do love you and I will protect you, baby."

She arched her body into his, craving his warmth and touch. She wrapped her arms around his shoulders and returned his kiss, deepening it and responding passionately.

"I need you so much, Caleb," she whispered, yearning evident in her voice.

"I need you every bit as much. I need you to believe that, Ramie. If you believe nothing else."

"I do," she said, her voice aching with emotion. "Make love to me. Show me what you feel for me."

His kisses grew more heated, more urgent as his big body moved over hers, parting her thighs with his knee. He bent his dark head to her breasts, tonguing them until they puckered and tiny goose bumps dotted her torso.

He kissed her neck, sucking at her earlobe, sending shivers cascading over her skin. He left no part of her untouched, unloved. He took his time, making her feel utterly cherished.

Then to her surprise, he turned her over and nibbled at her exposed nape and then licked a path down her spine that caused her to tremble uncontrollably. He nipped playfully at her buttocks and then kissed the small of her back, sucking lightly at the spot he'd licked.

He reached for a pillow and then lifted her enough to put it underneath her pelvis, elevating her behind so that he had better access to her pussy.

He played for a while, driving her insane with his probing fingers. He alternated between stroking the damp skin and gently thumbing her throbbing clitoris and sliding a finger inside her, pressing against her most sensitive spots.

She was mindless under his ministrations, her fingers digging into the sheets and holding on as the storm overtook her.

A gasp escaped her when he lifted her just enough to fit his cock to her opening and then slowly, with reverence, he pushed into her from behind. He was so much bigger this way and it took him several attempts before he gained full depth.

She moaned at the fullness, how she stretched to accommodate his width. He paused when he was all the way in.

"You okay?" he asked in a strained tone.

"Yes, God, yes! Please don't stop."

"I have no intention of going anywhere," he ground out.

He withdrew then and slowly pushed inward once more, eliciting another groan from her. She needed more. So much more. She didn't want him to be gentle right now. She wanted everything he could give her. She didn't want him to treat her like she was breakable.

She bucked upward, trying to tell him without words what she wanted—what she needed.

He responded to her silent plea and began to thrust harder, deeper, until her need was a desperate, tangible thing.

His fingers dug into her hips, lifting her higher to meet his thrusts. He began to move fast and furious, driving them both to the brink of insanity.

"I want you with me, Ramie."

"I'm with you!" she gasped. "Please, Caleb, don't make me wait. I'm there!"

Her words spurred him to action and he began plunging harder and harder until he drove her upward on the bed, her entire body shaking from the force of his thrusts.

She spasmed uncontrollably and let out a cry as her orgasm crashed over her with a force she'd never experienced. On the heels of hers, he lunged forward and blanketed her with his body, his warmth and strength pressed firmly against her back. They were both spent, their breaths coming in gulping gasps.

Finally he rolled off her, disposed of the condom and then pulled her into his arms, his hands stroking over her entire body as they both shuddered in the aftermath of their releases.

He kissed her forehead, her eyes, her nose, cheeks and finally her mouth. He lingered there, stroking his tongue inward, his movements so much more gentle than they'd been just moments ago.

"I love you so damn much," he said in an aching voice. "I hope one day you can love me, Ramie. But I'm willing to wait as long as it takes and I'll never give up on you. I'll wait forever if that's what it takes."

She cuddled into his embrace, burying her face in his chest, wishing for all the world that she could give him those words now, when he sounded so vulnerable. But she wouldn't say them just to say them. Not until she was sure she could come to him whole. Healed. And able to give back to him every bit as much as he'd given her.

The room was dark and Tori could sense she wasn't alone, but she had no idea where she was. Too terrified to make a sound, she huddled inwardly, praying that she wasn't seen or heard.

The smell of blood was acrid in her nostrils, assaulting her senses. She gagged, the scent overwhelming. She was all too familiar with the odor of blood. Particularly her own.

She clamped a hand over her mouth when her stomach revolted again. Silently heaving, she closed her eyes and tried to breathe through the nausea.

And then a sound, close to her. She forced herself to open her eyes and slowly let her gaze drift over her surroundings. She frowned when she realized she didn't recognize her environment. Blinking, she drew a shadow several feet away into focus, straining to make out who or what was in the room with her.

The shadow moved closer. Her breath caught as she realized it was her brother. Relief hurtled through her body with dizzying speed. Oh God, she'd been so terrified. But Caleb was here. He was with her and he wouldn't allow anyone to hurt her.

He took one step closer, the shadows suddenly gone from around him. Her heart thumped hard against her chest and her mouth opened in a silent scream and she kept screaming as she stared in horror at the gruesome sight in front of her.

Caleb was drenched in blood. It covered his hands, was smeared on his chest and splattered across his abdomen. His eyes were empty and hollow, soulless pools of ice.

Tori screamed again and again, desperation seizing and twisting her insides in a panicked frenzy. She shut her eyes in a frantic attempt to block out the sight of Caleb soaked in blood, but it was as though his image were imprinted on the backs of her eyelids because it was as vivid with her eyes closed as it was with them open.

Her head wobbled back and forth and she

became aware of someone *shaking* her and urgently calling her name.

"Tori! Tori, wake up, damn it!"

She pushed outward at the offending person, shoving so hard she tumbled backward. Her head cracked against the headboard of her bed and she saw a burst of colors. Pain yanked her from her seeming state of paralysis, and she didn't waste any time scrambling from the bed on the other side, prepared to flee for her life.

No one would take her again. Never. She'd *die* first.

When strong hands grasped her arms again, she lashed out, swinging her fist. A muffled curse and cracking pain in her knuckles told her she'd connected with a very firm jaw.

"Damn it, Tori, wake the hell up. It's *Dane*, for God's sake."

Her knees buckled and she sagged, hitting the floor with a resounding thump. Again she heard curses but the hands that touched her were gentle and nonthreatening.

Fingers carefully pushed her hair from her face and back behind her ears and then warm thumb pads smoothed away the tears silently tracking down her cheeks.

She flinched and made a guttural sound as she tried to slide backward on the wood floor. Much like an animal backed into a corner. She shoved the hair from her face so she could at least see to defend herself.

"D-don't t-touch me."

He immediately released her, holding his hands up where she could easily see them. She regarded him warily, the remnants of the horrible vision still lingering like a ghost in her mind. Her pulse roared in her ears and she blinked trying to bring her surroundings into focus.

"I'm just going to turn on the light, okay, Tori?"

The soothing pitch to his voice served to calm her. Gradually the red mist faded and Caleb's bloodied body no longer confronted her when she opened her eyes.

"Dane?"

The quivery jitter to her voice made her sound like a terrified little girl. Not an adult woman who'd seen the harsh realities outside the privileged existence she'd lived for twenty-three years.

"Yes, Tori, it's Dane. Are you okay now?"

Tears flooded her eyes and sobs welled from her throat as she slumped in relief.

"Oh God, Dane. You have to check on Caleb. I think he's *dead*."

Dane's head jerked up and his gaze narrowed, causing the hard lines of his face to seem even scarier than he normally was.

"What are you talking about?" he asked sharply. "Talk to me, Tori. Did you have a vision?"

Her mouth fell open and she stared at Dane in absolute shock and dismay. "What are you talking about?" she whispered.

"I know," he said. "So does Eliza. But no one else. Not even your brothers' other security experts or hired muscle. Now tell me what happened, Tori. Is Caleb in danger?"

She scrubbed her face with her hands, her eyes burning like they had sand and grit blown into them.

"I don't know," she said in frustration. "Ever since . . . *him* . . . I don't know what is a vision or simply a nightmare brought about by what happened to me. Oh God, I thought I was past this. I thought everything was going to be okay but I swear I think I'm losing my mind. The other night I dreamed that someone shot me. And now I dreamed of Caleb covered in blood."

Carefully Dane pulled Tori into his arms, slowly easing her against him as if he were afraid she'd freak and bolt away.

"Shhh, Tori. You aren't losing your mind. You've undergone a lot of trauma both physically and emotionally. That isn't going to go away in a week, a month or even a year. It takes time but you'll get there."

"You believe in my abilities?" she blurted out, peering up at him from underneath her lashes.

Dane had always intimidated her and if she was completely honest he scared her to death. There was a harshness to his features that made him look extremely dangerous. And he never missed the slightest detail.

He certainly hadn't treated her like she was damaged goods as everyone else did. Not that she blamed them because that was what she'd fostered. Because it was easier that way. If she gave the impression she could break at any time then no one pressed her. No one made her do more than she wanted to do.

Only, Dane hadn't particularly cared whether he upset her or not. He'd coldly told her to stop acting like a spoiled child and stop treating Ramie like she was the enemy. And Ramie wasn't the enemy. But she was Tori's past. The only person who knew precisely how close Tori had come to losing her very soul.

Shame crowded into her heart and she winced as those terrible days came back in a rush.

"Please. Go make sure Caleb is all right," she begged.

"He's fine," Dane soothed.

"How do you know?" she demanded, anger replacing the bone-deep sorrow she was immersed in.

"Because he went to bed with Ramie hours ago," Dane said. "And all is quiet on the home front. No one makes a move on this property without us knowing about it. Trust me when I say that he's just fine."

"What if it *was* a vision?" she whispered, giving voice to her greatest fear. "What if they were *both* visions? What if Caleb and I die? I don't want to die, Dane. Maybe once I did but not now. I'm scared to death that I'll die before *doing* anything with my life. I've never had to do anything for myself. It didn't used to bother me until I saw just how much my brothers protected and shielded me. Do you know how ridiculous it is that I can't go to a movie or a restaurant without a contingent of security? Who the hell lives like that?"

"All I know is that at least for tonight, nothing is going to happen to either one of you," Dane said matter-of-factly.

For some reason she drew comfort from the fact that he hadn't offered her blind assurance by saying nothing would ever happen to them. Just that it wouldn't be tonight. If he'd claimed anything else she would have known he was simply placating her and spouting nonsense.

For that matter he was the only person who didn't handle her with kid gloves. Everyone else was determined to protect her from the slightest upset as though her mental state was so fragile that any stress would cause her to have a nervous breakdown.

And maybe she *was* just that close to the edge.

How did Ramie do it time and time again? Once was horrific enough. Tori narrowly escaped with her life, even if she'd lost pieces of her soul in the process. But to endure such atrocities over and over? Who the hell was that selfless? It damn sure wasn't Tori.

Tori hadn't been fair to Ramie. She knew it. Acknowledged it. Even if she couldn't quite make herself blindly accept Ramie's presence here, Ramie was a stark reminder of every single painful thing Tori wanted to forget.

Tori blinked, yanked from her thoughts as realization dawned that she and Dane were sitting on the floor beside her bed, the sheets and comforter in a tangle, barely hanging from the bed.

She suddenly felt very exposed and vulnerable and she hated that feeling more than anything. But neither did she want to freak out on Dane and drive home the fact that she was hanging on to her sanity by a single thread.

"I'm sorry," she apologized in a low voice. "I didn't mean to wake you. The vision—dream, whatever it was—scared me. It was so . . . *real*."

"No apology is necessary."

The interlude was over. Dane stood and extended a hand down to help her up. She pretended she didn't see and turned to drag the sheet over her body to shield her from view.

"Will you be all right or do you want me to stay up with you? We can go in the living room if you'd prefer the brighter light."

Her brows scrunched together and she shook her head. "No. I'm fine. Really. You should get back to bed. I'm sure you have a full day ahead of you tomorrow. Thank you."

"You're welcome," he said after a brief pause.

He seemed to be studying her, perhaps to determine the veracity of her words. Evidently he was satisfied that she would truly be okay because he headed for the door.

Once there, he turned back, one hand on the knob.

"Sleep well, Tori. Try not to kill anyone in your dreams."

Her mouth fell open in surprise when she saw the teasing glint to his eyes and heard the sardonic drawl in his voice.

Dane had a sense of humor. Who knew?

His eyes opened and he stared sightlessly at the ceiling. Without making a sound, he eased from the bed and walked robotically to the closet. With

precise, measured movements he selected a pair
of jeans, picked up one of his neatly pressed and
folded polo shirts and quietly dressed in the dark.

A sense of alarm prickled down his spine but it
was quickly stifled as he turned to walk back by the
bed where Ramie lay sleeping. His gaze caught on
Ramie and he hesitated a brief second before stum-
bling forward. A stabbing pain in his head caught
him off guard. His jaw was tightly clenched and a
nerve twitched in his cheek.

His steps reluctant, as though he were fighting a
battle not to leave the room—not to leave *Ramie*—
he walked haltingly into the hallway. Once he
cleared the doorway, his steps became jerky, the
distance from Ramie tugging him lesser and lesser
until finally he moved with ease.

He descended the stairs, pausing at the bottom
as he glanced furtively right and then left.

Quiet blanketed the house. It was eerily silent
as he headed toward the audio/visual outpost next
to the safe room where surveillance cameras moni-
tored the grounds.

He punched in the security code to gain access
through the sliding wood panel built into the wall.
As soon as he was in he went straight to the bank
of monitors on the far left side of the room.

His gaze flickered up and down and then settled
on the monitor he was looking for.

An unwilling smile that felt all too wrong slashed his lips upward, making it more of a grimace than anything else.

Gotcha . . .

The word whispered through his mind followed by distant laughter and triumph.

His gut tightened and a sense of foreboding gripped his insides. The muscles in his neck twitched spasmodically. His eyelids drooped and then began to tic.

Wrong. All wrong. And yet he was powerless to do anything but obey the overwhelming compulsion that gripped him. *His mind was not his own.*

He was engaged in a battle of wills. One his own, buried beneath this . . . creature he didn't recognize and hadn't known existed, the other wrapping icy cold fingers around his heart. Sweat formed on his brow, his pulse thudding hard and fast in his neck. The silent tug-of-war over his level of consciousness raged, hard and strong.

He was being pulled in opposing directions. His heart raced, his breaths rapid-fire as sweat gleamed on his skin, visible in the low light of the monitors.

Pain seared through his chest as he finally turned his back to the damage he'd done. He left the security room as quietly as he'd entered.

Moments later he carefully undressed and arranged the clothing just as it were before. Then he slid back into bed with Ramie, carefully arranging the sheet and comforter over both their bodies.

A sense of dismay warred with the part of his subconscious that urged him to relish victory and fall into sleep.

His jaw tight to the point of pain, his pulse twitching in his neck and temples, his eyelids fluttered and then finally closed. Laughter once again sounded in the distance but then grew fainter and fainter before finally subsiding as Caleb drifted into a troubled sleep.

TWENTY-SIX

CALEB looked as though he hadn't slept at all the night before. He'd been quiet and withdrawn ever since he and Ramie had gotten up. For that matter no one was setting the world on fire. Tension boiled in the kitchen, the silence yawning like a chasm.

This whole situation was wearing on them all. Dane and Eliza looked drained. Tori was pale and listless and she sat in a silent stupor at the breakfast table. Quinn and Beau sat on either side of her, eating quietly, their attention focused on no one in particular.

Ramie sighed and pushed her food around her plate with her fork, stabbing at a clump of eggs. Her stomach revolted at the idea of putting anything down and so she toyed idly with her utensil while she waited for the awkward silence to end.

Her fork clattered loudly on the plate when

Dane's phone rang. Her gaze swung upward, a knot quickly forming in her throat. Just because his phone rang didn't mean the worst had happened. He got calls at all times of the day. As Caleb's head of security, it was his job to ensure everything ran smoothly. He and only he reported to Caleb while the rest reported to him.

Dane tensed when he checked the incoming call. He tried to school his features, but Ramie saw his jaw go rigid and the sudden burst of frustration was nearly a tangible thing in the room, flowing between them like an electrical current.

Shaking, she pushed herself off the bar stool and instinctively moved closer to Caleb, seeking the shelter of his much larger frame. A betraying tremor quaked through her body and she reached blindly for his hand, preparing herself for the worst.

"It's him," she said in a small voice, turning her chin upward so she looked Caleb in the eye. Her mind screamed at him to tell her she was wrong, but she knew the truth for what it was. Could see it reflected in Caleb's gaze as well.

Nausea coiled low in her belly, gliding sickly through her veins. Her mouth watered and she swallowed convulsively. The nightmare was about to begin all over again.

"He has another victim already, doesn't he?"

Caleb secured his arm tightly around Ramie while

his other hand was laced with hers as they waited for the revelation Dane would deliver. Ramie's entire body shook and jittered. Color had fled her cheeks, leaving them pale and washed out, her eyes enormous against the delicate bone structure of her face.

How the hell was he supposed to just let her leave the safety of his home and not know what the hell was waiting for her at the crime scene? If there even was a crime scene.

Dane was speaking in a low voice, his features a mask of angry concentration. He swore vividly and Caleb tightened his hold even further around Ramie. If he wasn't careful, he'd leave bruises on her skin. He forced himself to ease up a little but as soon as he did Ramie closed the small distance he'd opened between them and molded herself against his side.

He left her there, content to have her nestled in the crook of his arm.

Dane lowered the phone from his ear, resignation in his eyes.

"He's getting bolder," Dane said grimly. "He called it in again. This time he gave the police the woman's name and address and asked them to send his regards to Ramie St. Claire and said that any time she wanted to arrange a trade he'd be willing to show mercy toward his most recent victim."

Ramie went utterly still against Caleb. Only the soft puffs of her breathing registered any sort of life from her. Then slowly she tilted her chin up, seeking his gaze.

"We should go," she whispered. "Now, while it's early in the game. Before he has time to act out his plan."

Caleb had never felt so uncertain in his life. It was evident that he was the only one who objected to Ramie trying to establish a connection between her and the killer instead of the reverse.

He swept his gaze between Dane and Eliza and directed his question to them.

"Who do you have on tap for this?"

Ramie looked confused, her brows knitting together above her shadowy eyes. Did she honestly think he'd send her into the unknown without enough firepower to invade a small country?

"I have a six-man team assembled. If you want more, I can get them. But in this case, less is more. We don't want to draw too much attention and if we're moving a dozen security specialists along with Eliza and me, plus you and Ramie, we're going to get noticed," Dane said.

Caleb remained silent a moment as he contemplated the situation they were in. He trusted Dane's judgment and Eliza's too for that matter. And up until now he would have said that he had absolute confidence in their abilities to protect.

But it had never been personal before. Only with

Tori did he assign someone other than himself or Quinn or Beau and even then he'd only trusted Dane and Eliza. Tori didn't go out much at all, so she was never in a position to need more than minimal protection. He frowned, realizing just how little Tori had left the house in the year since her abduction and rape.

The million-dollar question was whether he trusted his multimillion-dollar team of security experts, all versed in personal protection and services, or a bodyguard to keep Ramie safe at all costs.

He could drive himself crazy with second-guessing himself. He locked gazes with Eliza, who coolly returned his, completely unruffled by his apparent hesitation.

Fuck it. He'd made damn certain he and his brothers hired the best. Beau had overseen most of the hiring, although no decision was made until Caleb and Quinn both signed off on it.

"You're taking lead on this, Dane and Eliza," he said, including them both in his address. He'd never offer Eliza the disrespect of placing Dane above her. She was every bit as capable and cool under fire as Dane was. They made an excellent team and they were both natural leaders.

"I'm trusting you both to make sure nothing touches Ramie," he said in a low voice. "Take on whatever you think you'll need. This is why I pay my employees a salary instead of doing contract work. I don't want guys who do a side job for extra money. I want unwavering loyalty and for them to be here whenever and however I call them out for a job."

"She'll be safe," Dane said.

Though he directed his statement toward Caleb, he was looking at Ramie the entire time as if trying to offer her the same reassurance he was granting Caleb.

Ramie nodded her acknowledgment of his promise but she swallowed noticeably and she still trembled against him.

"How soon?" Caleb asked.

"Now," Dane replied. "Detective Briggs wants us to meet him and Detective Ramirez there. It'll buy us a little more time. Not much but it could be all we need. Nobody in the department is thrilled with having civilians on an unprocessed crime scene but at this point they're willing to exhaust all available options."

Left unsaid was the fact that they most likely had doubts about the validity of Ramie's abilities even if the two detectives who'd visited Caleb's home had witnessed Ramie's accuracy in locating the body.

Detectives Briggs and Ramirez likely *did* believe Ramie's capabilities but they were only two detectives in an entire department of skeptics. And the two detectives probably didn't advertise the fact that they had anything to do with Ramie's trek to an unsecured crime scene.

Caleb had to curb his mounting hope. How many times did the police ever have a completely sealed, by-the-books crime scene that hadn't had relatives of the victim or concerned acquaintances stomping through the area before realizing what had happened and called 911?

"Who's staying here with Tori?" Quinn asked. "Surely it's not a good idea to leave the house so unprotected by sending so many of our men with you, Caleb."

"Dane has it well in hand," Caleb said calmly.

Then he turned to Ramie as the others prepared to depart. He pulled her into his arms, ensuring he was at his most serious as he turned her to completely face him. He framed her face in his hands, his thumbs feathering over her cheekbones.

"Promise me, Ramie. Promise me you'll do exactly as instructed at all times and nothing more. Don't try any heroics. Got me?"

She cracked a small, rueful smile. "We've already covered that I'm not particularly brave or heroic. So let me say that, while I may not be any of those things, neither am I stupid. I have no intention of doing anything that puts me or any of you at risk."

"Let's roll then," Dane said.

TWENTY-SEVEN

RAMIE shivered when they pulled up to an over-grown single-wide trailer that looked as though it was falling down. They were north of Houston, right on the fringes of a rural community where houses were spaced large distances apart and big pieces of acreage were used in farming and to keep cattle.

It had taken them almost an hour to get there, though it wasn't a great distance as the crow flew. Traffic in the bustling area called the Woodlands had slowed them considerably and all Ramie could think was that the killer had done it on purpose.

Nothing he did could be considered random. He thought everything out to the minutest detail and he planned for every contingency.

Why then had she even bothered to come? She already knew it would be too late for the victim.

That the killer was toying with her in an effort to push her over the edge. The women he abducted were merely instruments used to torture her. Nothing else. Their only crime was their accessibility.

The killer wouldn't have chosen someone who would pose a challenge to him. Because they weren't who he was after. He would have needed easy conquests so he could act fast and then have the police involve Ramie.

In essence, she, Caleb, his security and the city and county police were his puppets, dangling from strings while he directed their actions. She couldn't even imagine how many resources were being utilized in the hunt for this madman or the toll it was taking, both financial and psychological.

The two detectives looked haggard, like they hadn't slept in several nights. Dane and the men he oversaw all had determined, focused looks on their faces. There was an air of expectancy that hovered over the crowd of people standing in the front yard and then she realized that they were all looking expectantly . . . at her.

The pressure she was under, the expectations and demands placed upon her, weighed heavily on her heart and soul. Her feet dragged as she took a few steps closer to the rickety front porch of the trailer. They were so heavy it felt as though her feet were encased in lead.

"Do I just go in?" Ramie asked, staring in bewilderment at all the people staring back at her.

Their stares left prints on her skin. She fidgeted underneath their scrutiny. She lifted her gaze to Caleb in a silent plea for help. Did they expect her to perform like a circus monkey in front of them all? It felt as though this were some gruesome party where she was expected to entertain everyone by acting out a vicious crime.

"Detective Briggs?" Caleb said, raising his voice to be heard. "If you want Ramie to go in then the rest of you need to stand back and give her breathing room. Have you cleared the trailer yet? Is it even safe for her to go in?"

As he spoke, he put his arm in front of Ramie as if protecting her from whatever was inside.

Detective Briggs nodded shortly. "I realize that we can't ask you not to touch anything given that your gift manifests itself through touching, but if you could limit it to only what's necessary, perhaps we'll be able to collect fingerprints or DNA."

Ramie knew that was a tenuous hope at best. The killer was getting smarter, not more careless, as he escalated. Most killers probably did get more out of control and more convinced of their invincibility as time went on. But not this one. And Ramie found this kind of killer to be the most frightening of all. What could be worse than a man who couldn't be found or apprehended? Free to kill and torture at will. How could any woman ever feel safe again with men like this out there? He could be a neighbor, a member of the same church, a schoolteacher or even a pastor.

There was no limit to the possibilities and Ramie already knew the killer looked ... ordinary. Good-looking even. Neat and clean. Precise in his movements and meticulous in his dress.

Most women would find such a man harmless in appearance and would be liable to feel comfortable and at ease around him. He was, no doubt, charming and likeable.

What kind of world was it when such monsters lurked in seemingly benign waters?

"I'll take her in," Dane said. "One of our men and one of the county sheriff's deputies. Touch as little as possible but as much as you need, Ramie. We want to nail this guy for good this time."

Ramie nodded, her chin trembling with the effort.

"Not without me," Caleb bit out.

Ramie turned, resting her fingertips on his wrist. "It will be easier if you don't. I need to focus. It could look ... pretty bad." She grimaced and then lifted her gaze to meet his. "You wouldn't like it. You may even interrupt or intervene."

"Damn right," he said vehemently. "The minute this goes south, I'm getting you the hell out of here."

She gently shook her head. "No. We need to catch him this time. I have to try to look deeper than the surface. I have to see beyond what he *wants* me to see and see the things he *doesn't*. It's our only chance of taking him down. He's too smart to slip up and make a mistake."

Before he could argue further, and because he would argue the point into the ground, she turned and hurried toward the dilapidated wooden steps that were built onto a small square front landing.

The bottom step cracked as soon as she put her weight on it and her hand flew up to grasp the railing to prevent her falling. Dane gripped her other arm.

"Are you all right?" Dane demanded.

A loud roar burst through her ears, as though a hundred freight trains collided at seventy miles per hour. She swayed precariously and then sagged to her knees, her arm stretched upward because she still had a death grip on the metal handrail and her knuckles were white and straining.

A barrage of images, messy and chaotic, flashed rapid-fire in her mind. They were jumbled and confusing, no apparent rhyme or reason.

Fear had a chokehold on her. Not her fear. The victim's fear.

Pain. Also the victim's.

Triumph. The killer's.

Unfettered glee and satisfaction. Also the killer's.

She honed in on the killer, regretfully shoving aside the tumultuous explosion of the victim's cries for help and justice. She knew, as she'd known with the last one, that it was too late. There was no sense in focusing her energy there when she needed all she could get to unravel the layers surrounding a maniac. A very intelligent, cunning psychopath.

Each random flash was like having still photos cataloging the entire gruesome crime. She studied and quickly absorbed each, much like she was thumbing through a photo album containing memories. Only these were not meant to be saved, cherished or remembered.

Underneath the thin overlay of each chronicled step the killer had taken with his victim was a hazy image that Ramie couldn't quite make out. She concentrated harder, trying to bring it into focus.

Every time it seemed she'd manage to go beyond the carefully orchestrated façade, pain seared through her head, choking her with nausea.

It was camouflage. Despite the intensity of the pain and overwhelming nausea, excitement lit a spark inside her. One that couldn't be extinguished by the killer.

Where before she would have been deterred by the macabre sight of blood, suffering and death, she now braced herself and forced herself to push past it. He was hiding traces of . . . one of his thoughts? What was it he didn't want her to see?

She sensed victory and it imbued her with strength she hadn't imagined she had.

Her head ached so vilely that she was afraid one of the blood vessels would burst. She shoved her face into her hands, scrubbing, trying to refocus on the blurry memory strategically hidden behind the images of the victim, bloody, eyes glassy with the knowledge of her own demise.

Then she smelled blood. Felt it on her hands. She frowned because that wasn't what she was seeing. It took a moment to realize that she was the one bleeding. From both nostrils.

The pressure in her head was mounting. The pain was becoming unbearable. And yet she refused to back down and retreat. Not when she was so close to . . . something. She just had no idea what.

In the silent battle of wills, Ramie was determined that this one time she wouldn't lose. She wouldn't fail.

Damn it, what did he not want her to see!

And then the images covering his secrets shattered, sending shards of agonizing pain blistering through her skull. Warm blood spilled from her nose, but she ignored it, knowing this was it.

She went utterly still, refusing to even breathe as she waited for the pieces of the puzzle to assemble.

They coalesced and took shape right in front of her very eyes until the pieces were one solid image hanging in the air for her to see.

It was like pushing back a curtain and seeing the unthinkable.

Oh dear God!

"No!" she screamed. "Back! Get back! There's a bomb!"

TWENTY-EIGHT

CALEB froze when Ramie's scream rent the silence.
There was a split second when *everyone* seemed
frozen, looks of absolute *what the fuck* reflected in
their expressions.

Then everyone dove in opposite directions, rolling and scrambling for cover. To Caleb's horror,
Ramie tripped in her haste to descend the fractured
wooden steps of the trailer. Time slowed and he
hoarsely yelled her name as he dove for her, trying
desperately to get on top of her.

He grabbed her wrist, yanking her against his
body before turning and propelling them both
behind the Hummer they'd driven to the scene.
And then an explosion rocked the earth beneath
them.

An orange fireball erupted around them, heat
scouring their skin. The very air seemed to be on

fire and the smell of smoke choked Caleb, making it impossible to breathe.

Debris rained down on them from the sky, pelting the vehicles and their exposed bodies like a storm from the bowels of hell itself.

"Ramie!" he shouted.

They'd been separated in the blast. Smoke was so thick that he couldn't see her. He felt frantically along the ground in front of him, to the side and then behind him. She'd gone down underneath him but the explosion had ripped him away from her and flung him several feet.

He heard coughing but couldn't be sure who it was.

"Caleb!" Dane yelled.

"I'm here!" he yelled back. "I can't find Ramie!"

"Here," Ramie croaked.

He followed the sound of her voice, crawling on hands and knees until finally he fell on her as he nearly mowed right over her. Rage overtook him when he saw that a burning piece of wood had hit her square in the middle of her back. He wrenched it away from her and then rolled her frantically over.

"Ramie, thank God. Are you all right? Damn it, I can't see anything!"

"I'm okay," she said faintly. "Or at least I think so. I can't really feel anything right now."

The woozy note to her voice worried him. He waved the smoke from his vision and then placed a hand over her forehead, lowering his head so he could better see her.

"Don't move," he said urgently. "We don't know the extent of your injuries."

Damn it, he shouldn't have been so rough when he rolled her over, but he'd been desperate to make sure she was breathing, that she was *alive*.

As the smoke began to clear, Caleb got a better picture of the area and he stared in horror at the leveled space of land where the trailer used to stand. One of the vehicles that had been parked too close to the home had been blown over on its side. Men were sprawled in every direction. It looked like a military zone that had just been air raided.

Trees were on fire. The long grass around the trailer had been flattened by the force of the explosion. Windows were busted out of the remaining vehicles and a tree had been knocked over, T-boning another SUV.

"I need help over here!" Eliza yelled. "Man down!"

"You help her!" Caleb hollered at Dane. "I'll take care of Ramie!"

Where the hell was everyone else? With bodies scattered everywhere it was impossible to tell who was okay and who wasn't.

Several groans, mutters and curses arose as everyone began stirring. Then to his relief he heard Detective Ramirez urgently calling for backup and ambulances, radioing their location to dispatch.

Detective Briggs crawled to where Caleb was hunkered down over Ramie. Blood streamed from a cut in his forehead and a large bruise was already forming on his jaw. He spit blood on the ground and then asked, "Is she okay?"

Caleb's eyes narrowed. "I think she's a hell of a lot better than you. You should lie down, man. You're spitting blood and even I know that isn't good."

"Just a busted lip," Briggs said in disgust. "This son of a bitch has to go down. Now he's conspiring to take out an entire police unit?"

Caleb made a sound of agreement. As he glanced back down at Ramie, his hands began to shake. He touched her cheek and then ran his fingers down her body, checking for any bleeding wounds that required immediate attention.

God, he'd come so close to losing her. If she hadn't touched the railing. . . . He closed his eyes, unable to continue with the current direction of his thoughts.

She wouldn't have been the only one to die. Thanks to her everyone looked as though they were moving at least.

Dane crouched down next to Caleb for a brief moment, his gaze assessing Ramie's condition.

"Shock," Dane said grimly. "I'm going to help Lizzie triage the rest so that when the ambulances start rolling in the higher-priority cases will go first."

Caleb nodded. He was in shock himself. He couldn't get his shaking extremities under control. Every time he tried to touch her to reassure himself that she was alive, he had to pull back or risk injuring her with twitching hands and complete clumsiness.

Once Dane disappeared, Ramie's eyes moved, her head turning slightly so she found his gaze.

"Go help with the others, Caleb," she whispered. "I'm all right, I swear. I don't even hurt anywhere."

"I think you're hurt worse than you think," he said grimly. "There's blood all over your face and I can't figure out where it's coming from."

She blinked in surprise and then lifted a hand, wiping it over her nose and mouth. When she did so, he saw that blood covered both her hands too.

"Jesus," he swore. "That's it. You're taking the first ambulance."

She shook her head and he swore again, immediately framing her face so she couldn't move her neck again.

"Be still, Ramie," he said forcefully. "You have

no way of knowing if you have a spinal injury or not."

"It's not from the explosion," she said, her voice louder and stronger this time.

He looked at her in puzzlement. "What isn't?"

"The blood," she said patiently. "It's not from the explosion."

"Then what the hell is it from?"

"Nosebleed," she said simply. "The pain was horrible." She grimaced as she said it as if recalling just how painful it was. "I had to fight hard to see past the images he wanted me to see. I was scared I'd have a stroke or an aneurysm or that my head would just explode from the pressure. My head has never hurt like that. My nose started bleeding heavily. My back must have been to you or else you couldn't have missed it. And then finally just when the pain was too much to bear any longer I saw the bomb through his eyes."

Caleb cursed viciously. "This is *enough*. You're done with this. I won't let you risk yourself anymore. I don't give a fuck if that means you live the rest of your life hiding. At least you'll *have* a life. You can't keep this up, Ramie. Even you have to see that."

"I was so scared, Caleb," she said in a dazed voice that told him she hadn't even registered his statement. "God, I thought you'd all die."

And that pissed him off even more. He was fuming, his fingers curling into tight fists because he didn't want to chance touching her and hurting her.

She hadn't said she was afraid *she'd* die. No, her only concern had been for the rest of them. He had enough panic for her for them both but damn it, if he couldn't instill that same vehemence when it came to her own life, how the hell was he supposed to make her start caring for herself?

In the distance sirens wailed, drawing closer and closer until they screamed in Caleb's ears. He remained on his knees, surveying the damage in an attempt to make sure everyone was accounted for.

The two detectives had taken the lead going into the trailer while Caleb's men had fallen behind Ramie. To his relief he saw Detective Ramirez bending over one of his fallen police officers but then his blood chilled when he realized the man Ramirez was tending to wasn't moving.

"Ramirez!" Caleb shouted. "He okay over there?"

"He's breathing," Ramirez called back in a pissed-off voice. "Unconscious and bleeding like a stuck pig. He was impaled by debris."

Caleb swore, his fury mounting with every passing second. Medics from three ambulances swarmed the area while multiple police cars screeched to a stop a short distance away.

"Caleb, how is she?" Eliza demanded as she crouched down next to him.

"I'm okay," Ramie said weakly. "My head hurts like hell though."

Eliza's eyes swam with concern. "Did something hit you? Or did you hit it going down?"

"She wasn't hit," Caleb said through clenched teeth. "She damn near gave herself a stroke fighting to pick up the image of the bomb underneath the crap he *wanted* her to see."

"So that's how you knew," Eliza murmured. "I saw your nose start to bleed, but I didn't know if that was normal or not."

"It didn't used to be," Ramie said drowsily.

"Baby, stay awake," Caleb said in alarm.

He exchanged worried glances with Eliza, whose sharp gaze was already scanning Ramie.

"Kind of hard to sleep when your head hurts this bad," she mumbled.

Caleb lifted his head up, looking quickly for an available medic. He was starting to get extremely worried. Ramie needed medical attention regardless of whether she thought so or not.

"You know they'll just think I'm crazy if you take me in and explain how and why my nose bled and my head hurts," she said dryly.

"There is that," Eliza muttered.

"No way am I not bringing her in just because

she'll have to explain why her head hurts," Caleb snapped. "They don't have to know she didn't hurt her head in the explosion. How do we know she *didn't*?"

Eliza held her hands up. "I'm not arguing. That's between you and her. Certainly wouldn't hurt to get her a prescription for those headaches after the one she had earlier."

He hated the idea that she suffered at all. And the idea that until now no one had ever been there to care for her when she suffered was more than he could stand.

"It's not normal for a headache to cause nose-bleeds," he said fiercely. "What if she has a brain bleed? With the kind of pain she was describing and the mental strain she was under, it certainly seems possible."

Eliza shrugged and then stood, motioning for one of the medics.

"Guess the best way to know is to bring her in and get her head checked out," Eliza said.

"Traitor," Ramie grumbled.

For some reason, that slight complaint completely unraveled Caleb. Maybe it was the fact that she was injecting levity in a situation fraught with turmoil. Whatever the case, his behind slumped downward to rest on the backs of his legs and he found his strength gone.

The adrenaline that had given him superhuman strength and focus just moments before was over in an instant and he felt too old and weary to even push himself to his feet.

Even after Ramie had been placed on a backboard and boosted upward to one of the stretchers, he remained where he was, hands shaking.

"Come on, I'll help you up," Eliza said, her voice gentle. "You'll need to go to the hospital with Ramie."

Caleb lifted his gaze to Eliza's, his gut churning so much he worried he'd end up being sick all over the ground.

"She almost died," he whispered.

"We all almost died," Eliza amended. "But we didn't. Ramie warned us quickly enough."

"Caleb? Where are you?"

Ramie's worried question spurred him to action. He allowed Eliza to give him a hand up so he didn't embarrass himself by face-planting on the ground. Then he went to the stretcher and leaned over to kiss Ramie on the forehead.

"I'm right here, baby. Now let's get you to the hospital so I know that you're truly all right."

TWENTY-NINE

BY the time Ramie was discharged from the ER, a battery of tests run to ensure she had no serious injury, including a CT of her head at Caleb's insistence, she was exhausted and feeling the aftershocks of the bomb blast.

The only injuries she sustained were bruising and a feeling of being hit by a train. She was sore and stiff, every muscle protesting the slightest movement.

Caleb stopped by a twenty-four-hour pharmacy to have her prescriptions filled since it was an obscene hour of the morning the next day, and Ramie figured he had likely scared the poor pharmacist to death with his appearance because the script was filled in a matter of minutes.

"He likely thinks you're a prescription drug

addict," Ramie said in amusement as they drove away.

He glared darkly at her, his scowl making her giggle, which only served to make him glower more fiercely.

"I'm so glad you find this so funny," he muttered. "Do you forget you could have gotten killed today—yesterday? Whenever the fuck it was."

"But I didn't," she said gently. "And you could have gotten killed too but I'm not biting your head off for daring to be in danger. You didn't have to go, you know. I had to be there but you didn't."

"Stop right there," he snapped, his mood as black as his expression. "Swear to God if you suggest one more fucking time that I should just leave you to your fate and not give a crap where you go or the danger you're in I'm going to throttle you."

"I was merely pointing out the hypocrisy of you being pissed at me for almost getting killed when you did the same," she said in a mild voice.

"I'm not pissed at . . . Okay, maybe I'm pissed," he grumbled. "Give me a break. I was scared, all right?"

"So was I," she said, reaching over to squeeze his hand. "Do you have any idea how badly I panicked when I realized there was a bomb inside and didn't know if I'd be able to warn everyone in time?"

He sighed and lifted her hand to his mouth,

pressing his lips to her palm in a tender gesture. "I know, baby. I'm sorry. I don't deal very well with feeling helpless and right now that's exactly how I feel. I'm not used to other people controlling my happiness, my mood or my decisions. But you do."

"I do what?" she queried.

"You have complete control over my happiness, my mood and my decision making," he said starkly.

"Ah, the control freak in you frowns on that, huh."

He shot her another glare. "What I would like is for you to stop making light of this. You aren't helping."

She smiled back at him, ignoring his scowl. "One of us has to not take things so seriously all the time. Otherwise we'd both be hot messes."

He pulled through the gate at the end of his winding driveway and Ramie could see that every light in the house was on.

"Guess they waited up," Ramie muttered.

"It's not every day their brother nearly gets blown to hell and back," Caleb said dryly. "Did you think they'd just go to bed and catch up with me in the morning?"

"One could hope," she said under her breath.

The last thing she wanted right now was to be the recipient of their anger and disapproval over the fact that Caleb had nearly gotten killed because of her.

Caleb parked the vehicle in the garage and then stared at the cracked windshield, shaking his head. Every single vehicle at the bomb site had incurred damage. One of Caleb's company SUVs had been totaled by a fallen tree. Yesterday's blast had put a serious dent in his fleet of vehicles.

She groaned when she started to climb down from the passenger seat.

"Your ass stays put," Caleb ordered.

"You know, you've got to work on your disposition, Caleb," she grumbled. "Would it kill you to ask me something rather than hand down a command from on high?"

He appeared just behind her and then simply scooped her into his arms and headed for the door leading into the house.

"I find barking orders to be more satisfying."

She snorted. "Ya think? I can't imagine why you're still single."

He stopped short just inside the house, a frown seemingly tattooed on his face.

"I'm not single," he growled. "And neither the hell are you."

She lifted an eyebrow when he resumed walking toward the living room. "I'm not? You're not?"

"Just shut up, Ramie," he said in an aggravated tone.

She sighed and relaxed in his arms. Her lips

twitched from trying to keep her laughter in, but one, he'd just get more pissed, and two, he'd wonder what the hell was wrong with her that she could laugh at a time like this.

What else could she do, though? The last year and a half of her life was a calamity of disaster and close calls. It was either laugh or start crying and never stop, and while Caleb might be pissed over her laughing, he'd freak if hysteria took over and she cried all over him.

Pissing him off seemed the lesser of two evils, and well, poking him amused her because the man had no sense of humor. She wouldn't have thought she did either, but how else to explain her finding so much amusement in the fact that she'd very nearly been incinerated by a bomb blast.

He set her down on the sofa and it was then she saw his siblings—all three of them—standing across the room, their expressions drawn and worried. Relief was all over Tori's face. And for some reason Ramie finally lost the battle and began laughing.

"What the hell?" Beau demanded.

"You think this is funny?" Quinn said in an incredulous voice.

Caleb made a sound of exasperation but then lost all semblance of anger when he looked at her.

"Shit," he murmured.

"What's wrong with her?" Tori asked sharply. "Is she okay?"

"No," Caleb said quietly. "She's not."

"Don't be angry, Caleb," she said with an odd hitch in her voice. It sounded like she was gulping or making some other strange noise she couldn't identify. "I have to laugh or I'll start crying."

"Baby, you *are* crying," he said gently.

"I am?"

She lifted her hand to her cheek, astonished to find it wet. She became more aware of the odd noise emanating from her chest and throat and realized it was her. *Sobbing.*

"She's hysterical," Beau said unnecessarily.

"What was your first clue?" Caleb snapped.

"Y-you r-really n-need to learn to c-control your t-temper, Caleb," she stuttered out between each gasping sob.

Her chest was tight, squeezing her insides to the point of pain. She was precariously light-headed and spots appeared in her vision.

"Get her some water," Caleb demanded of no one in particular.

Tori scurried from the room and Caleb went to one knee in front of her.

"Ah, baby," he said, all anger and annoyance wiped from his face and eyes. "I'm all right," he said, accurately guessing the source of her hysteria. "I wish you'd be this concerned over your own well-being, but I'll make you a deal. You look out for mine and I'll look out for yours."

"D-deal," she said, her teeth chattering almost violently.

Tori hurried over, a glass of water in her hand, thrusting it at Caleb. There was actual concern on her face as she looked at Ramie.

Caleb ripped open the pharmacy bag and pulled out one of the bottles. She had no clue what the ER doctor had even prescribed. Caleb had been the one who talked to him because she hadn't been able to keep her focus for any length of time during the seemingly interminable visit to the emergency room.

"Can you swallow this?" Caleb asked, holding a tiny peach-colored pill out to her.

"What is it?"

"Something to help you calm down and sleep. Take it," he said firmly.

He nudged open her lips himself and carefully put the pill on her tongue. She made an immediate face and recoiled from the horrible bitter taste.

"I'm going to take her upstairs," Caleb said over his shoulder. "We'll talk in the morning. I have no idea what the hell we're going to do next, but I don't want Ramie involved any longer. She could have died today."

"So could you have," Beau said quietly.

Caleb glanced at Tori, who was as pale as death, her eyes wide with fear. Then he glanced back at Ramie.

"Give me just a second, honey."

He rose to his feet and then held his arms out to Tori, who flew into them, landing against his chest. She buried her face against his neck as he hugged her tightly.

"I'm okay, Tori," he soothed. "We all need to get much-needed rest and then we'll decide what is to be done in the morning."

A prickle of unease had Ramie rubbing her chest. His words sounded so ominous. As though he was going to discuss something life-changing with his brothers and sister.

"Where are Dane and Eliza?" Quinn asked sharply. "Did we have any serious injuries on our side?"

"They're fine," Caleb replied. "They're assisting in cleanup and evidence gathering. I don't trust the police to share important information with us so I made sure I had men on the scene."

He let Tori go, squeezing her hand before allowing it to fall from his grasp. Then he gently helped Ramie to her feet as though she were a breakable piece of glass. Judging by the expressions on the others' faces it was too late for her not to end up a hot mess, which only left Caleb to be the relatively sane one.

Still, she couldn't help the apology that formed on her lips. She lifted her gaze to Caleb's two brothers and then swept it to Tori.

"I truly am sorry," she said quietly, scrubbing back the stupid, endless tear trails from her cheeks. "If I had known, if I'd had any idea this would become so dangerous and out of control for Caleb—and you—I would have never called him."

Caleb went rigid with anger. His jaw bulged from the strain of clenching his teeth.

Beau stared at her a long moment, his expression softening into a look of apology.

"I'm glad you did, Ramie. I believe my brother needs you every bit as much as you obviously need him. You certainly can't be blamed for the actions of a cold-blooded murderer."

Ramie offered him a tremulous smile, though he was blurry through a sheen of tears. If only she could quit crying, for God's sake.

"Thank you," she said sincerely.

"I believe we all owe you an apology," Beau said, including his brother and sister in his stare. "But we'll wait to give it to you when you're in better shape to hear it."

THIRTY

CALEB wrapped his arm around Ramie's waist and slowly walked her up the stairs. As soon as they reached the top, he swung her up into his arms and carried her the remaining way to the bedroom.

He leaned over the bed, easing her down, and then sat on the edge turned sideways to her as he wiped at more tears that streaked her cheeks.

"We make quite a pair, don't we?" he asked with a sigh.

"I don't know why I can't stop cr-cr-crying," she said through chattering teeth.

Her jaw quivered and a fresh surge of hot tears trickled down her temples and into her hair. He lowered his head and pressed his lips to her forehead in the tenderest of kisses.

Without a word, he began to undress her, though

her skin was ice cold and goose bumps dotted her body.

"Cold," she fretted.

"I know, baby. Give me just a minute and I'll get you warm."

She went silent, only a hiccup escaping her when she evidently tried to swallow back another sob.

When he was finished undressing her, he hurriedly divested himself of clothing as well and climbed into the bed with her, pulling her flush against his body so his heat would warm her.

She gave a drowsy sigh then yawned broadly as she nuzzled her face into his chest. He hoped the medicine was taking effect and that she'd soon drift off to sleep.

"Caleb?" she whispered.

"What, baby?"

"I realized something today."

"Oh? What's that?"

She hesitated a moment, her cheek resting on his bare chest, her soft breaths blowing over his skin.

"That I love you."

His heart surged and his pulse began racing.

A fresh torrent of tears wet his chest.

"Ramie? Baby, why does that upset you? Hey," he said, nudging her chin up with his fingers. Her eyes were glossy wet. Not exactly the reaction he'd hoped for when she made such an admission. "What's wrong? Why does that upset you? You have to know that I'm pretty damn happy about the fact that you love me. I'd sure hate to be in this alone."

"Because it scares me," she said baldly. "If you don't love anyone then you can't be hurt. If something happened to you I couldn't bear it, Caleb. I've never loved anyone before and I have to tell you it sucks."

He laughed softly at her mournful tone and then he gathered her up in his arms, squeezing her tightly against him. He kissed the top of her head, smiling against her hair.

"I agree. It totally sucks," he said, still grinning.

"If I didn't hurt so bad I'd so jump your bones so I'm going to hang on to the sorry-honey-I've-got-a-headache line from last night."

"I'll let you get by. Just this once."

"Caleb?"

"Yes, baby?"

"I really do love you."

He squeezed her again, unable to control the urge to hold her as tightly as possible.

"I love you too, Ramie."

"Caleb?"

He chuckled. "What, you imp?"

"That medicine you gave me made me loopy."

"I see that," he observed dryly. "Go to sleep, baby. I'll be here when you wake up. I promise."

"I'm afraid to close my eyes," she whispered.

"Why is that?" he queried.

"What if I wake up and you're not here and this was all just a dream?"

Again he nudged her chin upward and then fused his mouth to hers in a deep kiss. For several long moments, he did nothing but kiss her. It wasn't overtly sexual and that was what he liked about it. It was just a sweet and innocent kiss, one shared by two lovers who were both in need of comforting.

"Does that feel like it's all just a dream?" he whispered against her mouth.

"If it is then I never want to wake up."

"Me either, baby. Me either."

He held her in silence, simply stroking his hand up and down her slender spine. She made a deep sound of contentment and went limp against him. He continued his slow caressing until he was certain she slept.

Long after she had fallen into deep and dreamless sleep, Caleb lay there, awake, her in his arms, her soft body molded to his.

"Keep the people I love safe," he whispered. "It's all I'll ever ask for."

THIRTY-ONE

THE explosion rocked the entire house, yanking Caleb from deep slumber. He jackknifed up from bed, his pulse hammering in his neck and wrists.

"What the ever-loving fuck?"

He shook the fog of sleep from his mind, positive that he'd been having his own nightmare about losing Ramie in the explosion. But no. It was too loud. Too real.

Panic slithered up his spine and he reached desperately for Ramie, trying to rouse her from her drug-induced sleep.

His bedroom door flew open and Beau burst in.

"Get up!" Beau yelled. "You have to get out. The house is on fire."

Caleb scrambled up, dragging Ramie's limp body with him.

"Come on, baby. I need you to wake up. Come on, Ramie. Wake up!"

"Where are Quinn and Tori?" Caleb demanded. "What the fuck is going on, Beau!"

"We don't have time for questions," Beau yelled. "We have to get out now! Quinn's getting Tori."

Caleb threw Ramie over his shoulder in a fireman's carry and surged into the hallway to see Quinn herding Tori toward the stairs. Quinn quickly recoiled, thrusting Tori behind him and then shoving her in the direction of Caleb's bedroom, which was at the very end of the hall.

"Stairs and the safe room are out!" Quinn hollered. "We'll have to go out a window."

"We're on the second fucking story," Beau bit out.

Caleb didn't waste time going over the logistics. Already he could see flames licking up the stairway. To his horror the ceiling collapsed at the other end of the hall where Quinn's and Tori's bedrooms were, and smoke came billowing up through the opening.

"Son of a bitch," Caleb swore. "Everyone in my room. Now!"

Beau herded his younger brother and sister into Caleb's room. Tori was obviously shell-shocked, her eyes wide and haunted.

"Get the window, Quinn," Beau ordered. "Caleb's got his arms full. We'll have to do the best we can and hope we don't break our damn necks getting out."

"Let me go first," Quinn said quietly. "I can try to break Tori and Ramie's fall."

"No, wait," Caleb said. "Slow down and let's think about this before we do get ourselves killed. We can get on the roof outside my window dormer and then make it down to the garage roof. It's only one story there and much less distance to fall."

"Let's go then," Beau barked. "We don't have much time before the whole place goes up."

Quinn slid the window open and then climbed out, hanging on to the eaves as he inched out onto the roof.

Beau helped Tori through the window and Quinn held his hand out for her to grab so she didn't fall.

"You go," Caleb directed Beau. "I'll have to hand Ramie to you. She's out cold."

Beau ducked out after Tori and after making sure she was in a secure place on the roof, Beau reached back and carefully hooked his arms underneath Ramie's shoulders. Caleb eased her legs out so that Beau was dragging her along the rooftop in the direction of the garage.

Already Caleb could feel the heat of the fire. Below them might already be consumed and it was only a matter of time before the roof they were standing on fell in as well.

"Quinn, you get Tori," Caleb said. "Beau and I will have to manage with Ramie."

They inched along the roofline as fast as they dared. Caleb's forehead was beaded with sweat. Fear for his family gripped him in a vicious hold. Just an hour ago he'd prayed for his family to be safe and they were anything but right now.

And then another fear utterly paralyzed him.

"Nobody move," Caleb ordered.

"What the fuck, Caleb?" Quinn demanded.

"We don't know if that son of a bitch is on the grounds or how the hell he managed to plant a bomb. For all we know he's waiting to kill us as soon as we get off the roof."

Tori let out a whimper but Caleb couldn't afford to spare her fears. Not when he could possibly be stating an absolute truth.

"I've got to go back and get the gun out of my nightstand," Caleb said. "Nobody move until I get back."

"*Hurry!*" Beau urged.

"Just in case something happens to me," Caleb said in a steady, serious tone, "you and Quinn get Tori and Ramie to safety and do not look back for me."

"Shut up and move!" Quinn hissed.

Caleb slid on his ass down the roof incline as fast as he dared and then swung himself around

and into the window, holding on to the overhang.
Smoke was already filling his room and surely it
would not be long before fire consumed the entire
house, including everyone on the roof.

He yanked open his nightstand drawer, grabbed
his pistol and an already loaded clip, shoved it
in and jacked a shell into the chamber. Then he
climbed back onto the roof and crawled back to
the others.

Together they inched their way to where the roof
dropped off to the garage. Quinn went first and
then Beau helped Tori over the edge, holding her
hands while her feet dangled toward Quinn.

"Let go," Quinn called up. "I've got her."

Tori squeezed her eyes shut and then dropped
down to where Quinn had landed.

"Give me one of her arms," Beau said. "I'll help
you lower her down to Quinn."

Positioning Ramie between them, they each held
her wrists and guided her down to Quinn's waiting grasp. Beau and then Caleb slid over the edge,
holding on to the overhang and dropping the few
feet onto the garage roof.

Caleb surveyed their options and decided going
down the left side was their only route. The con-
crete garage apron in front and the sidewalk to the
right prevented them from being able to drop the
distance from the roof to the ground.

Again, Quinn went first. Caleb eased Ramie down, praying she didn't wake and panic and slide off while he helped Beau lower Tori over the edge.

Once Tori was safely down, Caleb and Beau took Ramie's hands and then carefully slid her legs over the edge and inched her forward very carefully so her weight didn't suddenly plummet.

And she picked then, when she was dangling several feet above Quinn's head, to open her eyes.

She screamed and began to struggle, her legs thrashing and rotating wildly in the air.

"Ramie! Ramie!" Caleb yelled. "Stop! You've got to stop. I've got you. You're safe. But you have to stop fighting us."

She went still, a low whimper working its way past trembling lips. "Caleb?" she choked out. "This is a dream, right? Tell me this is a dream."

"It's just a dream, honey," he soothed. "A nightmare. Close your eyes and it'll all be over."

She went limp and relaxed and as soon as she did, he and Beau let her go and she dropped into Quinn's arms, sending them both crashing to the ground.

Once Beau was down, Caleb tossed the gun to his brother. Then he swung his legs over and lowered himself to hang from the eave and then dropped the remaining distance, rolling the moment he landed to absorb some of the impact. The breath was momentarily knocked from him and he sucked in steadying breaths.

Immediately he crawled over to where Ramie and Quinn lay in a tangle of arms and legs.

"Quinn, are you all right?" Caleb asked.

"Yeah, just got the breath knocked out of me is all. What about her?"

"Can I open my eyes now?" Ramie asked in a small voice.

"Yes, baby. Open your eyes. We have to get moving."

"What's happening, Caleb?"

The tremor in her voice clutched at Caleb's heart. The last thing he wanted was to tell her what had happened.

"The house is on fire. We had to get out through my window," Caleb said gently.

"What about the others?" she demanded, scrambling to her feet. She shook her head several times as if clearing the drug-induced cobwebs from her mind.

"Tori, Beau and Quinn are here. Everyone is fine."

"Eliza and Dane?" she asked anxiously.

"They aren't here tonight. The team was coming back in the morning to discuss our next step. It's just us and we need to get the hell out of here."

"Is he *here*?" Ramie whispered.

Caleb knew exactly who *he* referred to.

"We don't know," Beau cut in. "But we aren't going to take any chances. We have to get you and Tori someplace safe."

"And you as well," Ramie said pointedly.

"Yes, us too," Caleb agreed.

"We can't take any of the vehicles," Beau said. "We can't be sure they aren't wired too."

"How the fuck did he get a bomb into this house?" Caleb bit out.

"We don't know that he did," Quinn said in a low voice. "We don't know what the fuck happened here. For all we know he shot an RPG at us. All I do know is that there was an explosion and now the house is on fire. His proximity to us is completely unknown so I vote we get the fuck out of here as quickly as possible."

"That gets my vote," Beau said.

Caleb's gaze followed Ramie as she walked over to where Tori stood, shaking like a leaf from head to toe. Ramie gently took Tori's hand in hers and squeezed. To Caleb's surprise, Tori sent her a look of gratitude and kept her hand in Ramie's as they set out quickly through the woods surrounding the house.

THIRTY-TWO

"THIS has gone on long enough," Caleb said coldly. "I want the son of a bitch taken out and I don't care how it's done, legally or illegally."

Dane stood in Eliza's kitchen, pouring cups of coffee for the ten men assembled in Eliza's home. Aside from Caleb, his brothers, Eliza and Dane there was also one of the two six-man teams that Caleb and his brothers employed. They only hired the best and it was time for them to do what they did best. Take down a killer.

Before anyone could respond to Caleb's decree, Eliza walked into the kitchen and Caleb immediately turned his attention to her.

"How are they?" he asked in a low voice.

It had been a hell of a night and morning for Ramie and Tori. They'd trekked through the woods in the dead of night, and Ramie had been terrified that they were being followed. Hunted. Every noise had set them on edge. Their nerves had been wound so tight that by the time they'd made it to a place where Caleb could call Dane to come get them, they'd been utterly exhausted.

Caleb had felt no guilt whatsoever in giving Ramie medication to ward off an imminent panic attack. She'd been hyperventilating by the time Dane had arrived. Tori was every bit as distressed and had hovered anxiously over Ramie, evidently worried about the other woman.

"Ramie finally agreed to lie down and try to get some rest," Eliza said grimly. "And she only agreed because Tori didn't want to be alone and asked her not to leave the room."

Caleb blew out his breath in rage. When would people he loved stop suffering? When would they be safe, or would they ever truly be safe? He ran a hand raggedly through his hair.

"Thanks, Eliza."

"No need to thank me. Now, do we have a plan of action yet?" she asked pointedly.

"I'm setting up a safe house for them to stay in tonight," Dane said. "It'll take me until this afternoon to get surveillance and all security measures in place. Until then I think they should stay here and out of sight."

Eliza nodded.

"We'll split the team into threes and twelve-hour shifts," Dane continued. "First shift gets seven P.M. tonight until seven A.M. tomorrow morning. Second shift will pick up seven A to seven P."

Caleb couldn't stomach the thought of sitting back, allowing his security team to babysit him and his brothers while he himself did nothing. He was pissed off and ready to take the bastard apart with his bare hands. If the murderous rage in his brothers' eyes was anything to go by, they were every bit as frustrated as he was.

Fuck the rules and fuck the law. If Caleb ever got his hands on him he was a dead man.

"I'll consult with the police and set up times for you to give statements," Dane said to Caleb. "For now I don't even want the police to know where you are."

"It does you no good to hide if Ramie's stalker still has an established link to her," Eliza pointed out. "Won't he know exactly where you are at all times?"

"Maybe you should keep her drugged until we take this bastard down," Beau said in a serious tone.

"For God's sake. I'm not going to keep her doped up so she doesn't disclose our location," Caleb said in disgust.

"No," Eliza said thoughtfully. "But you could make it so even she doesn't know where you are."

Dane pointed a finger at Eliza. "That's perfect. I don't know why the hell I didn't think of it before."

"Because women are smarter?" Eliza smirked.

"Smarter assed," Dane muttered.

"What are you suggesting?" Caleb asked impatiently.

"You blindfold her," Eliza said simply. "Make sure no one talks in front of her. Keep her quiet and in the dark and you do the same to him. Ramie can hardly broadcast what she doesn't know."

"True," Caleb said slowly. "The speed in which he's escalated leads me to believe that we shouldn't stay here any longer than absolutely necessary. He's displayed an ability to act fast. If we keep Ramie in the dark then there's no reason we can't move to the safe house while you're still installing security measures, right?"

"Right," Dane confirmed.

"Then right now is better because she's already out," Caleb said. "If we move her now, he'll never see anything but the inside of whatever room we stash her in at the safe house."

"If we're moving now then tomorrow's seven A to seven P team needs to cover the safe house until seven P tonight," Eliza said.

"We're on it," Eric Beckett, part of the security team present, replied.

"Let me get something for you to wrap around Ramie's eyes," Eliza said. "Make sure and explain to her when she wakes that she needs to keep her mind as blank as possible. The less this asshole knows, the safer you all are."

"I'll keep her occupied," Caleb said.

Eliza stifled her smile—almost. Caleb groaned when he realized what he'd said.

"Dirty-minded woman," he grumbled.

Ramie frowned her displeasure over being jostled around like a sack of potatoes being tossed in the air. Then she realized that despite the fact she'd opened her eyes, she still couldn't see a single thing.

Her fingers dug into solid flesh and then the jostling stopped abruptly.

"Ramie, I need you to trust me."

Caleb's voice instantly relieved her, soothing her fears.

"What's going on, Caleb?" she whispered.

"Trust me, baby, okay? I need you to just lie still and keep your mind as blank as possible. Can you do that for me?"

Her brows knitted together in confusion. What on earth was he doing? Despite his reassurances, she couldn't help but tense up in his arms. He was carrying her. Where she had no idea. He'd blindfolded her. Again, why she had no idea.

In light of the insane happenings over the last several days, this suddenly didn't seem so crazy.

Deciding to go with it, she rested her cheek on his shoulders and allowed some of the tension to flow out of her. And then she marveled that she actually trusted another human being.

But in order to love someone you had to trust them, right?

And to think she'd once thought she would never be able to forget what Caleb Devereaux had done to her. It was funny how life turned out sometimes. If someone had told her six months ago that she'd be involved with someone much less fall in love with him she would have laughed her ass off.

"Almost there, baby," Caleb murmured against the top of her head.

The sound of a door opening and then closing alerted her senses. Then Caleb eased her down onto a bed. A moment later, he tugged the blindfold from her eyes and her gaze met with his.

He looked tired. She slid her hand over his cheek and brushed the pad of her thumb over the dark shadow underneath his eye.

"Going to tell me what's going on now?" she prompted.

He smiled. "The way we figured it, if you don't know where you're at and haven't seen where you're at then our bomber can't very well tap into your mind, which means that he won't know where you are either."

She blinked in astonishment. "I never thought about that. It's . . . genius!"

"As much as I'd like to take credit, Eliza is the one who came up with this one."

"She's a smart cookie," Ramie said with a smile. But then she rapidly sobered as the prior night's events came crashing back around her. "Caleb, what about your house?"

He sat on the bed next to her and laced their fingers together between their thighs.

"It's just a house," he said. "Houses can always be rebuilt. But people can't be replaced. I'm just thankful that we all got out alive. This entire situation has escalated out of control. He's got to be taken down soon or there's no telling what he'll do next. He's getting bolder, and that's the last thing you want from a savvy, extremely intelligent, cunning serial killer."

"I didn't like your house," she said honestly.

He chuckled. "By all means don't spare my feelings."

"It was so cold and austere," she said, pursing her lips. After a moment she added, "There wasn't any . . . warmth there."

"Well, what do you say the next house I build you oversee construction and decoration. You can knock yourself out making it a home."

She pretended to give it thought. "I may have to take you up on that."

Smiling, he leaned over and kissed her. "Are you hungry? I can go rustle up something to eat and bring it back so you aren't alone in solitary confinement."

"Am I allowed to take a shower and change?"

"Of course. Just don't stick your head out of this room. I made sure and gave you the only room in the place that doesn't have a window so there's no possibility of you giving our location away."

"You make it sound like I do it intentionally," she muttered.

He kissed her again. "Nope. But intentional or not, the same result is achieved. I'm not taking any chances with any of our safety."

When Caleb left the room, shutting the door behind him, Ramie leaned back on the bed and forced her gaze to focus on the ceiling. Then she closed her eyes and purposely blanked her mind.

Sudden pain in her head made her gasp. Faint laughter echoed, leaving her to wonder if she'd imagined it.

You think you can hide from me?

"Caleb!"

Within seconds of her cry, Caleb threw open the door and charged inside. When he saw her sitting on the edge of the bed where he'd left her, his brow furrowed in confusion.

She shook from head to toe and she hugged her arms around herself.

"Ramie, what is it?" Caleb demanded.

"He laughed," she said, uncaring how crazy it made her sound. "I was lying here staring up at the ceiling and trying to keep my mind blank like you said and he laughed and said, 'You think you can hide from me?'"

Caleb sat back down beside her and pulled her into the crook of his arm.

"He can't see what you can't," he said matter-of-factly. "He can't know what you don't know. So yes, I'd say we do think we can hide from him. At least until we formulate a plan to take him out for good. Until then, I'm keeping you under lock and key and absolutely ignorant of your surroundings."

"Okay," she said hoarsely. "I'll quit freaking out, I promise."

He pushed a strand of hair behind her ear. "Having another person in your head gives you the right to freak out."

"Don't mollify me. I'll stop being such a complete scaredy-cat. Now go get me some food and leave me to my imaginary friend. Or rather not so imaginary killer," she said, pulling a face. "God, I can't believe I'm joking about this. I really am losing my mind, aren't I?"

He cupped her chin and smoothed his thumb over her cheek. "Glad I'm not the only one with an inappropriate sense of humor."

THIRTY-THREE

THIS was a piece of cake. Hardly worthy of someone as skilled as he. His father had always said, "Charlie, the early bird gets the worm. Everyone else gets the dirt. Remember that and you'll go far in life."

His fucking name was Charles. Not Charlie. Charlie was a child's name, not a man's.

He pushed through his rage, locking it away so he could focus on the task at hand.

His breathing calmed as he stepped from the shadows of the trees. Calm settled into place. Not a single muscle in his body twitched. He was disciplined and patient. Qualities that were rewarded in life.

He approached the parked car under the cover of darkness. When he was close enough to be seen in the rear or side-view mirror, he got down on his belly and inched the remaining distance to the driver's side door.

It was long, painstaking work designed only for those with infinite patience and eye for detail. One wrong move, one tiny slipup and he was a dead man. Instead of frightening him or making him wary, the idea of him being a marked man gave him a heady, euphoric high like none other. Only killing provided a bigger rush.

Carefully he raised up, positioning the gun with its silencer in such a way that as soon as he rose, the so-called security specialist sitting in the car keeping watch over the house and occupants would be a dead man.

When he popped up, he smiled at his adversary's startled expression. He didn't give the victim a chance to react. The glass folded inward, the bullet creating a hole in the spiderwebbed surface. Blood and brain matter splattered the opposing window.

Pleased with his initial success, he hurried toward the well-lit house and his next victim.

Who needed to see through Ramie St. Claire's eyes anyway? This was much more satisfying. He was salivating over Caleb Devereaux's reaction when Caleb realized he was the tool used in Ramie's destruction. Such pleasure was almost unbearable.

He slid around the side of the house, gun up and

ready to shoot. One never knew the unpredictability of others. It paid to be on constant guard.

When he stole a quick peek around the corner of the house, he saw his target standing guard by the back door. Charles nearly giggled but caught himself in time, remonstrating himself for the near careless slipup.

No reason to be stealthy. Dead men couldn't stand in your way. He swung around the corner, arm raised, left hand supporting the stock of the pistol. His aim was highly accurate, never off target by more than a centimeter. The guard crumpled without a sound, dead before he ever hit the ground.

Charles stepped over the fallen body, eased the door open and slipped inside. From what information he'd been able to glean from Caleb Devereaux he knew the sole remaining guard was in the hallway just outside Ramie's door.

He could hardly contain his glee. Better not to celebrate prematurely. There would be plenty of time to celebrate later. With Ramie!

Charles knew that when he rounded the corner into the hall he'd only have a tenth of a second to find his target and shoot or risk discovery. He was so close to his ultimate goal that his hand shook, bobbing the gun up and down.

Angrily, he tempered his reaction, forcing himself to take deep steadying breaths. He closed his eyes, inhaled deeply and then did a mental one . . . two . . . three!

He swiveled, planting his foot and turning rapidly into the hallway. His current aim was off by six inches. Adjusting upward in that flash of time he squeezed the trigger. The bullet smacked the guard right in the middle of the forehead and dropped him like a stone.

Yes!

It was all he could do not to rush into the bedroom, put a bullet into Devereaux's head and be done with it. But that would ruin everything. Charles had meticulously planned this down to the nth degree. The other night inside Caleb's head was a mere test run, one that he'd been delighted with the results of.

He fumbled, with shaking hands, for the cell phone in his pocket. He had to set up quickly if he was going to get it all on video. Wouldn't Caleb be shocked when he watched this footage? He smiled and then closed his eyes to summon Devereaux.

Caleb sat up in bed, the comforter and sheet falling down to his lap. There were whispers in his mind, demanding he act. He slowly rose, walking to the doorway in measured steps. *Quiet! You don't want to wake Ramie.*

He entered the kitchen and opened a drawer before shutting it again. Then he went to the next and this time he reached into the open drawer, his fingers curling around the handle of a wickedly sharp carving knife.

How appropriate to have a carving knife when he planned to carve Ramie up like a Christmas turkey. She would be the best Christmas and birthday present all rolled into one that he'd ever had.

Gripping the handle of the knife with a firm hand, he retraced his steps to the bedroom and quietly pushed the door open, slipping inside where Ramie still soundly slept. For a long moment he stood over her next to the bed drinking in the sight of the woman he'd hunted the last eighteen months.

A smile curved Caleb's lips. "There's no one here to hear you scream," he whispered.

Still, he clamped one hand over her mouth, put the blade against the soft skin of her abdomen and sliced from one side to the other, angling slightly downward to follow the curve of her belly.

She let out a muffled shriek against his hand and he quickly straddled her writhing body. She bucked upward, trying to unseat him, but he followed her back down and then slid the blade in a vertical line between her breasts.

Blood rose and dripped down her body in rivulets. She was wild beneath him, clearly hysterical and not yet comprehending who was doing this to her. The anticipation of her discovery was so keen that Charles was practically bubbling over.

And then her gaze locked with his and horror contorted her features. He let his hand slip from her mouth because it was too good an opportunity to pass up. He nearly clapped his hands together in the corner but if he did so it would mess up the video he was recording. And he wanted Devereaux to see every single cut he put on her body.

"Caleb!" she screamed. "Caleb, stop! Oh God, what are you *doing*?"

Two more cuts in quick succession. Her eyes went glassy with shock, her speech slurred from that same shock and blood loss. She tried to fight back, but she was no match for Caleb's strength. Oddly she would have had a chance against Charles. Caleb was much bigger and stronger. Experiencing a kill vicariously through another's eyes was deliciously addictive. It was something that now that he'd done once he'd want to do it again and again.

Tears streamed down Ramie's face. Her voice was nearly gone from the force of her screams. The next came out in an ugly hoarse rasp when he made another cut, this time on her hip.

"Please don't do this," Ramie begged, her chest heaving from her pants of pain. "I thought you loved me," she whispered. "You promised . . ." Her voice trailed off and her bowed body sagged back onto the mattress. She finally passed out. She'd earned a measure of respect from Charles. Not many people would have been able to stay conscious for as long as she had under such horrific conditions.

Charles frowned. Caleb's eyes flickered. Turmoil shone in features creased with pain. Charles knew he had to get Ramie out now before Caleb broke free from his hold on him, but he felt like a pouty child deprived of his favorite toy.

Caleb's movements were jerky, spasmodic almost as he leaned down and scooped Ramie up into his arms. Smiling, Charles followed along, continuing to film. The blood dripping from Ramie onto the floor was a nice touch. It added authenticity, but Charles was careful not to step in it.

Charles was sure to film Caleb stashing her in the backseat of his SUV. After the police saw this video, there would be no doubt as to who Ramie St. Claire's murderer was. They wouldn't even need the body to gain a conviction!

THIRTY-FOUR

CALEB'S eyes opened and immediately slammed shut. What little he'd seen of the room had been like a crazy Tilt-A-Whirl, spinning so rapidly it had made him instantly dizzy. His temples throbbed. Pain speared his skull and radiated down to the base of his neck. His mouth was dry, and he licked his lips, trying to moisten them.

His nostrils flared, the sickening sweet smell of . . . blood? . . . overwhelmed his senses. It was unmistakably blood.

His stomach balled into a knot and he sat up in bed, eyes flying open to the unthinkable.

Blood bathed the sheets, the mattress, the pillows. Oh God. It bathed *him*, covering his hands, arms, chest and legs.

He rolled off the bed, landing on the floor as his

stomach heaved and he gagged at the overwhelming stench.

"Ramie!" he yelled hoarsely. "Ramie!" Oh God, where was she? What had happened? Why couldn't he remember? Surely he would have remembered her bleeding this much. Why wasn't she in bed?

He pushed himself off the floor and stumbled into the hallway, only to trip over the dead body of one of his security specialists.

"Oh Jesus," he said with growing horror. This was a nightmare. It had to be. It was the only reasonable explanation. None of this was *real*.

"Ramie!" he yelled as he ran down the hall, throwing open every single door in an effort to locate her. Where the hell was everyone?

His blood ran cold when he saw the back door was ajar. He sprinted over, shoving the door open wider, and his gaze fell over the second dead body.

A chill slithered up his spine, a sense of foreboding so strong within him that it paralyzed him. He stared numbly at the dead man. A hole was punched through his forehead. His eyes were glassy with death and the back of his head had been blown off by the bullet.

He leaned over and vomited on the patio. His stomach clenched viciously, curling into knots, forcing more of the contents of his stomach out onto the ground.

He had to find Ramie. He had to call someone for help. He couldn't remember what had happened here. Shouldn't he know what occurred? Ramie couldn't have disappeared and two men killed without him knowing, could they?

He stumbled back into the nightmare of the bedroom and stared at the blood-covered bed. Then he reached for the phone, his fingers shaking when he punched in Beau's number. Tori, Quinn and Beau had to be all right. Maybe Beau would know where Ramie was and what awful thing had struck here.

"Caleb, where the hell are you?" Beau barked into the phone after the first ring.

"At the safe house," Caleb said faintly. "Something terrible has happened, Beau. Is Ramie with you?"

"Don't move," Beau said curtly. "Don't touch *anything*. You understand me? We'll be there in three minutes."

Caleb frowned at the disconnected phone in confusion. He was missing something vitally important, but what? Why couldn't he remember anything of the night before?

Mindful of his brother's command not to touch anything, Caleb walked to the front door of the house, stepping outside into the bright wash of sun. He squinted and then shielded his face from the sun with one hand. And then he stared transfixed at the dried blood that covered his outstretched hand.

Two vehicles screeched to a stop in front of the house. Beau was out and running from one while Dane and Eliza jumped from the other and bore down on him, their expressions grim and . . . furious.

"Get down!" Dane barked, drawing his weapon and pointing it at Caleb. "On the ground!"

Caleb stared at Dane in bewilderment. Was he serious? Had the whole world gone mad?

"Jesus, Caleb," Beau said, his face pale as he stared back at Caleb. "What have you *done*?"

"Make sure he isn't armed," Eliza said from a distance, her own weapon drawn and trained on Caleb.

He was starting to get pissed.

"Someone want to tell me what the *fuck* is going on?" Caleb erupted. "Where's Ramie? And why the hell are you pointing your goddamn guns at me? *Where is she?*"

"That's what we want to ask you, Caleb," Dane said in an even tone.

Caleb narrowed his eyes impatiently. "Ask me what?"

"Where Ramie is," Eliza said. "Tell us what you did with her, Caleb. Tell us now before the police get here and we can't help you anymore."

He shook his head in confusion. Then he stared down at his hands, as if for the first time realizing that he was covered in blood. He began to shake convulsively, his vision blurring with tears.

"I don't know," he said, his voice cracking. "God, I don't know. What have I done?"

Eliza dipped her head at Dane, who quickly closed in on Caleb while Eliza hung back, her gun trained.

"On your knees," Dane commanded.

Numbly Caleb slid to his knees.

"Hands behind your head."

Slowly Caleb laced his fingers together at the back of his head. He flinched when the cool metal handcuffs surrounded his wrists, clicking into place. He lifted his gaze to his brother, who stood there staring at him, tears in his eyes.

Beau looked . . . devastated.

"Let's go," Dane said, pushing Caleb to his feet. "Get in the car."

Eliza opened the backseat door and Dane unceremoniously stuffed Caleb inside while Beau got back into the vehicle he'd been driving. Dane and Eliza slid into the front seat of the vehicle he was riding in and slammed the doors.

Dane peeled away, causing Caleb to bump his head on the window before righting himself.

"Damn it, Caleb. You don't have anything to say for yourself?" Eliza said in disgust.

"What am I supposed to say?" Caleb asked wearily, some of the shock finally wearing off. Anger was quickly replacing his bewilderment but at the same time, dread gripped him by the balls, squeezing the very life out of him. "I wake up to find Ramie gone, blood covering the bed where she slept. Two men supposed to be guarding the house are dead. I can only assume the third one is as well. It seems to me that you need to be the ones talking and fast," he snapped.

Eliza turned sharply in her seat, her brows furrowed as she stared hard at Caleb.

"What do you last remember doing before you woke up?" she asked.

Caleb was silent a moment as he thought back through the night before.

"Ramie and I went to bed early. We were both tired. And then I woke up a few minutes ago and Ramie was gone and blood was everywhere."

"Jesus," Eliza muttered. "Could he really not know?"

"Maybe he blocked it out," Dane said, his jaw ticking with fury. "I know I sure as hell would if I'd done that to an innocent woman."

A prickle of unease skated down Caleb's spine. An elusive memory taunted him, so close and yet out of reach. Why did his head hurt so goddamn bad? Had he been drugged?

"Blocked what out?" Caleb demanded. "Goddamn it, talk to me and stop speaking in riddles. This has gone on long enough!"

Dane slammed on the brakes and turned in his seat to level his furious stare at Caleb.

"Tell me what happened last night, Caleb. Tell me *why* you did it."

Caleb stared down at his hands, red with dried blood, the smell sickening. He just wanted it off. He rubbed his palms up and down his pants leg but the blood remained. Was this what it meant to have blood on your hands literally?

"Dane, *where is Ramie?*" Caleb asked, fear curling through his stomach and clenching his insides.

"Not here," Eliza said in a low voice. "We don't need him going bat-shit crazy and bailing out."

Dane punched the accelerator and roared down the winding road on the back end of the subdivision toward a more rural area of the county. Away from the city.

It just didn't make sense. Why had Caleb cracked? How could Dane have so grossly misjudged the man he worked for? The man he gave his absolute loyalty to. Worse, why wasn't Dane driving him straight to the police station so he could be taken into custody? Sorrow was etched in Eliza's eyes as she stared sightlessly through the windshield.

Dane's cell phone rang, and he glanced down to see Detective Ramirez's number pop up on the screen.

"Shit," Dane swore. "We're busted. They must have gotten to the house already."

"They may have," Eliza said, "but they can't know *we've* been there. He likely just wants to know if we've seen Caleb. Not many guys are going to hang around the crime scene and wait to get busted."

"It doesn't add up," Dane bit out. "He's not stupid. And I can't have been so wrong about someone. What did he have to gain? Why kill her?"

"Kill who?" Caleb said flatly. "I want some goddamn answers and I want them now."

To Dane's relief, they were nearly to one of the many off-the-grid properties he owned. This would buy them some time, and hell, if Caleb was guilty, Dane would turn him in himself.

He roared into the garage and parked. Beau roared in beside him and Dane immediately shut the garage door.

Dane got out and yanked open the door to the backseat. "Get out," he ordered. "And walk slowly into the house."

Frustrated by this stupid game they were playing, Caleb stalked through the door and into the living room.

"Sit," Dane directed, sweeping the barrel of his gun downward to indicate Caleb was to sit on the couch.

With a sigh, Caleb sank onto the edge of the couch.

Beau strode in behind Eliza, his eyes haunted as they traveled the length of Caleb's body, taking in the gory sight of so much blood.

"Would everyone stop looking at me like that and tell me what the fuck is going on?" Caleb roared in frustration.

"I'll do you one better," Beau said grimly. "I'll show you."

With shaking hands, he punched a series of buttons on his phone and then turned, shoving the screen into Caleb's line of vision.

"I can't watch this again," Eliza said, turning away but not before Caleb saw the sheen of tears glistening in her eyes.

Caleb focused his gaze on the LCD screen, his dread growing with every passing second. His brow furrowed when he realized someone had filmed him and Ramie in bed, asleep.

Movement from the bed silenced him when he would have demanded an explanation.

"What the fuck?" he murmured when he saw

himself get up and exit the bedroom. Time on the video continued to elapse and he frowned, wondering who the hell had been in the room with him and Ramie. His eyes caught movement again and he leaned forward, shocked to see himself return, carrying a wicked-looking blade.

"What the . . ."

He went deathly still, every muscle painfully contracting in his body. Bile rose in his throat as he stared in utter horror at the events that played out on the screen. No. No. No. This could not be happening. No goddamn way. They couldn't think . . .

He glanced at his brother, who was looking at him with such disgust that it staggered him. And Dane, who looked as ill as Caleb felt.

They *did* think . . .

He bent over and dry-heaved on the floor, nothing left in his stomach to come up. He'd never been so sick in his entire life. Sick at heart.

"Get it out of my sight," Caleb choked out. "Dear God, you can't think I did something so horrific. I *love* her!"

Dane's gaze was fastened on the screen, his features ice cold.

"That says right there you did," Dane spit out. "You want to tell us where you took her?"

"I didn't take her anywhere, goddamn it! Why won't you listen to me?"

"Because we have overwhelming evidence to the contrary," Beau said, his voice shaking.

Sick fear twisted Caleb's insides. His own brother was convinced of his guilt. For the first time, Caleb considered the very real ramifications of that damning video. This would be a slam-dunk case. Nothing Caleb said or did would make any difference. Everyone who saw the footage would immediately convict him in their minds—and in a court of law.

And then like a floodgate giving way, memories of last night—and of others—crashed through his mind with dizzying speed. Indescribable pain flayed his chest open, leaving him bleeding on the inside.

Huge, welling sobs choked him, cutting off his oxygen. He staggered and fell to his knees. "No!" he yelled hoarsely. "Oh God, no, no, no!"

He buried his face in his hands and rocked back and forth, so utterly sick at heart that he'd never be right again.

"Caleb, what is it, damn it?" Beau demanded.

Eliza and Dane exchanged worried glances, for the first time uneasy, worried that maybe somehow they had been wrong? But the proof didn't lie.

Tears streamed down Caleb's face in a never-ending river of grief. Oh God, how could he have done it? He wanted to die. He deserved to die for his sickening betrayal of an innocent.

He'd killed her. No one else. She'd died by his hand, the man who loved her. The same man who'd sadistically carved her up at the behest of a madman.

Caleb had been responsible for the bomb that had destroyed his home and could have killed his family. He'd worried about protecting her from evil when it was him who proved to be the monster.

"Arrest me," Caleb said in a hollow voice that in no way sounded like the same man. "I did it. Take me to the police."

Beau glanced worriedly up at Dane and Eliza.

"The poor bastard," Dane muttered.

"I don't think he did it," Eliza said slowly as she reached for the phone in Dane's outstretched hand. A phone that Caleb refused to even look at now.

Beau yanked his head in Eliza's direction. "What? You saw what I saw. What on earth would make you say something like that?"

"I didn't want to watch—I stopped watching when it began," Eliza said, her eyes dark and haunted. "But just now . . . Oh God, it's sick but I don't think he did it. Or maybe that's just what I want to believe or not believe."

"You aren't making any goddamn sense," Beau

snarled. "Now, if there is a chance, *any* chance that my brother didn't do this then you need to tell me what you know before it's too late for him."

Her hands shaking, she took the phone, pain and grief swamping her eyes. She hit a button and winced when the video began playing just as Caleb brought the knife down and Ramie screamed.

"T-there," Eliza stammered, pausing the video clip. She turned the phone around and shoved it in Dane's face. "Tell me what you see."

Dane frowned, studying the still shot of Caleb kneeling over Ramie's body. Then his heart slammed against his chest and his breath expelled in a rush, as though someone had just sucker-punched him.

"His nose is bleeding. Sweet mother of God," Dane said in horror. "A psychic bleed. The bastard was controlling him the entire time and Caleb was trying to fight back. Just like Ramie did when she saw the bomb."

"What?" Beau said in disbelief.

"He's fighting the compulsion. Fighting himself and what he knows he's doing," Dane said quietly.

"You're saying Caleb wasn't cognizant of doing this?" Beau demanded.

"Dane, look," Eliza hissed.

Dane and Beau swung around to see Caleb on his knees, his face drawn in a black rage, blood streaming from his nose and over his mouth. It was a macabre sight but not as gruesome as the video footage of Ramie being systematically carved up by an unwilling hand.

Caleb's face was stony, his features rigid, his eyes glazed over with a faraway look to them.

"I think he just went after the bastard," Dane murmured.

THIRTY-FIVE

CALEB was pale and sweaty, his hands shaking, his head throbbing from the effort of trying to trace the mental pathway back to the killer.

Realization was slick and oily with fear. His head pounded, his heart broken into a million pieces.

"Dear God," he whispered. "It was him. God-damn it! That fucker used me to get to her."

"What the fuck is going on, Caleb?" Dane shouted.

"He bumped into me on the street. I didn't think a thing of it. How could I have? Psychic links are hokey bullshit. He set me up. He established the link when he grabbed my arm and then he used me to turn off parts of the surveillance system so he could get in to plant the bomb. He used me to torment Ramie and hand her over to him on a silver platter," Caleb choked out, grief consuming him.

Eliza, Dane and Beau stared at Caleb in abject horror. Then Eliza stepped forward, her expression determined as she got down on her knees in front of Caleb. She framed his face in her hands and shook him fiercely.

"You have to find her, Caleb. If the killer established a link to you then you have a link to him as well. Just like Ramie had. It will enable you to see into the killer's mind and through his eyes."

"I can't do what Ramie does," Caleb said in frustration. "I'm not psychic like her."

"You're not doing anything," Eliza said impatiently. "The killer is. All you have to do is use the already established pathway into his mind."

"Do it, Caleb. What have you got to lose?" Beau said tersely. "If we don't get Ramie back, you'll go to jail for her murder. Time is of the essence. We may already be too late."

"Don't goddamn say that!" Caleb roared. "We aren't too late. We can't be too late."

He closed his eyes and tried to shut down everything around him. Frustrated by his inability to trace any sort of pathway back to the killer, he rammed his fist into the floor.

Eliza slid her cool hand over Caleb's shoulder and squeezed. "You're trying too hard," she said softly. "Relax and let it happen. Think only about finding Ramie and then open your mind."

He huffed breath in and out, rage blowing like a firestorm inside him. The realization of just what he'd done, unwittingly or not, sickened him. It was a burden he'd bear for the rest of his life. That one night would haunt him forever.

He tried to relax, focusing on Ramie's image. Her smile. Her beauty and resilience. She deserved better than a weakling who could be bent to another's will.

There was a brief moment of peace and then he was assaulted by a bombardment of images. Ramie bruised and bloodied, arms tied over her head, legs spread-eagled and tied to posts thrusting upward from the floor.

The killer taunted her, demanding that she beg for mercy. She remained quiet, her eyes defiant as she stared him down. The killer flew into a rage, kicking and lashing out at Ramie, her body jerking from the multiple blows.

Then she lifted her gaze, hatred glittering in the depths of her eyes.

"Go to hell," she said through swollen lips, blood spitting from her mouth with the effort.

Caleb curled his fingers into tight fists until his nails dug into the skin of his palms. *Baby, no. Do whatever it takes to stay alive, even if it means surrendering. Please, stay alive for me. I'll come for you. I don't care how long it takes, I'll find you.*

Tears burned the edges of his eyes and carved a path down his cheeks.

Knowing the sight of her distracted him from his main purpose, he reluctantly blocked her out, focusing his entire energy on her captor. Images blurred and raced chaotically through his mind. Caleb's view of the inside of the killer's mind was a view of insanity. Utter derangement. Evil emanated from him in waves.

His head ached vilely but he pressed on, determined not to give up until he knew where Ramie was being held. He'd free her if it was the last thing he did, and then he'd get as far away from her as possible. Never would she live in fear of him again.

The barrage of images abruptly stopped and silence blanketed the pathway between Caleb and Ramie's tormentor. Caleb floated, detached from the immediate surroundings of a maniac. He leaned forward, anticipation making him eager.

Caleb had managed to push through into the killer's subconscious. He was in.

He absorbed the knowledge as if they were actual memories of his and not the killer's. It was an eerily spooky sensation to be inside the head of another, to see the world as they saw it.

His head popped back, pain snapping him back to himself. Back to Eliza, Dane and Beau, who all stood staring while Eliza popped him again in the face to get his attention.

"Snap out of it!" Eliza yelled. "Get your ass back here and tell us where to find Ramie."

The edges of his consciousness began to fade and grow dark. He panicked for a moment because back there was where Ramie was and he didn't want to leave her alone. She had to be terrified, no hope of anyone coming for her after what Caleb had done to her.

He closed his eyes as grief consumed him once more. He swayed, nearly toppling over as he opened his eyes to see the others all standing around him.

He stared bleakly up at Eliza, his chest so tight he couldn't breathe. When he tried to speak, he choked on the words, bile rising up his throat.

Tears slipped unheeded down his cheeks. Eliza's gaze was as grief stricken as his own.

"I hurt her," Caleb whispered. "I did this to her. How can I ever get past something like this? I don't deserve to go unpunished. I hurt her. She deserves justice."

"She does, indeed," Eliza said quietly. "And that's why we're going to give her justice by going after that son of a bitch and taking him down once and for all."

Caleb struggled to his feet and then blurted out where the killer—and Ramie—were located. Eliza gently pushed him down onto one of the sofas. "It's probably best if you don't come."

Caleb shot to his feet again. "The fuck I'm staying here! Ramie is mine. I love her. And I can't for one minute let her continue to think that I did this to her! That it was me who handed her over to a psychopath."

"I understand," Eliza said in a placating tone. "But you have to see it from Ramie's perspective. If we go in and rescue her and she sees you, there's no telling how she'll react. She's already damaged enough. Seeing you right now would likely crush her."

"I can't stay here and do nothing," Caleb seethed. "Not when she's out there dying an agonizing death. Because of me," he said bleakly. "Because of me."

His words ended in a whisper and he lifted his haunted gaze to Eliza, Dane and his brother. "I put her where she is right now. It seems all I'm capable of is hurting her. First Tori's captor and all I forced her to endure so Tori would be saved and now I hand her over, bloodied from wounds I inflicted. How is she ever to believe I love her? Or that I'd never do something so horrific? How can I even believe it myself? Do you know how it feels to watch yourself do the unthinkable to someone you love and be absolutely powerless to stop it?"

Eliza's expression softened, and a glint of sympathy flashed in her eyes. Beau's face was a wreath of torment as he watched his brother completely break down.

Caleb didn't bother to wipe the tears away. "I have to go. I can't stay here. I can't allow her to think even for a moment that I wouldn't come for her."

Eliza looked clearly torn but Dane shook his head at her. "Think if it were someone you loved, Lizzie. You wouldn't stay back no matter what."

Eliza sighed. "No, you're right. I wouldn't."

"Then let's get the hell out of here," Caleb said in a tortured voice. "You can call the police for backup on the way, but I have to get to her first because they're going to arrest me on sight. And I'm not waiting on them before we go in and take this guy out. He signed his death warrant when he used me to hurt the woman I love."

THIRTY-SIX

IT took everything in Caleb's power not to burst through the doors of the ramshackle cabin on an old hunting lease, thirty miles outside the Houston city limits. Only the knowledge that the killer could kill Ramie if he were threatened held him back.

He and Beau positioned themselves at the back door, making sure to keep out of the line of sight for any of the windows. Dane and Eliza took the front door because Caleb was sure the killer wouldn't have stood anywhere in the pathway of the front. It was instinctual to fear entrance from there. And he wanted to be the one who came across the bastard first.

"On my count," Dane whispered through the phone into Caleb's ear. "One ... two ... three!"

Caleb crashed through the back door and straight into hell. His gaze found Ramie, who was tied in a grotesque manner to a metal bar suspended from the ceiling. Rope was wrapped tightly around her ankles, blood seeping from the abrasions, and her legs were secured at an odd angle.

Every time she strained against her bonds, the rope cut deeper into her flesh. Her head sagged weakly, her chin resting on her chest as blood dripped from her nose and mouth.

Caleb forced his focus away from Ramie and he locked on to her tormentor, who looked shocked to see Caleb standing in the open doorway.

"Didn't think I could find you, you arrogant, sick fuck," Caleb hissed.

A ghost of a smile glimmered on the man's face. Then he laughed, the sound sending shivers down Caleb's spine. It was a laugh that would haunt Caleb the rest of his days. The killer had laughed while Caleb had systemically carved Ramie up.

Dane burst into the kitchen from the living room, where he'd gained entrance, he and Eliza both holding their guns up and trained on the killer.

Dane and Eliza would want to do it by the book. They'd want to take the bastard in, throw him in jail. But Caleb knew that as long as this man lived, Ramie would never find peace. She would be forever bound to him by the psychic link connecting them. And Caleb would never know a night's sleep.

He'd forever live in fear of doing the unthinkable once again.

Caleb would already be arrested when the police arrived for attempted murder. He may as well go down fighting. He'd gladly sacrifice his life in prison if it meant Ramie would finally be free of a monster's hold.

Caleb didn't waver or hesitate. He raised the gun, ignoring Dane's and Eliza's alarmed cries for him to stop. He put a bullet between the killer's eyes and watched without remorse as the man crumpled and folded.

Caleb stared for a long moment, tears burning his eyelids. He already mourned what had been lost. Ramie's trust. Her laughter. Her love. He'd never find those things again.

He dropped the gun and ran to where Ramie was tied. Her bound wrists were bearing the brunt of her weight. She was literally hanging by them. Her fingers were white and bloodless. He lifted her with one arm, to alleviate the strain. With the other hand, he tore savagely at the ropes and then Beau was there, slicing through the bonds. Ramie dropped into his arms and Beau finished cutting the ropes around her ankles.

Caleb cradled her body to his chest, rocking back and forth as tears slipped hotly down his cheeks.

He pressed his lips to her hair, his arms wrapped around her as though he'd never allow a single hurt to get to her.

Dane squatted down in front of Caleb, his expression dim. "We've got a mess here, Caleb. That video was sent to the police. They're looking for you even now. There's three dead bodies at the safe house and now another here."

"Tell me you wouldn't have shot him too," Caleb ground out. He rocked Ramie harder, holding her head against his chest as he buried his face in her hair. "As long as he lived, Ramie would also be connected to him. I would always worry that he was using me to hurt her. I don't regret killing him. The only regret I have is that he didn't suffer more."

"He's speaking the truth," Eliza said grimly. "The only way to end this was with his death. That's the only way Ramie or Caleb could ever be free."

"I thought you'd done it," Beau said painfully. "I actually believed my brother had done this."

Caleb slowly lifted red-rimmed eyes to Beau. "I *did* do this," he whispered.

Beau shook his head. "No. No! You didn't. He did. You were merely the instrument of his choosing."

Caleb ignored Beau's outburst and resumed his rhythmic rocking.

"Caleb, we need to get her to the hospital," Eliza said gently. "She's lost a lot of blood and she finally passed out. Don't have done all this for nothing and let her die anyway."

Panicked, Caleb pulled Ramie back, allowing her head to loll and tip backward. He pressed two fingers into her neck, relieved to find a weak pulse.

Dane rose and reached into his shoulder holster to retrieve one of his pistols. He wiped it completely clean with a handkerchief and then picked up the killer's hand and wrapped his fingers around the stock. He was certain to put one of the fingers on the trigger so a partial print would be found there. With his hand covering the killer's but not touching any part of the gun, Dane lowered the hand holding the gun to the floor.

"Too bad he drew his weapon," Dane murmured. "Caleb had no choice but to shoot him." Beau's mouth quirked, the corners drawing up in amusement.

"Yeah, that's a real shame."

"Let's go, Caleb," Eliza gently urged. "We have a lot of explaining to do before Ramie can come home."

Caleb closed his eyes in grief because he knew Ramie would never come home to him. Who could blame her? Obviously somewhere in the deepest recesses of his soul he must be capable of the horrific or his mind wouldn't have been so easily controlled.

THIRTY-SEVEN

THE steady beep of the heart monitor reassured Caleb that Ramie's heart still beat. In his darker moments, he'd feared that he had been too late and that she'd die of blood loss from all the knife wounds to her body. Cuts he'd inflicted. He still couldn't look at her without his stomach knotting viciously.

He'd been her constant shadow in the days following her rescue. She hadn't yet regained consciousness but the doctor had told Caleb that she had a lot of healing to do and it was best done while sleeping. It was the body's natural way of ensuring its recovery.

Only by the grace of God was Caleb not in jail at this very moment. The two lieutenants who'd witnessed Ramie's psychic abilities had gone to the D.A. and at least stalled any action until Ramie could herself be questioned about the incident.

Caleb stood by her bed, stroking his knuckle down the still-bruised skin of her face. He touched her loose curls, twining one around his finger and then letting go, it jiggling like a Slinky down the stairs.

He wasn't in any hurry for her to wake up because when she did, she'd look at him with the knowledge of his betrayal in her eyes. Until such time, he was content to stand here and watch over her while she slept so peacefully.

As it was, it happened when he wasn't the least bit prepared for it.

The fingers of her right and his left hand were laced together and rested on the bed next to her side. He was sitting in a chair next to the head of the bed and he'd leaned over, resting his cheek against the reassuring pitter-patter of her chest.

He'd drifted to sleep, into sweet forgetfulness, when he felt her stir and then stiffen. He lifted his head, expecting the worst and yet still gutted when fear chased the color from her face.

A panicked whimper slipped from trembling lips.

He stared at her a long moment and then simply backed away from the bed, his hands up where she could see them.

"I just wanted to make sure you were really okay," he whispered, his heart breaking wide open. "I'll go now. Eliza or Dane will be in to take over."

He lifted one tiny hand and brought it to his lips, pressing a gentle kiss to the palm.

"I love you, Ramie. I'll always love you."

And then he turned and walked away, closing her door carefully behind him.

THIRTY-EIGHT

RAMIE stared at the opposing wall of her hospital room and once again practiced making her mind go completely blank. She was getting more adept at the skill, which gave her hope that her future would be nothing like her past.

So much pain and devastation. Lives wrecked, ruined. It didn't make any sense to her why people like Charles Bloomberg were even born. The sole legacy he'd left behind was one of pain and misery, not only for her and Caleb, but for so many other victims.

She was overcome with sadness, the weight becoming heavier and heavier with each passing day. She was sliding helplessly into a void she might never get out of. She couldn't muster the energy to care.

Caleb hadn't been back to see her since the day

she woke up and he'd kissed her goodbye. Even after she'd absolved him of the horrific charge he was facing with the police, he hadn't returned.

Warm, salty tears burned her eyelids and she sucked them back, taking several deep, steadying breaths so she didn't cry. Again. So far everyone who'd come to see her had been cried all over by her.

Especially Tori, Quinn and Beau Devereaux. She'd cried so hard that they'd instantly retreated, apologizing for traumatizing her.

She wearily closed her eyes, uncaring that all she did these days was sleep. The doctor had asked her if she was ready to go home and she'd merely shrugged. She didn't have a home so it didn't really matter if she stayed or went.

A soft knock sounded at her door. As with all her other visitors, they didn't wait for her to offer a summons. Eliza barged in a few seconds later, her eyes bright and cheerful, her sunny demeanor making Ramie want to hold her down and choke her with her own hair.

How could anyone be that friggin' happy? Especially when Ramie was so friggin' miserable.

She glowered darkly at Eliza, but Eliza didn't look like the happy, chipper Eliza Ramie had been subjected to for the last week. She'd lost count of the days she'd spent recovering in the hospital. Just as she'd lost count of the stitches they'd had to give her. She was a veritable Frankenstein's Monster these days.

"I need to talk to you, Ramie," Eliza said firmly. "And since I know you can't go anywhere, I'm taking advantage of you being a captive audience."

Ramie raised one eyebrow, wondering what had gotten up Eliza's behind.

"Can you not bring yourself to forgive Caleb? Or at the very least offer some understanding? I'd think you of all people would know what it felt like to be at the mercy of someone else and their bidding. For God's sake, Caleb killed him in cold blood . . . for you. So you'd never be linked to him or anyone else again."

Ramie went utterly still, her pulse pounding like a freight train in her head.

"What?" she croaked. "What did you say?"

"He's dead!" Eliza snapped. Then her eyes widened and her mouth dropped open. "Oh shit, no one told you, did they? They were probably all tiptoeing around you and not wanting to take you back to a place so painful."

"No one told me what?" Ramie asked impatiently.

"Charles Bloomberg is dead," Eliza said quietly. "Caleb shot him. He knew that unless Charles died, you'd still have a connection to him. And likely so would Caleb."

It was automatic for Ramie to seek out the mental pathway that she'd lived with for over a year. Something she'd avoided ever since she'd been rescued, but now she opened her mind, seeking the very evil responsible for putting her here. She felt . . . nothing. Just a blank void as if he'd never existed. He truly was dead!

Ramie closed her eyes as sweet relief billowed over her body. This time her tears were ones of relief. Staggering, overwhelming relief.

She was free.

Caleb was free.

"I'm free," Ramie whispered.

"Yes, hon, you're free," Eliza said, patting her hand. "Now about Caleb."

"Where is he?" Ramie demanded. "I need to see him here right now."

Eliza's expression became somber, sadness glittering in her eyes. "He's gone."

Ramie couldn't help the stab of pain that speared her heart. He'd just left her?

"Why?" she croaked out.

Eliza's eyes dimmed with sympathy and she moved to sit on the bed next to Ramie, taking her hand and squeezing.

"He didn't think you wanted him here or to see him," she said gently. "After what happened . . . He thinks you blame him for what he did. He's not in good shape, Ramie. He's gutted by what he was forced to do to you."

"Do you know where he went?" Ramie asked desperately. "I have to find him. Make him understand. I don't hate him. I love him."

"I was hoping you'd say that," Eliza said with a smile.

"Where is he?" Ramie asked in frustration. "And when can I get out of this place?"

"Whoa, you aren't going anywhere for a couple more days. You nearly died. Caleb will wait and he likely needs time to sort out his own feelings of guilt."

Ramie closed her eyes, tears slipping down her cheeks. "I did this to him," she said painfully. "I was afraid of him when I first woke up. I didn't understand everything. It was all too muddled and all I could remember was him c-cutting me," she choked out. "And I was trying to protect him. I didn't know the killer was dead. And I guess I was trying to protect myself because I didn't know if he still had a link to Caleb and could compel Caleb to do his bidding. I should have trusted him more."

Eliza leaned over and gently hugged Ramie, mindful of her injuries.

"Your reaction was perfectly justified. But now that you know everything you can make things right with Caleb. *After* you're discharged from the hospital," she said firmly.

THIRTY-NINE

THEY kept Ramie in the hospital another frustratingly long week before they finally released her with strict instructions to take it easy and not to overtax herself. She had no intention of heeding their instructions.

Surprisingly it wasn't Dane or Eliza who collected her from the hospital. Beau, Quinn *and* Tori all showed up and drove her to a house they were renting in the Woodlands. As soon as she got inside the house she shrugged off their demands that she go immediately to bed and faced them, having no intention of backing down until she got the information she wanted from them.

"Where is he?" she demanded.

"I don't know if it's a good idea for you to know," Beau hedged. "He'd have our asses if you went after him. He's not in a good place right now."

"I don't blame him for what happened," Ramie said softly. "I *love* him and I can't make things right with him if I don't know where he is."

Beau and Quinn exchanged uneasy glances but it was Tori who spoke up.

"He's in Colorado. At the cabin where he first found you. He's like a wounded bear. I think you're exactly what he needs."

"Damn it, Tori," Beau growled. "The very last thing she needs is to make that trip in her condition. Caleb will come around. We just have to be patient."

"I don't have to be anything," Ramie argued. "I have no home. Nowhere to go. Caleb is the only home I have if he still wants me."

Quinn looked at her in shock. "Surely you don't think we're going to put you out on the streets. Ramie, you're free to stay with us as long as you need."

She shook her head. "I appreciate what you—all of you—have done for me and I'm sorry for all the turmoil I've put your family through. If I could go back and undo it all I would. I would have never called Caleb for help if I'd had any idea the consequences of my request."

"Bullshit," Beau swore. "You aren't responsible for that bastard's actions. You did exactly what you should have done and came to Caleb for help. I once told you that we all owed you an apology, an apology you never got. But I'm offering mine now. We owe you far more than you will ever owe us. You saved our sister at great cost to yourself."

"I owe you an apology too," Tori said in a stricken voice. "I was awful to you, Ramie."

Tears filled Tori's eyes. "I owe my life to you and what I gave you in return, the way I acted toward you is unforgiveable. I can only hope you can find it in your heart to forgive me—us—for the way we treated you."

"I'm sorry too," Quinn said in a somber voice. "Caleb loves you and that you love him is all that matters to us. He's been alone for so long, shouldering the responsibility of this family on his own."

"Then you can make it up to me by booking me a flight to Colorado and arranging a rental car because I'm going with or without your blessing and I'm bringing Caleb home."

Not a single member of Caleb's family argued further after her passionate, determined declaration.

Ramie drove the winding, bumpy road to the cabin she'd stayed in all those months ago, the irony not lost on her that Caleb had made a similar trip to track her down. Only this time she was doing the hunting and she was going to be every bit as forceful as he'd been when it came to demanding he see her.

She parked beside his SUV and sat a moment gathering her courage for the impending confrontation. What if Caleb refused to see her? What if she'd waited too long, her irrational desperation to feel safe overriding all else? When she thought back to her reaction when she'd awakened from the grasp of a nightmare to see the very man who'd starred in the terrible memory there, in front of her, she cringed all over again. It had been a rejection. A cold one at that.

She was more afraid than she'd ever been before. Even when she'd awakened that horrible night with Caleb above her, slicing through her skin. She closed her eyes, banishing the disturbing image from her mind.

Those memories had no place in the here and now. The man who'd done so much damage to so many people was finally dead and she and Caleb could be at peace. Finally at peace.

Wiping her damp palms down the legs of her jeans she carefully got out of the Jeep Beau had rented for her. She was still in a lot of pain and had to move slowly, but determination got her to the door where she knocked with every bit of the force Caleb had once knocked on this same door.

It opened within seconds and Caleb stood there, brows furrowed, fury glinting in his eyes.

"What the fuck are you doing out of the hospital? Are you out of your goddamn mind? Do you even *know* how close you came to dying? That I tried my damnedest to kill you?" he asked hoarsely.

"I was released two days ago," she said lightly.

"Then you need to be in bed, not traipsing across the country to some godforsaken cabin in the middle of fucking nowhere!"

Then he seemed to realize that she was here and *not* where he'd ranted that she should be. Confusion clouded his eyes and his features went rigid, as though preparing himself for more hurt. Hurt she'd unwittingly caused him.

They'd hurt each other over the course of their short but volatile time together. It was time to move past that. To look ahead and forget all that was behind them. Looking back did neither of them any good. If either one of them refused to shake the grip their past held on them, they had no chance at all. Their relationship was well and truly doomed. It was up to her to make him put it all behind them both.

"What are you doing here, Ramie? Haven't I hurt you enough?"

"Are you going to invite me in or let me freeze to death out here?" she asked pointedly.

Her words galvanized him to action and he quickly ushered her in and sat her down in front of the fireplace, his touches so gentle that her chest ached. It was obvious he was working hard not to touch her at all and yet still ensuring her absolute comfort.

But as his hands slid away, his fingertip brushed over one of the stitches on her arm barely peeking out from the long-sleeve shirt she wore.

Sorrow swamped his face as he brushed his thumb upward, pushing the sleeve to bare even more of the twelve-inch slice he'd inflicted down the length of her arm. And then as if realizing what he was doing—inspecting the injury he'd caused— he yanked his hand back as if burned.

"Eliza said you killed him," she said casually to take his focus off his obvious self-loathing.

Sorrow shone in Caleb's eyes and he looked away as though he were unable to bear it if she condemned him for what he'd done.

"He's dead," Caleb said flatly. "I don't regret killing him."

She wondered if he even heard the defensiveness in his voice. Did he think she would condemn him?

"*Good*," she said savagely. "Do you realize we're truly free now?"

His brow arched and furrowed in obvious confusion. He nodded as if not trusting himself to speak. Or perhaps he simply didn't know what to say. He looked as though he were afraid to say anything at all because he was still trying to sort out why she'd come all this way to tell him something he already knew.

She was waiting no longer. They'd suffered long enough. Suffered too long a separation even if it only had been two weeks.

She reached her hand out to him, praying he wouldn't reject her. He stared at it for a long moment until something shriveled and died inside her. She started to lower it, already bracing herself for his rejection and then to her profound relief, he caught her hand before it rested on her lap and slid his fingers over hers, lacing them together.

She pulled desperately at him, wanting him near her, close, touching her. He stumbled forward, a deep frown on his face. She reached up to him with her other hand, practically climbing him in her effort to pull him all the way down to where she sat on the couch.

"Hold me," she whispered. "Please, Caleb. I need you to hold me. Banish the painful memories and replace them with new ones."

The absolute lack of hope in his eyes gutted her. Had she done this to him? She'd been afraid before, not wanting to place Caleb in the untenable position of having to ever hurt her again. But now, they were free. There was no threat. No one to control either of them ever again.

"Come here," she choked out, holding up her arms to him.

With a tortured sound of agony, he enfolded her in his embrace, wrapping his arms so tightly around her that she couldn't breathe. She didn't want to breathe. Not another breath unless she shared it with him.

"I'm so sorry, Ramie," Caleb said brokenly. "I'm so damn sorry."

"Shhh, Caleb," she soothed, clutching his head to her breasts where his cheek rested. "Never be sorry for killing that son of a bitch."

"I'm not sorry I killed him," Caleb said coldly. "I'm sorry for what I did to *you*."

"I'm sorry for what he did to *us*," Ramie gently corrected.

She pulled him closer to her, resting her cheek atop his hair as she stroked his face with her hand.

"I love you," she said tenderly.

He went rigid against her and would have bolted back up, but she caught him and held him tightly to her.

He found her wrists with his hands and carefully pulled himself away from her, holding her wrists on either side of her. His eyes glittered and his jaw was pulled tight as he stared down at her.

"Don't say something you don't mean," he said hoarsely.

She smiled, allowing the full light of her love to shine. So he could see it. *Feel* it.

"I'm not in the habit of telling guys I love them," she said wryly. "And I have to say I don't like it much. So if you could just say I love you back then I'd feel much better."

He stared at her in absolute befuddlement.

"Do you forget what I did to you? That I took a *knife* to you and cut you to ribbons? That I could have *killed* you?"

Tears glittered brightly in his eyes and he didn't even make an attempt to call them back. They trickled down the hard line of his jaw. There was so much grief and regret in his eyes that she wondered if he'd truly ever heal after such a grievous injury to his soul.

No, she wouldn't think like that. Love could heal all things. She had to believe that.

"*You* didn't hurt me," she corrected firmly. "It took me longer than I'd have liked to figure that out. But given that I know well what it's like to be controlled by another, I could hardly blame you for the same thing that has happened to me."

He looked stunned. "You knew it wasn't me controlling my actions before . . . *before* we got to you?"

She nodded, her smile a little quivery. Her chin wobbled as she herself was precariously close to tears.

"When I came to and that monster was gloating about you handing me over to him, I knew you would have never willingly done that. You love me," she said simply.

He hauled her into his arms, his chest heaving and body trembling from head to toe.

"God yes, I love you," he said. "Desperately, hopelessly, absolutely in love with you until the day I die."

She reached up to cup his face when he finally pulled back, his gaze raking over her as though he was having to convince himself that this was all not some cruel joke being played on him.

"I like that notion," she said in a loving voice. "But what do you say we save 'until the day I die' for a hundred or so years from now?"

He hugged her again, his hand buried in her unruly hair, his arms like steel bands around her body. She smiled, marveling at the fact that she and Caleb had weathered a storm no other couple would ever have to endure.

"Don't think for a minute any of this counts as an actual proposal," she huffed. "I expect bended knee, the ring . . . everything."

Caleb threw back his head and laughed, the sound joyous and carefree.

Then he sobered and dropped to his knees in front of where she sat on the couch. He took both her hands in his and looked at her with such love that she melted on the spot.

"Will you marry me, Ramie? Spend the rest of your life with me? Have my children and grow old together? I swear to you that no one will ever love you more than I will and that no one will ever be as loved and cherished as you will be."

She lifted her hands from his and framed his beautiful face, staring him directly in the eyes so there was no mistaking her sincerity.

"Oh yes," she breathed. "Yes, I'll marry you, Caleb Devereaux. I don't care how much money you have. I'd love you if you had nothing. I love *you*."

His eyes were suspiciously wet again and he swallowed as if he couldn't get the words out he wanted to say. Finally he gave up and pulled her into his arms, rocking her back and forth as he shuddered and shook against her.

"I thought I lost you," he choked out. "I thought I'd driven you away. Betrayed you in the worst way possible. I don't even know how you can be in the same room with me without being terrified after what I did. But God, I want a second chance. I want it more than anything else in the world. You won't regret this, Ramie. I swear I'll make you happy."

"You already make me happy," she whispered.

"I'll build you your dream house. One you'll be happy in. One with warmth, love and laughter and if, God willing, a passel of children born of our love."

"Home is wherever you are, Caleb. I don't care where we live or what kind of house. As long as you're there, I'll always be home."

Don't miss the other Slow Burn novels by

#1 *New York Times* and *USA Today*
bestselling author MAYA BANKS

Available now wherever books are sold!

IN HIS KEEPING

Abandoned as a baby to a young wealthy couple and raised in a world of privilege, Arial has no hint of her past or who she belonged to. Her only link lies in the one thing that sets her apart from everyone else—telekinetic powers. Protected by her adoptive parents and hidden from the public to keep her gift secret, Ari is raised in the lap of luxury, and isolation. That is, until someone begins threatening her life.

Beau Devereaux is no stranger to the strange. As the head of Deveraux Security, he's more than familiar with the realities of psychic powers. So when a family friend approaches him about protecting his daughter, he's more than ready to jump onboard. What Beau isn't prepared for is the extent of his attraction to his beautiful and powerful client. What began as a simple assignment, just another job, quickly turns personal as Beau discovers he'll do anything at all to protect Ari. Even if it costs him his life.

SAFE AT LAST

They say young love doesn't last, but a girl from the wrong side of the tracks with unique abilities and the hometown golden boy were determined to defy the odds. For Zack Covington, Anna-Grace—*his* "Gracie"—was the one. Until one night forever alters the course of their future, when a devastated Gracie disappears without a trace, leaving Zack to agonize over what happened to the girl he loved. As the years pass, his desperate efforts to find her uncovered nothing.

Now working for Devereaux Security, he stumbles across a painting featuring a special place only he and Gracie would know. The image is too perfectly rendered for it to be coincidence. His Gracie must be *alive*. When he finally tracks her down, he is shocked—and heartbroken—to discover the wounded shell of the girl he once knew and still loves. Her psychic gifts are gone, and worse, she believes he betrayed her all those years ago.

Zack has enemies, and once his weakness is discovered, Gracie becomes a target for revenge. He'll have to save her before he can earn her trust and her love. And he vows they'll never be torn apart again.

WITH EVERY BREATH

Eliza Cummings fought free of a monster who terrorized her when she was an innocent teenager and helped put him away for good. She took a job with Devereaux Security Services and devoted every hour to taking down the very thing she'd nearly become. No one, not even those closest to her, know her darkest, shameful secrets. But now the killer has been set free on a legal loophole and it's only a matter of time before he comes for her. Eliza's only choice is to run and lead the monster away from the people she loves.

Wade Sterling has always lived by his own rules, a law unto himself who answers to no one. He's never professed to be a good man, and he's definitely *not* hero material. Wade never allows anyone close enough to see the man behind the impenetrable mask—but one woman threatens his carefully leashed control. He took a bullet for her and the result was more than a piece of metal entrenched in his skin. She was under his skin and nothing he did rid himself of the woman with the courage of a warrior and who thinks nothing of putting her life before others.

But when Wade sees a panicked and haunted Eliza he knows something is very wrong, because the fool woman has never been afraid of *anything*.

And when she tries to run, the primal beast barely lurking beneath his deceptively polished façade erupts in a rage. She may not know it, but she belongs to him. This time, Eliza isn't going to play the protector. She was damn well going to be the protected. And as long as Wade breathes, no one will ever hurt what is his.

———————————

And coming May 2017

JUST ONE TOUCH

Pre-order it today!